Drifting Apart

BOOK TWO

DRIFTING apart

AMANDA BRYK

For My Daughter

No measure of time moves faster
than a mother watching her child grow up.

And Then You Were Gone

THE MIDDAY SUN hangs like a chandelier suspended from a cloudless pale blue ceiling. As I sit on my favorite rock, watching Croy build a sandcastle with our daughter, I can't help but be grateful for the perfection of this moment. She's gotten so big, and it's odd the way time seems to speed forward when we aren't looking. It reminds me I can't be a spectator in my own life or I'll miss out on moments that are impossible to get back.

My sandals fall away as I slide from the rock and dig my feet into the sand. No matter how old I get, this is still among my top ten favorite sensations even though Croy has taken over the top five spots simply by existing.

- The way he makes me feel protected when I'm in his arms.
- The sound of his voice calling to me in the darkness.
- The feel of his kiss against the side of my neck.
- The way he smells after he steps out of the shower.
- The way he looks when he's working out.

I find myself distracted by thoughts and overwhelmed by love for the man who saved my life, so much so that I never see it coming. Croy's back is turned. He's filling a red plastic pail with sand when the wave crashes onto the beach. The water stretches like arms, wrapping around our little girl's waist, and then, she disappears.

I scream her name and take off running, trying to locate her position before diving into the water. The panic is evident on her tiny face as she breaches the surface, further away than I expected. She must have been dragged into a rip current because she's a hundred feet from shore the first time I see her.

There's no time to talk or think or call for help. There's only time to swim. If she goes under the surface before I reach her location, I'll never again see her smile or hear her voice or feel the warmth of her embrace as she cuddles into my chest. She'll be swallowed by the silent darkness, and I'll be quick to follow.

Croy is already in the water, but I know this task falls on me. He's a proficient swimmer, but he isn't faster than I am. His metal framework and close-quarters combat training serve him well on land, but they're of little use to him here in the lake.

I push my body beyond its limit. Slowed, ever so slightly, by the clothing I lacked the forethought to remove. "It's going to be fine." That's what I tell myself as I steady my breathing. I only have to save enough strength for the trip back with her, and then I can die in the sand.

Hand over hand, my arms cut a path through the water as my legs kick hurriedly. When I sense I'm close, I shift my eyes and see her less than twenty feet away.

"Verlaine! Swim to mom." I locate a reserve of breath and call to her as I drive my body forward. There is no time to stop. "Keep swimming, baby. I'm coming."

A wave of relief washes over me once my little girl is within reach. I press her tiny body to mine as she trembles in my arms, using only my legs to hold us above the surface.

"I've got you. There's no more need for tears." If I had more time, I would attempt to comfort her, the way her father comforts me when I feel like I'm drowning, but if I don't start back, we might not make it. Slipping off my shorts, I leave them behind and roll my tank top into a sort of makeshift handle across my shoulder blades. "Hold on to mommy's shirt, and I'll take you back to the beach."

The current must have carried us further from shore as I was swimming. Now, safety appears impossibly far away when I look towards home. If I pace myself, I can make it. I have to make it. Failure is not an option when my daughter's life is on the line.

I fill my lungs with air, check to make sure my passenger is secure, and begin to frog swim. The condos remain straight ahead, but something is missing.

My heart begins pounding, and there's a burning at the back of my throat as I attempt to swallow the reality of my current situation. This panic is going to choke me if I can't get it under control. I need to focus on the task at hand. I need to concentrate on the things I can control. But how can I do that when Croy is absent from my vision?

I keep my strokes steady and increase the pace, counting out the reasons I've survived this long. One. His strong arms wrapped around me and the way his embrace felt like home. Two. The depth of his voice and the way it calls me back to him, as though that's where I was meant to be. Three. Impossibly delicate kisses he places against my neck that make my body hum and my soul tingle. Four. The lingering scent of his warmth mixed with body wash, and how much it reminds me of new beginnings. Five. Tattooed skin perfectly stretched over layers of muscle and a heart that beats in time with mine.

Finish strong.

My body exerts its remaining energy, dragging the pair of us ashore. Somehow, I'm able to get to my feet, but everything is spinning. The muscles in my legs have burned to ash and are about to give way.

Our daughter is safe. In that, there is comfort. But my husband is missing, and I don't know how to exist without him.

Croy is the reason I push through when I desperately want to quit. He's why I continue to endure the onslaught of demons threatening to tear me apart. My husband is everything I'll never be and all I've ever wanted. I love him more than I ever thought myself capable of, and I'm realizing now that I haven't told him that enough.

There's nothing left. The exhausted muscles in my legs give way, and I drop like a stone into the sand. Finally, I have found my way back to the darkness as a traveler without a home. Surrounded, once again, by the absence of everything. It's peaceful here, in this place where there is nothing.

I wonder if this time, I'm meant to stay.

One

"HEATHER, I need you to wake up!"

I open my eyes to find Croy sitting beside me on the bed. His mesh shorts and sleeveless t-shirt are soaked through with sweat, and concern is etched into the lines of his face. I must have slept through the alarm and missed our morning trip to the gym, though I doubt his unease is a result of my neglected workout. I toss my arm over his legs and reposition myself against him.

As he runs his fingers through my hair, I inhale deeply, filling my lungs with him. His body feels different when he first comes home from the gym. A little firmer. His muscles are still swollen with exertion, and I want to run my fingers over every line and curve.

"You scared me for a second." His voice is soothing, mirroring the lightness of his touch. "When I walked in, you were thrashing around, and then you stopped with such force I had to check to make sure you were still breathing. So, come on, you might as well tell me. What invisible monsters have I failed to save you from this time?"

"Oh, you know how it goes. A lovely day at the beach with

the family turns into a life-or-death situation. Verlaine got washed out to sea, and you disappeared. Then I fell into the empty place, and that's when I heard your voice." I try to keep my tone light, like a cocktail party joke that gets funnier as the drinks get stronger. There's no need for Croy to be upset along with me.

"Verlaine, huh? Have we finally settled on a name?" Croy lifts my hand to his lips and gently kisses my skin. "You know I would do anything to protect my girls? You're my whole world."

"Yeah, I know." I close my eyes and sink into him.

"Okay. Well, if you know, then why am I completely worthless in your dreams? Why don't you let me save you?" He slides into the bed next to me, wrapping me in his arms. The coiled muscles twist like a snare, crushing me against his chest. "Do you think I'm too weak to defend you?"

I let out a small laugh, unintentionally making light of his feelings. "I'm not in control of what happens when I'm asleep. You know that, right? And according to the baby book, vivid dreams are common during pregnancy. So, evidently, I'm perfectly normal, according to science."

I run my hand over his arm, stopping to squeeze his bicep. Every one of Croy's impressive features make my knees weak, but his arms make my mouth water. "I know how strong you are. You don't have to prove anything to me because I'm already convinced. You saved me when it truly mattered, and every day since."

"I would argue it was *you* who saved *me*." Croy kisses the top of my head, signaling the end of our time together. While he showers, I allow my mind to wander. How could he ever think, even for a second, that I would consider him weak? He's the strongest person I know, both mentally and physically. And what does he mean I saved him? I'm pathetic and worthless and weak. Far weaker than he even knows.

As of late, when I'm alone, peace seems impossible to come

by. My thoughts race at an overwhelming pace as I walk around the condo, dreaming of worst-case scenarios. I used to have vices and various self-destructive habits I could exercise depending on the direction of my mood, but I've recently given them up for the sake of those I love. It's a decision I stand by, even if it has left me feeling adrift in rough seas.

Croy is great at calming my nerves and pacifying the voices. Five months in, and everything about him still impresses me, even the way he falls asleep the moment his head touches the pillow. Croy sleeps as though nothing bothers him. There's not one nagging regret or irrational fear clawing through his memories, only peace. I curl up in his arms, allowing that considerable strength to shield me from the outside world. He has become my safe harbor. A steady island unshaken by rough seas. But he can't be home twenty-four hours a day, seven days a week, and his absence leaves me vulnerable.

Since falling into his arms, our whirlwind romance has felt more like a hurricane. My job at the jail and my life before Croy feels like someone else's memories. The only tangible things still tethering me to that time are a uniform shirt hanging in the closet and my friendship with Kelly.

Every morning, Croy and I wake up early, go to the gym, shower, have coffee on the patio, and share a kiss goodbye. He leaves for work, and I'm left at home, alone, wallowing in the absence of him. I've found ways to busy myself, but nothing keeps my mind from wandering into debilitating uncertainty.

When we talk at lunch, he asks how the day is going. Sometimes, I'm honest about feeling overwhelmed, lonely, and scared. Other times, I tell him everything is fine. I hate lying to him, but he worries too much, and I don't like the idea of adding more stress to his already piled-high plate. And anyway, it's only a struggle when we're apart.

In typical Croy Jepsen fashion, he takes it all on his back without complaint, but I see the things he doesn't say. I know he's exhausted, wanting everything to be perfect. I can hear it in his voice. His omnipresent smile has faded slightly, and I'm making it my personal mission to fix whatever is broken. Regrettably, I've yet to figure out what's bothering him. Maybe I'm the anchor weighing him down, even though he assures me that could never be the case. It could be work-related, a family issue, or the house.

We're currently four months into our six-month lease at the condo, so we don't have much time left to enjoy our view of the lake. I'll miss this place, but it was meant to be temporary. Thankfully, knock on wood, the progress on our house has been moving ahead at full steam. My strict attention to detail and manic overthinking have resulted in the running of a tight ship. My respectful but firm work voice has come in handy on the job site, and it doesn't hurt that my better half looks like a professional cage fighter.

Croy was crystal clear with everyone on the job site. "My wife calls the shots. Questions and concerns need to be directed her way. Whatever she says, goes. There's nothing I can tell you that she can't, so don't bother me."

Overall, I try to be pretty good to the teams of people working hard to build the life Croy and I dreamt of over dinner. I make the crew lunch a few times a week, and the fridge in the gym is fully stocked with drinks and snacks. For the most part, Croy doesn't get too involved with projects, drama, or decision-making at the house. Not that he doesn't care, because I know he does, but lately, he seems to be getting pulled in a lot of different directions beyond the scope of my awareness.

As a couple, we've naturally fallen into a synchronized rhythm almost effortlessly, but something outside of the relationship has him distracted. If Croy were anyone else, I would assume he was having an affair. The usual telltale signs remain absent, but something is drawing his focus, and it would be stupid of me not to consider the possibility. Cheating doesn't seem like something he would be capable of, but I've been wrong before.

Would Croy actually throw away the future we promised and the life we're building? Seems unlikely. Then again, it's not impossible to believe a little part of him might want to find someone on his level.

He's doing better now than when we met, and I'm doing worse. I bring nothing to the table, yet he constantly tells me how much he loves me. It doesn't make sense. I'll never be good enough to deserve him, but I know we're meant to be together, and it can be difficult to square those conflicting feelings.

As evident to anyone who cares to notice, I've been struggling even more than usual with questions that drive me further from serenity. I don't know what kind of mother I'm going to be. What if I'm not any good at it? What if I yell too much or forget to fake a smile? What if I can't force myself to be okay? It's harder to be convincing around people who truly see me.

The constant pestering of my self-doubt keeps happiness beyond my reach, and stress follows me into the world of dreams, finding me defenseless. At least once a week, I have a nightmare about Croy being killed and our daughter being kidnapped. I awake with my heart pounding, swimming in a pool of sweat.

A few nights ago, I dreamt Croy and I were back at the old house. It was like we had never left. The three of us were happy, and everything was fine until it wasn't. Kelly called to tell me there had been a breach at the jail, and all one hundred fourteen inmates from the minimum-security block escaped.

One hundred fourteen. Why did that number feel so significant?

Before I could process the information, Croy was hauling me up the stairs as I called 911. The line was busy, and the inmates were already at the door. It was as if my beating heart were the beacon calling them there. We did our best to fight, taking out wave after wave, but eventually, Croy was stabbed in the chest, and I was tied to a chair in the office. They found our daughter hiding in her closet and took her. Leaving me to imagine the horrific fate that would befall her. Unable to endure the weight of my grief, I begged for death. Anything to escape the pain of my loss, but there was no relief to be found. I was left there, alone. Always alone. Alone with only my misery to keep me company.

Sometimes, I move around in my sleep, startling Croy and pulling him from his restful slumber. He wraps me in his arms, kisses my shoulder, and reminds me that he'll always protect his girls. But how can he protect us if he's gone? I'm not sure if it's pregnancy hormones causing these dreams or my fear of losing him. Either way, I'm starting to think I might need a therapist to help me sort through my new anxieties.

On our walks to the gym, I tell Croy about my current playlist of dreams but omit several of the darker details. Since moving here, I've had to watch him die no less than a dozen ways while attempting to fend off hundreds of attackers. Without him, I'm nothing. Each time our daughter is taken away, I awake wanting to burn the world to the ground.

I think I might be losing it.

Thankfully, Kelly and I still talk. He works overnight at the jail, so he's my go-to distraction when it's dark and Croy is out cold. I haven't seen him or heard his voice since I left, but we text nearly every day. He's pretty much my only friend, so I value what we have and keep him permanently inked onto my priority list.

After Croy leaves for work, I take my phone and pillow to the living room and curl up under a blanket on the couch. I know my nightly conversations with Kelly border on inappropriate, and if I were smart, I would delete them. But I'm not smart. I'm lonely. I'll scroll through our previous discussions until Croy gets home from work, and then I'll smile and pretend everything is okay because sometimes it is.

Reading through last night's messages in the light of a new

day, I feel guilty. But not guilty enough to let go of the only person who understands.

: Are you working tonight?

Kells: Yes, ma'am. I'm in the blocks, but it sucks without you. I used to spend the entire night fantasizing about hidden areas in the jail where we could sneak off and make out. Too bad I never said anything, huh? You're up late. Another nightmare?

: Maybe I was dreaming of sneaking away and wondering who would come looking for me.

Kells: You know I would follow you anywhere if I thought it was what you wanted. I'd be your sexy stalker, watching from the shadows, convincing myself you were still mine.

: Watching my every move and not being able to touch me? Now that would be a nightmare. Hahaha. Tell me a story. I need someplace for my mind to go. Take me somewhere we can be together.

Kells: I knew a girl once. She was brave and strong, but also fragile and vulnerable. She was the most beautiful girl I'd ever seen. Every time her eyes met mine, I felt like the only person in the world who mattered. And then, one day, when I wasn't looking, she broke into a million pieces, and someone picked them up and stole her from me. Sometimes, I can feel her here, even though I know she's gone. When I'm lucky, I dream about her smile and her laugh. I try to imagine her, away from this place, happy. But I miss her so much. My life feels empty without her like no one will ever see me again, and I'll never matter.

: You matter!!! Why would you say that? But for the record, that was a pretty sad story. Don't you know any happy ones?

Kells: Well, I did dream that I came home and found her lying in my bed. She was wearing my favorite hoodie and a pair of my sweatpants. Everything about her at that moment was perfect. Seeing her there, that's the happiest I've been in my whole life because, for one brief second, I thought she was mine.

: I remember having a dream similar to yours, only mine had an incredibly attractive man in uniform standing in the bedroom doorway. That was a nice morning. And if I recall correctly, he was VERY excited to see me.

Kells: I would love to remind you how good it was. Come for a visit and stay at the apartment. Your keys are on the counter. Let me take you on a proper date.

: You know I would enjoy that, but I can't.

Kells: Why? Because he's got you locked away in that golden tower.

: Fire-breathing dragon, armed guards, moat full of sharks, the works. LoL. You know how it goes. Croy is a Viking, after all. They all have dragons... But Colborn is quite sweet. He keeps my feet warm at night.

Kells: Way to change the subject... And what color is Colborn, the fire-breathing dragon? I'd like to complete my mental image.

: Sort of dark gray and red, with flecks of gold at the tip of each scale. He's quite lovely when he's not eating the neighborhood cats.

Kells: And how am I supposed to compete with all of that? Castles and guards and moats with sharks. A Viking warrior with a dragon. The hero of damsels in distress.

: It's not a competition, you know. I'm not a trophy you two can pass back and forth, and I'm certainly no damsel… Croy isn't keeping me locked away. It's my choice to be here.

Kells: If I drive there, will you sneak out and go to lunch with me? We can go anywhere. Do anything. I just need to see you.

: If you drive here, I'll go to lunch with you, but I won't sneak around. Croy knows we talk. I'm allowed to see you. I can be honest with him.

Kells: If you're so honest with him, why don't you wake him up and tell him about the monsters? Why do you message me in the middle of the night if he's the one who's there?

: I messaged you because I was thinking about you, but if you'd rather I not text you, then say so.

Kells: Stop. That's not what I want. I hate when you're upset, and I can't do anything because I'm three hours away. I miss holding you. I miss making you laugh. I think about you constantly... Babe, I wish you would talk to someone about what happened that night. I've been in therapy since you left, trying to sort through a mountain of regret.

: Is it helping? Being able to say the words out
loud. Does it make the guilt a little less heavy?

Kells: It's a process. Or so they keep telling me.
Talking helps with some of the feelings, but not
all of them. It doesn't bring back what was lost.

: I think I understand what you mean. That night
stole things from both of us.

Kells: Be honest with me. Do you love him?

: You know I do.

Kells: Do you still love me?

: That's different.

Sinking further into the couch, I close my eyes and snuggle
into the warmth of my blanket. I know Kelly wants me to love
him, and I do, but it's never enough. He wants more.

More than friendship. More than texting. More than what we
had. He wants to travel through time and space so he can be the
hero. He wants to change the night that altered my course and
knocked me off the path we'd only just begun walking together.
But I can't follow Kelly into the past. Not today. If I don't shower
and get dressed, I'll waste away on the couch until Croy walks
through the door.

The phone feels heavy in my hand, weighted with the burden
of my ever-present guilt. I drop it on the table and retrieve the
remote. Being productive isn't in the cards, so I might as well
admit defeat and succumb to the visual distraction of unsolved
cold case files and serial killer documentaries. Anything to get
my mind off the decisions I refuse to make.

Eventually, Croy will come home and all will be right with
my world. We'll have dinner and talk about the day, glossing

over the parts that might sour the picture. Then, he'll hold me in his arms as we watch something on television and he'll fight to stay awake as I over analyze the motives of reality TV characters. I'll join him in bed, making an honest effort to sleep beside him, but eventually, I'll end up on the couch, phone in hand.

Part of me knows I should let Kelly go, let him drift away silently, but I'm selfish, and I still need him.

Two

IT'S 5:00 am when Croy's alarm begins singing, prompting the start of another day that's sure to be the same as those that came before it. Why we feel the need to torture ourselves with these early morning workouts, I'll never understand. My fingers trace over the outline of images inked into his skin as my thoughts wander, not ready to part from the warmth of our bed. In all my life, I've never come across a more attractive human being. He's tall and muscular, with ocean blue eyes and sandy blonde hair that gets darker the further we move from summer. The vast majority of his skin is decorated with intricate tattoos ranging from demon skulls to geometric patterns.

I'll never admit that Croy's inked tableau prompted me to fall in love with him, but it unquestionably pushed me down the path. Most of his tattoos are black and gray, whereas mine are a hodgepodge of colors. It makes for a nice juxtaposition when we're naked and tangled together.

And don't even get me started on his beard, or the size of his feet and the strength of his hands. Croy is every fantasy I've ever had, and more than I could have hoped for. The man checks off boxes I didn't even know I had. Truly, he's walking perfection, and that can be intimidating. More than once, I've convinced myself he's some kind of oversized sexy robot or a coma dream I refuse to wake from.

When he's feeling particularly playful, he'll grab me just below my ass and lift me off the ground to kiss me, and every time, it sends my heart racing. Croy is nearly a foot taller than I am, with muscle layered over a steel frame. When I'm in his arms, I feel tiny but also significant. Honestly, I'm not sure how much stronger the man can get, but he seems to have a goal in mind.

While my mind makes its way back toward reality, Croy shuts off his alarm and puts on his watch. "Have you slept at all?"

I run my hand down his arm and up his chest as he moves to face me. The tip of each finger gently brushes across his skin, conveying my intentions. "Why don't we skip the gym this morning, and find a more creative way to increase your heart rate." I slide closer, trying to remove the distance between us.

"What exactly did you have in mind, my love?" His hand follows the curves of my body.

"I'm pretty sure you know what I'm thinking. You usually do." I shift forward to kiss him. Croy's kiss never fails to excite me. The second his lips touch mine, I'm ready for more.

I'm a little sad to admit this, but my husband is the first and only man I've been with who has cared enough to satisfy me. It seems like most men are under the impression that because they got off, the woman must have enjoyed herself. As if they're doing her some kind of favor simply by showing up. I feel bad for the women who married my exes.

"Tell me you love me." He plants a row of kisses along the inside of my thigh. "I need to know you're mine."

"I love you. You know I love you." Each exhaled sentence is more pleading than the next. "Please don't stop. I need to feel you."

He continues to tease, pushing my body closer to its breaking point, and when I try to finish myself off, he pins my hand to the bed, denying my efforts. I lovingly refer to this as sexual torture because it's pleasurable in the most excruciating way.

What he doesn't know is that I can get myself off without using my hands, and that's exactly what I do. I open the catalog of dirty phrases I wish Croy would say to me and silently speak in his voice. His words are absolutely filthy, and the images they paint make my body tingle and shake. When it comes to bedroom fantasies, my husband's got no idea who he's married to. The threesome with Kelly was tame compared to the desires breeding in my subconscious.

Once I add my internal audio track to what he's already doing, it only takes a few seconds for me to tumble over the finish line. My body convulses momentarily and then liquifies. "Goddamn, I love you."

I've accepted everything he's given, and now it's his turn. As my skeletal structure returns and my muscle fibers reconnect, I extend my arm, but Croy retreats beyond my reach. He gets to his feet and begins getting dressed as though he's uninterested in anything I might offer. "Maybe that'll help you sleep." He stops to kiss my forehead on his way to the door. "I'm going to work out."

He can't be serious.

I'm not sure why this pisses me off so much, but it does. "Well, have fun at the stupid fucking gym." My legs are weak, and I'm out of breath, but I manage to get to my feet and grab my clothes from the chair.

I don't want to look at him, so I dress in the living room, slip out to the back patio, and stare at the lake. I've been awake all night, and I'm exhausted. It seems sleep deprivation has given me a short fuse, and even though I got off, I can't help but be angry. It isn't long before Croy joins me outside.

There's a lot going on as of late. Uncontrollable forces continue to stifle my happiness and it's not Croy's fault, but he's the only one here to bear the brunt of my spiraling emotions.

"Please don't walk away from me when you're upset. Let's just have a conversation." His voice is steady, without so much as a hint of anger. It's annoying how calm he is. I want Croy to fight with me, but he never does. "I'll always love you, and I'll stand beside you forever." He sits across from me and turns my face toward his. "So, come on. Tell me what's going on in that pretty little head of yours, and let me make it better."

The last time I sat on the patio alone, I placed two of the chairs close together, facing one another, because I wanted to elevate my legs. Now, I wish I had spaced them further apart, on opposite corners of the deck. I want Croy next to me until the bitter end. When the world burns, and we're surrounded by the ashes of our enemies. But I want to deserve him.

"Forget it. It's not worth discussing. I'll figure it out on my own." I'm being an asshole for no reason. I know that. But it's difficult to stop the boulder that is my depression once it starts plummeting down the hill. "I don't want to burden you with my emotional baggage."

"Figure what out? I did something to upset you and I'd like to know what it is so I can apologize and avoid making the same mistake in the future." He leans forward, placing both hands on my legs. We sit, face to face, with our secrets filling the space between us. "You're my wife, and you're the only person who truly matters to me. It's my job to take on your burdens and carry them for you. Hell, I told you from the beginning, I loved you so much I would've carried your bags even if you would've chosen the other guy."

"This has nothing to do with Kelly. I don't even know what you're talking about. Be honest with me. Was all of this a huge mistake?" My eyes flood with tears, and I'm seconds away from ugly crying and begging him to stay, even though he's not the one trying to leave.

"No! How could you think that? I can't... I... I don't even

know what you're talking about right now. Was all of *what* a mistake? Us being together?" Croy looks panicked and lost. He wasn't expecting me to ask *that* question, and the mere mention of us parting ways was enough to break his calm disposition. "What the hell is going on? Babe, I can't lose you. You need to talk to me. Are you saying you regret getting married to me?"

"You got me off and then walked away. You said *I'm going to the gym* like having sex with me was the furthest thing from your mind. If you're not attracted to me, I want to know." The words sound stupid coming out of my mouth, and I'm grasping at straws. He's never given me a reason to question him in this way. It's my lack of self-worth that nurtures this dread, and Croy isn't to blame for that.

"Okay." Taking a deep breath, he regains full control of his composure. "It would seem that I've been slacking in my husbandly duties, and for that, I am sorry. I know you've been struggling since the move, and I haven't been around as much as I wanted to be. I've been too focused on work, even though *you're* my top priority. I assure you that I am deeply in love with you and very much attracted. You're the only woman I see." Croy's eyes lock on mine, and there's an intensity building inside of him as he moves closer. His hands slide up my thighs as he leaves his chair to kiss me. "Let me show you how much I need you."

I run my hands over his flexed shoulder muscles, ready to accept whatever apology he has to offer. Not that he owes me anything. I'm the one who should be sorry. My laundry list of insecurities stemming from my looks isn't even what brought me out here in the first place, but it is the easiest thing to fall back on.

"Okay."

We move inside but never make it to the bedroom. The couch is so much closer, and I can't wait any longer. My desire for him is off the charts, and if I'm forced to wait even one more second, I might die from the throbbing pain of my need. Our clothes spread across the room as our bodies twist into a mini tornado, and we're thrown onto the couch. Croy has proven on numerous occasions that he's capable of taking care of me on his own, but again I decide to help things along. Silently, I count backward slowly from 10, giving my orgasm a measured timeline as the intensity increases. Once I make it to zero, my nails are practically piercing his skin as I drag Croy with me over the edge.

Three

SOMEHOW, I awake in bed, although I can't remember how I got here. I must have stumbled into the bedroom after we finished desecrating the couch, but Croy's side is empty and the sheets are cold. I angle my body and allow the cool emptiness to absorb into my skin.

Normally, if I wake up alone, I'm disappointed, but today the unmistakable smell of coffee hangs in the air like a breadcrumb trail leading me back to him. I breathe in familiar indulgence while locating my clothes, hoping for a chance at a fresh start.

The first thing I see when emerging from the darkened bedroom is my husband leaning against the kitchen counter. He's dressed in a pair of gray basketball shorts and a black t-shirt, with his hair still damp from a shower, and he's the image of perfection. Like a photo torn from the pages of a magazine, Croy is the type of guy I would have taped to the inside of my locker and fantasized about during class. It's still hard to believe he claims to be mine.

Croy is effortlessly handsome, though I know he works hard to maintain his exceptional form. Right now, he looks better than ever, with two cups of coffee at the ready. I'm not sure how he does it, but I swear he can either read my mind or see the future.

"Good afternoon, my love. How'd you sleep?" Something about the way Croy smiles at me reminds me of our first week together. I knew, even then, we'd spend the rest of our lives together. That first week of falling in love with him was the happiest I've been in my entire life. In the beginning, we felt like a matched set, each tailor-made to complement the other. In the months since, Croy's stock has skyrocketed, while my value has plummeted into the basement. None of this seems to bother him, but it weighs heavily on me.

My attention finds a trail back to the moment at hand as his words finally sink in. Did Croy say good afternoon? Surely, he's got to be joking. I look at my watch and find it's much later than I thought.

"You should've dragged me out of bed hours ago. I missed our morning together." I'm mad at myself for falling asleep. Of all the days for me to slip into a mini coma, why did it have to be on the weekend when he's home? Those are hours of missed time I can never get back.

"We still have plenty of daylight hours." Croy steps forward and wraps me in his arms. "You needed to recharge. You were in quite the mood this morning." He laughs and tightens his grip so I can't wiggle away.

"I was tired, but I need you more than I need sleep." I sink deeper into his embrace and squeeze. "I don't want to lose you." Instantly my eyes are filled with tears as images of my life without him flood my mind. I can't handle the thought of going on without him next to me. The second he caught me, Croy became the center of everything in my life, the star I orbit around. He's my rock when I need support and my home when I feel lost. Parting ways with him would be devastating on a cataclysmic level.

"Babe, you're not going to lose me. Ever." His arms pull me in, and it would be impossible for us to get any closer. Every muscle in my body is holding onto him as tightly as he's holding onto me. This isn't just a hug, it's a promise.

When I'm finally able to look at his face, I notice Croy's eyes are wet with tears. This is the first time I've seen him like this and it hurts my heart because I know it's my fault he's upset.

"I'm sorry. I'm being stupid, but I'm so afraid you're going to leave me for someone better."

"You're joking, right? You talk to Kelly pretty much every day, and I don't say a damn thing because I'm afraid of what would happen if I asked you to choose. And I get it, you miss him and your job at the jail and that's my fault. I was afraid I couldn't protect you, so I pushed for us to leave. But now you're standing here telling me you're afraid I'm going to cheat on you? You're not just a part of me, Heather. You're my whole life. I can't do any of this without you." The tears fall from Croy's eyes and sit like dew drops at the edge of his beard. He uses his shirt to dry his face before placing his hands back on my shoulders. For the first time, I feel like I'm the one holding him upright, while simultaneously being the one who broke him.

I had no idea he felt that way, but I should have. Croy is my missing half. Our brains run on the same frequency. If I were any kind of a wife, I would have seen that I was causing him pain. I mean, I knew something was off, but I thought we were solid. I can't believe I thought Croy could cheat on me, and now he's standing here telling me I'm the one who's being unfaithful.

"I'm sad and scared and lonely, but that isn't your fault. I'm afraid of being a failure as a wife and a mother." I hide my face behind my hands as the tears stream from my eyes. "I would never be unfaithful to you. I don't want to be with Kelly. It isn't like that. I talk to him because he's awake. He reminds me of who I used to be. Honestly, I didn't know it bothered you. I thought you didn't care."

My legs begin to lose their strength as the room starts to spin. "Can we please sit? I feel like I'm gonna fall over."

"I've got you." Croy lifts me into his arms before I have the chance to take a step. How could he think I would ever choose someone else? Kelly would never be able to carry me around like this.

"We need to have the doctor check your iron level." Croy props me against a pillow and puts my feet in his lap. "I noticed you started eating ice again and you're looking drained. I'm sure that's contributing to whatever else is going on."

Whenever I'm feeling tired or sick, Croy rubs my feet until I drift off. He's so good at knowing how to relax me. Why do I allow my thoughts of him to be poisoned by my past? Croy isn't anything like those other guys, and he's given me no real reason to question him. I need a place to check my baggage so I don't have to carry it with me through the rest of our marriage.

I sit forward, touching his arm. "I'm sorry I made you feel all of that. It was wrong of me to go to Kelly for comfort when you make every effort to offer me what I need. I should have talked to you. And I'm ashamed to admit, I never stopped to think about how it might look from your perspective. Babe, I genuinely am sorry."

"You don't have to be sorry. I know it was hard for you to leave everything behind. That job gave you a feeling of purpose you haven't been able to find here, and Kelly reminds you of that. He's important to you. I shouldn't let it bother me, but it does. I would do anything for your happiness unless it meant letting you go."

"I don't want you to let me go."

"There will never be anyone else. You know that, right? I've been busting my balls in the gym to look good for *you* because I don't want to lose you to that pretty boy, ex of yours. This whole life we're building means nothing to me without you." Croy rubs my feet as we continue to talk.

As it turns out, my husband has a secret of his own. He's been dealing with some family issues since the move and failed to mention it. Apparently, Croy's parents heard about him transferring here so he could be with a girl, and they don't think too highly of me. Interesting, since they've never even met me. His mother went so far as to call me a "leach" who's only with him for the money.

I can understand why he didn't want to tell me. I wasn't exactly thrilled with the initial reaction from my parents either. It sucks that the people we care about refuse to be happy for us, but even my parents didn't resort to name-calling and tossing around hurtful accusations.

"A leach? That's ridiculous! I'm not with you for your money. I'm with you because you're the hottest guy I've ever seen, and because you knocked me up." I give him a wink so he knows I'm being playful. I have hundreds and thousands of reasons for why I want to be with Croy. Looks and money might be on the list somewhere, but they sure as hell aren't at the top.

"Even better looking than your ex? The GQ model. Mr. I can't live without you." Croy sounds like he's half joking and half serious.

"You're the only man I see. And yes, even better looking than my fake ex." I don't know what I'm supposed to say. I want Croy to know, beyond all doubt, that he is my everything. Kelly could never get in the way of that, certainly not on my end.

"I know you're going to dwell on this whole leach thing because that's how you are, but honestly, you shouldn't waste one second worrying about my mother's opinion. I know why you're with me. And you know I feel the same way about you. So, please don't let this stress you out. I only mentioned the stupidity of my family because it has me on edge. I was short with you this morning and that wasn't fair. My parents are making me choose between them and you, which is exceedingly ignorant on their part and stupid. They created this hostile tension for no reason, and they're trying to place blame on anyone except themselves. They have no idea what's going on with us, except for what they see posted online."

This information leaves me in an awkward position. How can I not worry about what she said? Now that I've heard all this shit, it's not something I can forget. How am I supposed to look these people in the face and smile when I know what was said behind my back?

So many things make sense now. I finally understand why Croy never wanted a big wedding, and why I've yet to meet his family. Maybe the reason we've kept our life a secret is because he's embarrassed of them, and not me.

I get up from the couch and walk over to the console table near the front door where there are two framed photos of us and a tray where we drop our keys. One frame holds the picture of Croy and me in front of a waterfall in Hocking Hills. The other photo is of us on our wedding day. I retrieve the wedding photo and carry it back to the couch.

Handing it to Croy, I ask, "How do we get back to this?"

"The apple orchard? I think it's just off Mapleton, by that winery you like," he says with a smile, trying to be funny.

I sit next to him and snuggle against his arm. Looking at the photo, I'm transported back to the picture-perfect moment in time when we committed the rest of our lives to one another, for better or worse.

We originally planned on getting married at the beach behind the condo, but a friend suggested having a small wedding at her family's apple orchard. Megan is a photographer and offered to take the photos. Neither Croy nor I cared much about the details of the wedding, we just wanted to be married. She could have suggested saying *I do* on the back patio and we probably would have gone along with it.

"This was one of the happiest days of my life. In fact, every good memory I have, you're beside me, or on top of me." My momentary smile is quick to fade. "Seriously though, this photo was taken five weeks ago, and already we each admitted to being scared. As if losing each other was a possibility. How did we get here?" I hold onto his arm like a teddy bear and bury my face to hide my eyes. I don't want to cry again, but I can feel it coming.

"We're still the couple in that photo. Nothing's changed. I've been afraid of losing you since the moment I saw you, and I'll probably feel that way forever. I can't imagine my life without you, but I promise you that happiness and love will always outweigh my fear and self-doubt. To hell with my parents and the stupid shit they say. You and our daughter, that's my family. You're my wife. You're the one person I will fight for from here until the end. We're on the same team." Croy kisses the tops of my head and locks his arms around me.

We have both allowed things outside of our relationship to cloud our minds and persuade our thoughts. Things that, in the grand scheme, are pretty insignificant. Eventually, fear will stop invading my dreams and my friendship with Kelly will fade. As for Croy's parents, they'll either take the opportunity to get to know me, or they'll allow their stubbornness to persist, causing them to miss out on a relationship with their son and grandchild. Either way, I can't lose sleep over people who don't live under my roof.

I wish we would've had this conversation weeks ago. Lesson learned, I suppose.

Four

WITH THE AIR in the condo polluted by the stink from our metaphorical dirty laundry, a change of scenery feels in order. I suggest driving to the house to check on the progress, hoping it might alleviate any lingering tension. I've been working on a secret project all week and I'm excited to be the one surprising Croy for a change.

It's October, so I dress in jeans and a hoodie. Autumn is my favorite time of the year, probably because I'm obsessed with hooded sweatshirts, multi-colored trees, apple cider, and Halloween.

Croy gets into the shower just as my phone goes off.

Kells: Hey beautiful, are you good to talk?

: What's up? Everything alright?

Kells: I'm sitting on the patio thinking about you.

: Nothing bad, I hope?

Kells: There is nothing bad. I mean, your taste
in men is a little hit or miss, but other than that
you're pretty much perfect.

: Yeah, right. If I'm so perfect, why don't you
come and hang out with us for a couple of
days?

Kells: When your majesty's royal guard extends
the invitation, I'll be sure to accept.

: You're not as cute as you think you are.

Kells: Yes, I am, and you know it.

Eventually, I'll get Kelly to come here so he can see the new house, but now probably isn't a good time to push the issue. Best to avoid mentioning his name, and allow some space for things to cool down. Croy said he didn't want to make me choose, but his real feelings were distinctly implied.

As we drive to the new house, I keep my eyes locked on Croy, trying to read his micro-expressions while admiring his charming good looks. He normally dresses nicely, but right now he looks particularly tasty. I love it when he's casual because, in those rare moments, we match. Monday through Friday when he leaves for work looking like a professional, I feel like a lowlife loser in comparison, or a "leach" as his mother would say. I swear, that word is going to bounce around in my head from here to eternity.

As we approach a stop sign, Croy takes my hand and presses it to his lips. It warms my heart to see him smile in such a genuine way. The feel of his kiss on my skin sends a tingle up my arm and into my chest. Five months later, he still gives me butterflies.

"I haven't been here at all this month. I'm not even going to recognize the place. Hard to believe in five weeks we should be moving in." I see the anticipation in Croy's face as we coast closer to the driveway. He's like a kid on Christmas morning and I can't wait to see his reaction to my surprise.

When we moved to Vermilion and sold the house in Oak Falls, nearly everything went into storage pods that were later dropped off at the lot. Since then, our housing project has moved forward at breakneck speeds. In order to have everything completed within our six-month window, Croy used his scheduling skills to hire multiple companies. Working in tandem, each was responsible for building a piece of our overall dream. At one point, five different crews were here at the same time. A building crew for the house and one for the outbuilding that contains the pool pumps, Croy's gym, and a full bathroom. On a whim, my husband decided he wanted a pond dug, so a company came in for that massive undertaking, and another did the pool and hot tub. Last but not least, Croy found a company to properly lay out the landscaping as well as my backyard fruit orchard.

I've asked a few times, but he still refuses to show me the total cost. While I can assume it's a lot, I wouldn't be able to venture a guess and expect it to compare to the actual numbers, so I try not to think about it. I wonder if his parents have seen the price tag. Maybe that has something to do with why they think I'm over here spending all his money. Even still, I wish they would have reserved their negative opinions until after meeting me.

At this point, four of the five work crews have all but finished their assigned projects. All that remains to be completed is the interior. If push comes to shove, we could move into the house and stay out of the way while they finish, or set up a makeshift bedroom in the gym for a few weeks. Extending our lease on the condo is out of the question since there's already someone set to move in after we leave, but we can survive without it.

"I hope you're happy with everything since you were kind enough to put *all* of the decisions squarely on my shoulders." I feel a lot of pressure to make everything perfect for him. Croy works unbelievably hard, and I want him to be proud of the life we've built together. The life he's paid for all on his own. "No worries though, it's just your wife's ego and self-worth on the line."

"I thought you wanted to call the shots? If you need a break, tell me. I'm happy to take over." He squeezes my leg, adding emphasis to the offer. "I'm sorry I put so much of this burden on you. I should've been here more, you're right. From here on out, I'll be a better partner. Unless it's too late?"

I shake my head in silent disapproval. "How could it be too late? We're at the beginning of our lives together, and you're already an amazing partner. I appreciate everything you do for us." Leaning over the center console, I plant a kiss on his shoulder as we pull into the driveway. "I love you, more than everything."

"Damn it, I was just about to say that and you beat me to it." When Croy laughs, it fills my insides with marshmallows and hot chocolate, in a feeling I can only describe as pure joy.

How do you know when you've found the One? Well, when that person's happiness is your happiness, you're probably on the right track.

I've been coming to the new house nearly every day to check on the progress, but the reality still hasn't been fully absorbed. In five weeks, give or take, this is going to be our home. Croy and I met five months ago when he saved my life during a prison fight, and now here we are. How is that even possible?

The first twenty-eight years of my life, leading to our meeting, were such a disaster. I kept dating the worst people and making all the wrong choices. I even found myself in a weird situationship with my favorite co-worker, which I've yet to fully remove myself from.

When I fell into Croy's arms, everything changed. I was in love with him before I saw his face or his checking account balance, and I knew we belonged together. Crazier still, he felt the same way. Everyone freaked out when we got engaged after a week, which is why we decided to get married in secret. Five months ago, we were strangers, and now we're family.

The start of our life together could have been so much simpler had we stayed in central Ohio, but Croy couldn't stand the thought of me staying there. After everything that happened, he was worried I would never be safe. Since he couldn't quit his job and protect me twenty-four hours a day, seven days a week, we moved away, where trouble couldn't find me. So, here we are. To say it's been a lot in a short period would be an understatement, and it's no wonder we're both starting to feel a little cracked along the edges.

"Babe, did you hear me?" Croy stands next to my open door with his hand outstretched. "I asked where you'd like to start the tour."

"Sorry. I was lost in thought, reflecting on when we met. The whole thing feels like it occurred so long ago, but also very recent." I take his hand and start in the direction of the pool. "Let's check out all the stuff that's finished, and then we can go in the house if you want."

"Sounds like a plan. Lead the way, this is your show." His words cause me to stop mid-step.

"No. We're not doing that anymore. All of this is *ours*, and I'm tired of feeling like I'm on my own." When we moved to Vermilion, we went into our new life with a divide-and-conquer game plan, but I dislike the idea of things being divvied up along those lines forever. I could never have accomplished any of this without him, so to call it *mine* would be a gross misrepresentation of the truth.

"Hey, I'm right here." Croy pulls me into a hug and we sway together for a long moment. "I have no intention of leaving you alone."

"Ever?" I laugh against his solid chest.

"Never. So, I hope you're okay with that." He cups the back of my head with his hand as I look up.

"I suppose I could learn to live with the idea." I smile before closing my eyes and puckering my lips, in the universal request for a kiss. An invitation he's eager to accept.

Instead of spending my days on the couch, wallowing in self-pity, perhaps I should start reading fairy tales. Those stories are full of girls from humble beginnings who found their place amongst princes. But how did they do it? What did they bring to the table? It doesn't make sense. What meager offering could appear worthwhile when placed beside the bounty laid out before them? What does Croy see in me that I can't seem to find?

When we get around the back corner of the house, he drops my hand. "This can't be real. I can't believe how good this stamped concrete turned out." Walking over to the edge, he dips his hand in the pool water. "We should come back tonight and go in the hot tub."

"Make sure you watch out for sharks," I say, jokingly.

As stupid as it sounds, that has always been an irrational fear of mine. Anytime I put my face in the water of a swimming pool, I imagine a door opening along the side and a shark being released into the water. I know it's ridiculous, but fear doesn't have to make sense.

"Do you know? Are they planning to cover the pool soon?" Croy splashes water in my direction before standing.

I have half a mind to cannonball myself into the water and soak him, but I can't imagine how cold it's got to be. The guys filled it the other day with water they brought in on trucks, and I'm trying to remember exactly what they told me about the winter cover. I know we have one, I just can't recall what day they're coming to close everything. I swear, I have been having the hardest time remembering things. I laughed when I first read about baby brain fog, but it's a legitimate condition. Nine out of ten times, when I walk into a room, I can't recall why I went in there.

"I'm thinking maybe this week sometime. That's what those screws are for. The ones in the concrete. Allegedly, the cover can hold an elephant, but I don't know how they test that sort of thing. Do they keep an elephant on hand or do they borrow one from the zoo?" The in-ground pool at my parents' house had the same cover. During the winter we would dare each other to run out and lay in the freezing water. Then we would jump back in the hot tub to warm up. I'm surprised one of us didn't have a heart attack. "Should we go check out the pumps and whatnot? I have my keys."

"You know they don't test it with real elephants, right?"

I ignore his question and jingle my keys. "Do you want to see the pumps or not?"

The builders finished this building weeks ago and I've been working on a little project in secret. I was able to recruit the neighbor's teenage sons and a couple of their friends to help me move Croy's gym equipment from the pods. I was able to get the television mounted on the wall and found time to fill the bathroom shower with all his favorite products. I even bought a new gym couch and stocked the fridge with Angry Orchard and bottled water.

"Yeah, I can't wait to get over here and set everything up. I miss having my own space to work out. The one at the condo is nice and all, but they could use some extra plates." Croy catches up to me and takes my hand.

He needs to stop talking before he ruins my surprise. I unlock the door and step inside, flipping on the lights as I go. My heart is pounding in my chest waiting for his reaction. When I turn around to see his face, he's standing there, not saying anything.

Well, shit! I think I messed up. Is he mad that I set up the gym without him? I never stopped to consider that he might want to decorate this area himself since he's the one who will be using it.

Finally, after what feels like the longest five seconds of my life, he walks over, takes my face in his hands, and presses his lips to mine. It's the kind of kiss that makes my knees go weak. Perhaps he can sense I'm on the verge of collapse because he lifts me from my feet and carries me to the couch.

The kissing continues, pausing only when we remove a layer of clothing.

Two and a half times in one day is not a record for us, but I'm certainly not complaining. I go into the bathroom to put myself back together, leaving Croy to take in my surprise. I splash some water on my face, fix my hair, and laugh about the stupid grin being reflected back at me, before going out to join him.

"I have the best wife ever." Croy takes a lap around the room, taking it all in. "How did you do all of this, and who did you get to help you? Brian and Nate? And where did this couch come from?"

"I did a lot of it myself with the dolly we brought from your garage, but I also recruited help moving some of the heavier equipment. Anything I wasn't able to take apart and reassemble, the boys next door gave me a hand with. The couch I ordered online and had delivered. One of the landscapers helped me carry it in."

"*One* of the landscapers? Meaning, you were on the other side? Babe, you can't be doing stuff like that. This is why you have me, so you don't have to carry couches and move gym equipment. You're five months pregnant. When are you going to slow down and take it easy?"

"Please don't start with me. I wanted to do something nice to surprise you." Thank You sex, I enjoy. Guilt trips, not so much. Sometimes, all I can do is shake my head. Croy is so forward-thinking when it pertains to finances and social issues, but when it comes to pregnancy, he seems to be hanging on to a few old-fashioned views. Or, maybe it's that he's new to all of this, like I am. He's someone who likes to err on the side of caution, especially when it comes to my health.

"Well, I'm definitely surprised. Everything you've done looks amazing. Why are you so good to me?" He wraps me in his arms and rocks me back and forth. Every time Croy touches me, I'm reminded of the first time, and I wonder if those memories will ever fade.

I can feel myself absorbing his happiness as we continue our silent dance, surrounded by the reality of our new life. It's overwhelming, but in the most amazing way.

Even though I hate to see this moment end, today has been draining and I could use some takeout food and a quiet evening on the couch. Thankfully, Croy is agreeable to my request to head back to the condo.

We can come back tomorrow. After all, we do own it.

Every hour I've spent trying to make things match the image we created in our heads has been worth it. Seeing the smile on Croy's face and feeling his energy when we got out of the car, you can't put a price on that. Maybe that's what I bring to our relationship.

I may not be contributing financially, but that doesn't mean I'm worthless.

Five

QUIET NIGHTS on the couch with the love of my life are my favorite way to pass the time. The conversations we've had throughout today have made a huge difference, and things are starting to feel more like they did in the beginning when we were still talking about hypothetical futures. Had I known it could be so easy to get back there, I would have articulated my concerns sooner. Though, there is still one issue left to resolve. I can feel Croy's body tense the moment a text alert chimes from my phone.

Kells: What kind of trouble are you getting into this weekend? I have to work tonight, so text me if you can't sleep.

Kells: I was thinking about what you said, about me coming to see you and us going to lunch. I want to know if you meant it. I have some days off and I would love to see you. Think about it and let me know.

: You know me, I don't do trouble. LoL. Just a quiet night at home. I'd love to hang out. Let's figure something out and make a plan.

Kells: I'm not going to get killed if I drive there,
am I? Does he still track your every movement?

: Don't be ridiculous.

Kells: I wish you would've stayed here. Then we
could see each other anytime we wanted. I
swear, when you left, everything changed for
the worse. Work sucks without you there and I
miss the way things used to be.

: I'm sorry.

Kells: You could always come back.

"Please tell me that's anyone but *him* texting you." Croy glances at the phone screen before I can respond. "What I wouldn't give for fucking one day without Matt Kelly in my life."

I silence my phone and toss it on the table without replying. "If you want him out of your life, then he's gone. All you ever had to do was say so." I lay my head against Croy's chest and wrap my arm around his waist. "You're the only friend I need."

"Don't say that. I want you to have friends. I just don't think it's a good idea for you to talk to him." Even when he's annoyed, he cares enough to soothe me. Croy begins running his fingers through my hair. This is my kryptonite. "You know you're playing with fire, and yet you continue like everything's fine."

"It is fine because I'm not going to talk to him anymore, and you won't have to be mad about it. Simple. I'm not going to keep doing something that bothers you." I knew eventually this day would come. It was stupid of me to think I could keep them both.

"No. That's not good enough. We need to talk about this. I know you think he's a good guy, but I've never seen that part of him, and I'm never going to forgive him for hitting you. Not to mention the bullshit he dragged you through when we started dating. I tried so hard to be nice while we were still living there because you asked me to, but at some point, you have to acknowledge that Matt Kelly does not respect me or our relationship."

"So, some horrible shit happened to me, and my husband gets to be more upset about it than I am?" I say, somewhat jokingly, although I realize this is not the time for playful teasing. When we were in the hospital, Croy said something similar to me. Only he was talking about Kelly's reaction to my nearly being murdered.

"Oh, I forgot you were so funny. Trying to use my words against me, huh?" Croy repositions me on the couch so I'm looking at him. "You're the most important person in my life, and it's my job to keep you safe. But how do I protect you from him, when you won't let me?"

"I hear you. I hear everything you're saying. You met Kelly at a chaotic time, and he left a terrible impression. I get it. I understand why you feel the way you do." I move so I'm sitting on his lap, my knees on either side of his legs. "I love that you protect me, and you're good at it. Trust me, I know. I've seen the video. Twice."

"So, what am I supposed to do? You want me to forget what he did? Pretend like it didn't happen? The guy's an asshole, who is actively trying to steal my wife, and you're asking me to be okay with that?"

"Okay, well. First off, he could never steal your wife. And secondly, if he were an *asshole* and nothing else, I would've never been friends with him. When that fight at the jail happened, I looked weak and helpless, you looked like a goddamn savage, and Kelly looked like an asshole. I get it. But when you look at me, do you only see that pathetic girl passed out on the floor?" I hate my memories of that night, even though most of them are in pieces.

"No. Don't be ridiculous. You're the strongest woman I know.

I've seen your complexity, from the very beginning, just like you saw me as more than some savage inmate. I only know Matt Kelly to be a disrespectful jerk, and that's putting it nicely." His arms lock around my waist, holding me in place.

"There's nothing left to say, and there's no point in having the same conversation. You hate him, and that's never going to change. So, I can't keep talking to him. I won't." I swallow hard and work to hold in my tears. "I'm sorry you never got to meet the man I know him to be."

"If it turns out this baby is his, are you going to leave me to be with him?" Croy moves one hand to my stomach and waits for my reply.

"What the fuck? Why would you even ask me that? I'm your wife. That's not a joke to me. I'm pissed you would even think that." I want to move, but Croy anticipates my wishes and tightens his hold on me.

"I'm not trying to piss you off. I know you love me and that you're committed to our marriage, but this stuff with Kelly messes with my head. Don't you get it? I'm scared shitless that I could lose my family? Some days, it's all I can think about."

"It sucks you don't trust me, but I'm glad I finally know where you stand. Kelly could never force me to leave you. I'd have to make that choice on my own. But you think that's something I would do because I'm a piece of shit for a wife. Awesome!" I push against him, but his arms are a steel cage. "I'll block his number and never speak to him again. Not that it'll change anything."

"Stop! I don't think you're a shitty wife and I'm not accusing you of anything. That being said, I'm not stupid. If you lose him, you'll never forgive me, and I don't want that. Just forget I said anything, and I'll learn to deal with it eventually." Croy finally loosens his grip.

I move from his lap and retrieve my phone from the table. I'm not going to have my husband pissed at me forever, and I can't pretend like the conversation never happened. I'm used to being miserable, and I can handle the pain of being unhappy. I've been suffering under its weight all my life. But what I won't do is sit here willfully ignoring the part I've played in upsetting the man I love. That's not okay with me.

> : Hey, I'm sorry to do this, but I have to put an end to our communication. I appreciate all the nights you've been there when I needed you, but this friendship is causing too many issues in my life. I really am sorry. After you stop being mad, I hope you can forgive me. I promise you still matter, and you're still seen. That's always been true. You never needed me for that. I was the one who needed you. Thank you for being my friend and standing by my side. I miss you already.

Kells: Wait! Don't do this.

Turning off my phone and setting it on the table, my heart dislodges from my throat. "It's done. There is no more Matt Kelly in your life."

Six

SUNDAY MORNING, and yet again, the bed is empty. I get
dressed and check what few rooms we have here at the condo,
even stepping out onto the back patio to glance at the beach, but
I can't find Croy. Before I make myself a coffee, I grab my hoodie
off the couch. It would be nice to sit outside, but the temperature
is starting to drop. Usually, he's back from the gym by 6:30, and
it's already after 7:00. I try to call, but it goes straight to voice-
mail, so I send a text.

: Message me back when you get a chance.

Croy: Sorry I missed your call. I'm finishing a
workout with Brian and Nate. I'll be home in a
few minutes. Love you.

I plop down on the couch, tuck the thick blanket around my
folded legs, and drink my coffee while I wait. When ten minutes
starts to feel like an hour and he still isn't home, I decide to take
a shower. The hot water and floral suds caress my senses but do
little to ease my growing concern. If Croy is still pissed at me
about last night, he might as well say it, and toss another log
onto the fire while I'm still burning.

When everything begins spinning, I figure it's probably a good time to retreat from the hot water. I don't want to blackout in the shower, especially when I'm home alone. My half-hearted attempt with the towel leaves me damp, but from the safety of our bed, I send another message.

> : Are you avoiding me? Aren't you the one who said we should be talking?

> Croy: I'm not avoiding you, my love. I'm walking in the front door as we speak.

He finds me in the darkened bedroom and takes a seat beside me on the edge of the bed. His fingers braid into my hair as he leans in to kiss me. "My dad called, so I sat by the pool while I talked to him. We made plans to meet at the new house around 9:00. I would love for you to come with me, if you feel up to it."

It's difficult for me to be excited about meeting people who hate me. However, this is Croy's family, and I need to make an effort. "I'll go with you if you think that's a good idea. I would love to hear what they think of the house, and it'll be nice to finally meet them."

There's a feeling of dread within my heart as I get dressed, but I hide it beneath my hoodie. I'm sure everything will be fine, and I'm worried for nothing. Most people know how to be polite in social situations. Hell, Croy was so good at pretending that he fooled me into believing he and Kelly could get along. Or maybe I was simply latching on to hope.

When Croy dresses in a nice button-down shirt and the jacket he reserves for date night, I quickly realize I need to update my outfit. Turns out, his parents are even more high-maintenance than I thought. I locate a knit sweater in my dresser and remove my hoodie. This will have to do. I feel like I'm getting dressed for a goddamn job interview, and I wonder if a person can choke to death on anxiety.

"Nope. Go change back. You don't have to impress them,

they're assholes. I know how much you love your sweats and I've already got you in jeans. I don't want you to be uncomfortable. And anyways, you know what I'm going to say. Comfort is key." Croy's hands come to rest atop my shoulders. "You always look beautiful, no matter what you wear."

While I appreciate what he's trying to do, I don't need to hear any of these sugar-coated white lies. I just want to go and get it over with. "Thanks, but I'll be fine. You look nice too."

Yesterday, my heart was bursting at the seams with excitement as we drove to the house, and today, I'm on the verge of a panic attack. Croy's hand is in its usual place on my leg, but my body is positioned toward the door instead of angled towards him. Maybe I should have stayed home. I'm not great at fixing my face into a convincing fake smile, and I tend to wear my emotions on both sleeves.

As we pull into the driveway, Croy sees the white car already parked by the house. "Damn, I was hoping we'd get here before they did." He squeezes my leg and offers a hesitant smile that does little to calm my nerves. "I promise, it'll be alright. Relax. And don't forget to breathe. I've got you. They're going love you once they meet you."

Croy's parents aren't at all what I imagined when we first met, but the reality facing me fits the picture he's painted as of late. They look like they've come from brunch at the country club, and my heart sinks. These kinds of people have never liked me. I understand now why they would hate me based on nothing more than a photograph. I'm sure when they imagine the perfect girl for their perfect son, I'm not at all what they had in mind.

Despite that, I do my best to hide my discomfort and smile. In five months with Croy, this is the first time I've gotten out of the car without waiting for him to get to my door. The look he gives me as he comes around to take my hand is adorable. It's a mix of *What the Fuck Babe* and *Let Me Take Care of You*. These are expressions I know all too well, and I can't help but to smile more genuinely.

As introductions are made, they hardly seem impressed, but I keep smiling and speak only when directly spoken to. All I want is to break into a million pieces and disappear. I already struggle with feeling worthless since leaving the jail, so I'm not the least bit surprised when the very first question that comes my way is, "And what do you do for a living?"

Of course! Because what possible value could a person hold without an income?

"Absolutely nothing." The words come out of my mouth and I don't even attempt to stop them. I drop Croy's hand as I blink back tears. My heart sinks into my stomach as I contemplate drowning myself in the pool. This whole thing is a setup to make me look bad. It's the Vermilion leach hunt, and I'm about to be burned at the stake in my own orchard.

"That's not true. Heather is an incredible project manager. None of this would have been completed without her." Croy can talk me up all he wants, but these people already see me for exactly what I am. Nothing. No, less than nothing. I am the absence of everything. I am the nothing place, where lost things go to disappear. I'm not Croy's missing half. I'm a parasite.

If they make me feel any smaller, I'm going to get lost in the gravel driveway.

Croy finishes the tour, which brings us back to the start. Had I known they were coming, I would have gotten the patio set unpacked. Their glaring might have been easier to tolerate if I had been seated comfortably by the pool.

Over the last half hour, Croy has tried to take my hand a dozen times, but I keep stepping away before he reaches me. It's not that I'm upset with him. I just don't want to pour gas on the fire and I'm unsure of my position.

"If you don't mind, we'd like to talk to our son. Alone." His mom has been throwing daggers for an hour, but this one hits me straight in the heart. What she means is, without me. They all have each other, and I'm the one who's alone.

"Sure. No problem." I choke the words out, but I'm so insignificant, I doubt anyone heard me. I'm a speck of dust, floating away on the breeze, when Croy catches my arm.

"Well, I do mind. Quite a bit actually." Croy's arm wraps around my waist as he pulls me against him. "Heather's not going anywhere."

And with that, the fuse is lit.

I can't process the vitriol his mother unloads on him. "What are you thinking? Why are you throwing your life away on this nobody? Your exes were all so attractive. This one's not even pretty. She's a fat little leach, sucking you dry."

Only a few sentences in and I'm shut down. There is no place to hide, and now Croy will have no choice but to see me the way they do.

With my body still pressed firmly against his, I can feel every molecule within him vibrating. Croy feels like a bomb about to explode in my arms. He's yelling something, but I can't listen anymore. I ceased to exist the second we parked the car in the driveway. It's time to let go and retreat.

The door closes and finally, I can let it out. Tears pour down my face like waterfalls, my breath catches in my throat, and there is a stabbing pain in my chest. I can only assume this is what a broken heart feels like.

I hear multiple raised voices, but I can't bring myself to look in their direction. Never would I expect anyone to choose me over their family. That's ridiculous.

Chances are, this is the last time I'll see Croy or this house, but I can't bring myself to look at either. I wasn't prepared for any of this, and I'm not ready to watch my dreams die.

Seven

NEITHER OF US speaks on the drive home. Not that Croy could hear me if I tried. He turned on the radio as soon as he got in the car and has been blaring the kind of music I imagine he listens to when he works out. I don't know the name of the band, but they would definitely be considered heavy metal. Hell, listening to this, even I want to lift weights and punch someone.

When we get into the condo, Croy heads straight for the bedroom to change, leaving me at the front door. I need air and a place to hide. I remove the only piece of jewelry I own and leave it on the table in front of our wedding photo. That ring wasn't meant for me and I have no right to keep it. Grabbing my keys and headphones from the tray, I head back to the parking lot.

I want to call Kelly but I made a promise I wouldn't talk to him, and I can't very well call my mom. I refuse to say anything negative about Croy, and hearing their opinions would only make things worse. Looks like it's me and my demons from here on out. I hope they're in the mood for a Sunday drive. I have no one to turn to and no place to go, but any place is better than here.

Without a destination in mind, I drive aimlessly until I start to feel drained. Once my eyelids begin to feel heavy and my vision is speckled with sunspots, I turn North. When all else fails, head for the lake.

In my rush to leave the condo, I forgot to grab my wallet, so stopping for food isn't an option. I might be able to find something at my parent's house, though I'm not counting much. They're still out west, in one of the Dakotas, and the cabinets and refrigerator were left empty.

I park in the driveway and let myself inside. First things first, I need to change out of this horrible sweater. Then, I can look for food. Thankfully, the contents of my bedroom are right where I left them, and my dresser is full of the clothes I convinced myself I no longer needed. Like so many other things in my life, I cast them aside and left them behind, as though they never mattered. But they did matter. They were some of my favorite pieces. The items that wrapped me in comfort when life became overwhelming.

I retrieve the phone from my pocket and find I have several missed calls and a couple of unread messages.

> Croy: Baby, please call me. I've already driven
> past your parent's house a dozen times and
> back to the property twice, looking for you.

> Croy: Where are you? When are you coming
> home?

> : I don't have a home.

> Croy: Why would you say that? Please talk
> to me.

> : Nah, I'm good.

> Croy: What does that mean, you're good? I'm
> not good. I need to see my wife.

> : Well, you should probably find a new one. I'm sure your mother knows some nice girls she can introduce you to. Find someone who's attractive and has a job. Someone you don't have to be embarrassed by.

> Croy: Where are you? I'll come to you.

> Croy: Why is your ring here?

> Croy: Please don't do this to me. I need you. I screwed up. I'm sorry. I never should have agreed to meet with them.

My phone begins ringing, but by this point, I'm done swallowing lies. I'm not capable of having this conversation with him, so I turn my phone off and throw it across the room. As soon as it leaves my hand, I regret my decision. I can't afford a new phone, and mine is currently shattered. Well shit, that was so dumb.

This, right here, is my new life. Better to accept it and forget the last five months ever happened. I mean, how great is this? I'm going to be a twenty-nine-year-old divorced, single mother with no job. And no cell phone. Can't wait. Why am I so stupid? Why did I ever allow myself to think that this time would be any different? I knew that it was only a matter of time. I was never going to be good enough for him.

This is starting to feel like the perfect time for that swim to Canada.

It's quiet at the beach, making it the ideal place to disappear. No one will bother to look for me, and I doubt anyone will miss me.

As the tears fall from my eyes, my arms wrap around my stomach. "I'm sorry I ruined everything before you got here. Truth be told, I don't think I'm going to be very good at this whole mom thing. Your dad, on the other hand, you're going to love him. I know I do."

I take off my shoes and socks, and drop my keys on the pile. I love the feeling of dry sand against my bare feet. Being here reminds me of my birthday. This is the exact spot where Croy told me he had zero doubt. I remember him saying he would have married me that day.

What a joke.

Five weeks. I got to be his wife for five weeks. Shit, I don't know. Maybe five months with Croy was more than I ever deserved. Today's been horrible, and now that my phone's broken, I can't even say goodbye.

Sand turns to rocks as I step into the shoreline and the water soaks into my jeans like a sponge, defying gravity as it travels upwards. The lake is warmer than I expected. Why did I ever move here with him? We should've stayed down south. I never should have allowed him to trade his life for me. I fastened all of my dreams to him, and now I'm going to lose everything.

As I take several steps back and sit in the sand, I can hear Croy's voice from the top of the hill. I don't look as he approaches and I don't speak. I'm at a complete loss for what to say. Finally, I settle on, "I broke my phone."

"I know, I found it at your parent's house. Your car was there and the door was unlocked, so I went in to look for you." Croy sits behind me in the sand wrapping me in his arms. "We need to talk."

"I don't have anything to say." I'm glad he's here, but I'm not ready to have a conversation.

"Then just listen, okay? I swear on our daughter, I did *not* know that was going to happen. My mother was out of line and I'm furious with both of them. I don't know if you could hear anything that was said after you went to the car, but…"

I sink deeper into his chest, wishing this day was merely another one of my nightmares. "I wasn't listening, and honestly, it doesn't matter." I heard as much as I could tolerate, long before that point. "I'm sorry I ruined the visit with your family." I'm too numb to cry.

"This is my family, right here," he says, holding me. "I've told you that."

"I'm not interested in being the reason you don't see your parents, so..." In this kind of battle, there are no winners.

"So, nothing. We're not getting a divorce. Ever. I'm not losing you. Do you know how many times my parents came to see me at the old house? Zero. I lived there for three years. Since college, I've talked to them a handful of times, at best, and most of those calls took place after we moved here. If I don't see my parents, it's not because of you. It's because they don't give a damn about me or my life. They pop in to tell me what a failure I am, then disappear for another year. It was stupid of me to think they could ever be happy for us. I am disgusted by the things my mother said to you, and I'm sorry I didn't scream at her sooner. I should've put my foot down after the first comment, but I bit my tongue like an idiot. I failed you, again."

"It's fine. It doesn't matter anymore. She didn't say anything I haven't already been thinking." I'm so tired. I want to close my eyes and never open them.

"Okay. We can't have this conversation right now. This isn't even you. I'm not going to let you throw our life away. Let's go home, get into bed, and talk about this after you've slept. Please, baby. I'm begging you. Don't make any decisions right now. I still haven't figured out how to protect you from yourself."

Eight

"MY BEAUTIFUL GIRL. Goddamn, I've missed you." Kelly's voice is barely above a whisper as it brushes across my ear. "Are you planning on waking up at some point, or do I have to watch you sleep all day?"

This is the best dream I've had in months. It's so vivid, I can feel his warmth against my skin. I lace my fingers into his and pull his arms tightly around me. His muscles tighten, locking me into place. "I wish this was real so I wouldn't have to miss you so much."

"But if it's a dream, we can do anything we want." Kelly's bedroom voice still makes me melt. "And there's a lot I want to do to you right now."

I flip around so I'm facing him and run the back of my hand along his beard. It's longer than I remember. "You can't be here. I wish you were, but it's not possible." I know this isn't real, even though the heat from his chest is soaking into my flesh and he smells like my memories.

"Would you like me to prove it to you?" Kelly angles forward two inches and kisses me as his hand travels from the small of my back down to my butt. He's everything I remember and more. This is starting to feel like four months' worth of kisses all rolled into one, and that's when it finally hits me. This is real and Kelly is in my bed.

"Oh my god! What are you doing here? How did you find me? Kelly, how did you get in here?" My head swims in confusion. Nothing makes sense. "Where's Croy?"

"Okay, take a deep breath and relax. I'll answer all of your questions if you answer some of mine. Deal?" I nod my head in agreement and he continues.

"Croy called me yesterday, in a panic. He accused me of convincing you to leave him and he was certain you were moving back to Oak Falls. After I told him, half a dozen times, I hadn't talked to you, he apologized and asked me to come to see you this week. Honestly, he wasn't making a whole lot of sense, but I wanted to be around you and I needed to know you were okay, so I told him I had the next couple of days off work and he gave me the address." Kelly pauses to brush a strand of hair from my face and kiss my forehead before continuing. "What the hell happened yesterday? For Croy to call me, it had to be pretty bad. I left work as early as I could this morning, but he was already gone when I got here. The door was unlocked, so I assume he knows I'm here." Kelly stops talking, and I assume that means it's my turn.

"I'm sorry, I don't know why he called you. Yesterday was a shit show, to say the least, but it didn't have anything to do with you. Croy's parents came by the house and told me what they thought of me. Per usual, he got into a big fight, defending me, and then, we came back here. I needed space to think, so I left, and by the time I read his texts, I didn't want to hear anything he had to say. I guess he must have panicked when he didn't hear from me, but eventually, he found me at the beach and we came home. No big deal. He never mentioned anything about talking to you." This is all so strange. My life is so disheveled, even I can't keep it straight.

When Kelly's phone begins ringing, he gets up from the bed and goes into the living room before answering, closing the door behind him. I can only hear one side of the conversation, but I can assume he's talking to Croy. I listen closely to everything he says and the way he says it, trying to imagine what Croy might be saying on the other end.

"Yeah, I was just talking to her!"

"Yes, I know. She told me all of that."

"Okay fine, but I don't know what you want from me! You steal my girlfriend, move her three hours away, and then call me to fix things when she leaves you."

"No. We didn't talk about that."

"Well, it matters to me!"

"Are you fucking kidding me? Belk and I are friends. We talk every day."

"No. Obviously, you don't know!"

"I'm not trying to fight with you. I came here because I care about her, and because you asked me to."

"Then I'm not sure why you even called me in the first place."

I can't listen to any more of this. Of all people, why would he call Kelly? What the hell was Croy thinking? I get dressed in a baggy hoodie and a pair of sweatpants and walk out to the living room.

"Kelly, let me talk to him." He hands me the phone and I sit on the arm of the couch.

"Are you on your lunch break already? Why does it sound like you're driving?" I check my watch. Croy's lunch break doesn't start for another 30 minutes.

"I'm on my way home. I'll be there in like 10 minutes, okay? I love you so much. I'm sorry I had to go in this morning, there was a meeting I couldn't miss. I hope Kelly being there didn't scare you."

"Yeah, a little heads up on that one might have been nice. I legit thought I was dreaming for the first few minutes." I almost mention the kiss, but decide against it.

"I hope he kept his pants on, and it wasn't a sex dream you thought you were having." Croy's tone lacks any hint of playfulness.

"I love you, but you need to stop." I watch as every muscle in Kelly tightens and the fire ignites inside of him. "I have to go. I'll see you when you get home." I disconnect the call and hand the phone back to its owner. "Kelly, please calm down before he gets here."

"Why would you stay with him, after everything that's happened? We can leave together. I want to come home to you. I miss you." His hands tighten around my arms, locking me in place.

"Kelly, I can't. You know Croy will never let me leave. Not without a fight." I want to move closer, but I'm not sure what response that might provoke.

"He would never hurt you." Kelly takes half a step forward, wrapping his arms around me. "Of that, I am one hundred percent sure."

"True, but I'm not worried about him hurting me. We both know he'd be more likely to kill *you*." This conversation is a perfect example of why I should've ended this friendship before it began. Kelly isn't thinking clearly.

"Tell me you love me." His arms lock around me, and I'm back in his trap. Croy's voice is already ringing in my head before he walks through the door.

"You know how I feel, but me saying that isn't going to help the current situation. I need you alive." I attempt to push back, but he doesn't budge. No matter how much time I spend in the gym, I'm never going to be able to push Kelly away.

When Croy enters the condo, the mood shifts, and again I'm in the middle. Kelly's arms crumble away as he takes one giant step back. All of this could've been avoided had I simply stayed home yesterday. My marriage seems to have one fatal flaw, and it's me.

Nine

IN ONE FLUID MOTION, Croy wraps his arm around my waist and half carries me into the bedroom, closing the door behind us. The second we're alone, he kisses me. Slowly, he backs me toward the bed and gently pushes me into a seated position. Then drops to his knees in front of me, resting his head in my lap.

I know this isn't the right time, but if I'm being honest, I'm getting a little turned on. I run my fingers through his hair and over the back of his neck. "Can we have sex and forget yesterday ever happened?"

"Is that what you want, because I'm more than willing to give it to you." Croy looks into my eyes as his hands slide under my shirt. Every place he touches, my body reacts. "Should we ask Kelly to join us?"

"Is that why you invited him here, for another threesome?" I bite my lip as my body tingles. "Did you race home from work, worried you were missing out on the fun?" This moment is not what I expected when I opened my eyes this morning. I feel like we're both playing a character so we can avoid having another depressing conversation. How far is he willing to take this?

"I came home because I needed to be with you, and now that I'm here I feel better. That means it's your turn, and you know as well as I do, Kelly won't say *no* to you. So, if I let him join us, will it make you happy?" When Croy isn't teasing me with his words, he's kissing my neck, making it impossible for me to think straight.

"I don't want to say the wrong thing. I don't need another man to make me happy. I only need you for that." It's getting to the point where I'm not sure if he's joking around or if he's serious. This can't be the reason Croy called him here. They hate each other. But I can't help laughing at the absurdity of this situation. "But if you're serious, I wouldn't say no. So, is it something you want?"

"Are you still my wife?" His hands make their way around my body.

My back arches away from the bed as he finds new ways to tease me. I could never need another man more than I *need* Croy. "So long as you still want me."

Whenever he's positioned on top of me, the muscles in his arms tighten in the sexiest way. I can't help but rub my hands over each one. "Damn babe, you're a beast."

Croy laughs, "did you seriously say that?" He kisses my neck before whispering in my ear. "I love you. I would do anything to make you smile."

There's a knock at the bedroom door, followed by quiet, and Croy responds before I have a chance to say anything. "Kelly, either get your ass in here and join us or sit on the goddamn couch and wait."

When the door opens, I'm not sure if the surprise on Kelly's face is prompted by what Croy and I are about to do, or the invitation to join. "You two are unbelievable. You're seriously going to have sex right now, while I'm here?"

"We're working through something. Don't you know, sex fixes everything?" When I'm nervous I tend to default to playful joking. "We'll try to be quick."

"I'm not agreeing to that." Croy kisses my neck and lowers his voice. "Whatever you want, is what I want."

I bite my lip again and soak in the sudden change in Kelly's expression.

He doesn't say anything, but I can see he's considering the options. "You can stay. Unless you don't want me anymore."

Now that the seed has been planted and the mood is set, I need this to happen. As much as I try to deny it, I'm selfish, and I want them both. Croy is the rest of my life and nothing is ever going to change that, but Kelly is important to me. How can I pass up the opportunity when it's staring straight at me with eyes ablaze with fire?

It only takes Kelly three steps, and then he's next to me on the bed. Before kissing me, he whispers, "you know I want you," and with that, the decision is made. All parties have signed on the dotted line and a mutually beneficial agreement has been reached.

"Now then, where were we?"

Ten

THE THREE OF us decide to stay in for the night, so Croy orders pizza and I scroll through Netflix looking for a movie. Kelly has the next few days off, so I think he might be sticking around for a little while. That should be interesting. I haven't had a chance to discuss it with Croy, but I'm not the one who called Kelly and asked him to come here. The guys are going to have to sort all of those details out on their own.

"This place is nice. I didn't get the chance to tell you that earlier. I've never been this far North and I wasn't expecting the lake to look so much like the ocean. Maybe tomorrow you could show me around." Kelly joins me on the couch while Croy runs out to pick up dinner. Once we're alone he moves closer. "Unless, you meant what you said, and you don't want to know me anymore. Were you having a moment or was that for real? You really don't think I'm worth the trouble?"

"I want to be friends, but not at the cost of my marriage. Croy tends to see the bad in you, and unless that changes, I'm not sure how you and I can keep this going. You have to find a way to win him over, or at the very least, show him you're more than a jealous guy who would get mad enough to smack a woman."

"You're joking, right? He let me have sex with you, but you

and I can't be friends because he hates me? That doesn't make sense. You've forgiven me. Why can't he?" Kelly puts his hand on my thigh and looks deeper into my eyes. "I'm willing to do anything to keep you in my life. You're my best friend. If I let Croy hit me, will that settle the score?"

"Maybe we could find a less violent solution. With my luck, he'd accidentally kill you and wind up back in jail. I'd like to avoid losing both of you, if possible." For a moment, I allow my mind to wander. Some women would love to see two men fighting over them, but not me.

I have a feeling Croy would win, and relatively quickly. Not only has he been lifting weights like it's his job, but he's also gotten back into taking classes on different fighting styles. When we moved into the condo, he made friends with a couple guys here who were around his age and they formed their own little 5:00 am gym rat squad. This month, Croy and the guys are doing kickboxing. Last month it was Krav Maga. I go to the gym with him in the mornings, but Croy never lets me lift weights anymore.

Kelly's hand burns into my thigh as he talks. "We've already had this conversation a dozen times, but I'm going to tell you again because I love you. I'm sorry for the way I treated you. I know it was wrong. That was the best and worst week of my entire life and time isn't going to change that. I was so happy the night I gave you my keys. Finally, working up the nerve to ask you out, in a sense. Being with you was the first time the apartment ever felt like home. But then I turned into an asshole, and I'm ashamed of the things I said and did to you, even before the fight. As soon as you met Croy, I knew I lost you forever and that shit tore me apart. We both know there's no excuse for my actions, and your forgiveness is more than I deserve. I do love you. And I get it. You and I are only meant to be friends. That's become abundantly clear. I'll admit, I'm jealous of what you have with him. I wish I could find my soulmate."

"Well, it'll be a lot easier to find her once you stop pining over me," I laugh, resting my hand atop his. I don't require any more apologies from Kelly, but I always accept them when they come. There are a lot of things in my past I'm not proud of. Words and actions that if taken in isolation, would make me look like a complete asshole. I truly believe we are more than our worst moments. Now, that's not to say we should blindly forgive the people who have wronged us. I'm a woman, and I can hold onto a grudge as tightly as the next. But my opinion of Kelly is based on a lot more than a few bad days.

"Kelly, get your hand off of my wife. I swear, I can't leave you two alone for five minutes." Kelly's hands shoot in the air as Croy sets the pizza boxes on the kitchen counter and walks over. "Did you find a movie?"

"I think I've narrowed it down. You know how it is though, too many options." I scroll over to my final selection. Usually, I let Croy choose the movie, because I've been a bit indecisive as of late. I think I'm burned out from being at the house so much, and then taking care of everything here. I need to convince my husband to start staying home more. There are times when I miss his face, and we live together.

"Ahhh. Having trouble choosing between your options, huh?" Croy gives me a wink so that I know he's joking.

I get up from my seat on the couch and walk over to where he's standing so I can wrap my arms around his waist. "No. Being with you was the easiest choice I've ever made."

I can't remember consciously choosing Croy. From the beginning, he felt like my destiny. And when he proposed after five days, I never needed to stop and think about what my answer would be. From the moment I heard his voice, I knew he was my forever. All I had to do was fall. "I love you."

"I know, babe. I was only messin' around. Come on, let's eat and see what kind of movie you picked for us."

Even though my final selection is one of those loud, non-stop action flicks, I fall asleep halfway through. The harder I tried to keep my eyes open, the heavier my lids started to feel, and eventually, the darkness came to claim me. Croy's arm must be laced with melatonin because more than once, I have fallen asleep using him as a pillow.

When I finally open my eyes, I'm still on the couch, but I've shifted into a new position. My head is against Croy's thigh and my legs are stretched across Kelly's lap. The sound of gunfire has been replaced by the voices I would recognize anywhere.

"The problem is, I can't forgive myself for not being there to stop you. I gave Heather my word. I swore to protect her, and I didn't. Sure, you've apologized to both of us and she pretty much forgave you instantly, but I'm not as easily won over. No matter what you say, you're the reason for my broken promise. I failed the woman I love, because of you." Croy's words hang in the air above my head, like a guillotine. After all, I'm the one who sent him away that day, and invited Kelly to the house to talk.

"I've failed her in all the ways that matter and yet she still loves me, so I think you're in the clear. I am sorry. I feel guilty about that shit every day. I have to live with the fact I hurt the best person in my life." Kelly moves his hand so it's resting atop my leg. "Heather should have written me off a dozen times, but for some reason she never does. You're lucky to have her. Even though she would argue she's the lucky one. Christ, all I ever hear about is how amazing you are. It's nauseating."

"These are only words, Kelly. You two have a history, and I try not to interfere with that. I've never asked her to stop talking to you. Or maybe I have, I don't know. Either way." Croy plays with my hair as he talks, taking me in and out of consciousness. I struggle to hold onto his voice. "My wife needs a friend. I don't necessarily like that it's you, but it's her decision to make. That being said, if you ever touch her in anger again, nothing she says will stop me."

I squeeze Croy's leg so he knows I'm awake. "I'm going to bed." Hopefully, Kelly doesn't mind sleeping on the couch while he's here because our condo is only a one bedroom and I get the feeling Croy is finished sharing.

I get a pillow and two blankets from the closet and set them on the coffee table. He's a grown man, I'm sure he can make himself comfortable. But before saying goodnight, I give him and hug. "Thanks for coming to check on me. I'm glad you're here."

I'm not sure why I thought Croy and Kelly could be friends. At this point, I'd be happy to have them not be enemies.

Eleven

NORMALLY, Croy is asleep soon after his head hits the pillow, but last night all he wanted to do was talk. Turns out I slept through most of his conversation with Kelly, only catching the tail end. Seems like it must have been productive, so that's a good thing, right? I would like for them to get along, but do I want them to be friends? If I'm being honest, probably not. Besides my husband, Kelly is the one person I know I can talk to. The last thing I need is for my only friend to spill my secrets. Croy worries about me too much as it is.

After our lengthy discussion, we did something that felt even better than sex. We laid next to one another like spoons melted together. Back when we first met, Croy and I connected in every way, big and small. The decision to move was stressful, but even with that, our bond continued to strengthen. Until recently.

It feels like we're being attacked from all sides, and instead of working as a team, we allowed ourselves to drift apart. Maybe we both started to take things for granted since so much of our instant connection had been effortless. Or maybe Croy's been too accepting of my selfishness.

During our talk, I finally broke down and told him how lonely I've been. I love going to the gym with him, but it gets annoying when he doesn't let me do anything. Don't get me wrong, I love watching him work out and it's admirable that he wants to be strong so he can protect his family, and I'm not mad about how ridiculously attractive he looks with his shirt off, but I didn't fall in love with him because of his muscles. I fell in love with his strength of character and the honesty in his eyes. I fell in love with his contagious smile and his jokes that weren't even that funny. From the very first moment, I knew our love had always existed and we could endure anything together.

I'm realizing so much can be solved with honest conversation. Sadly, I got used to dating guys who never cared to listen, but Croy isn't like any of my exes. I need to stop looking backward and adjust my thinking, but that's a skill set that takes time to master. Luckily for me, he's patient.

I awake to the sound of running water, which means it must be around 6:30 or so. Unless it's Kelly in the shower and I've already missed seeing Croy before work. I get out from under the blanket and poke my head into the bathroom. "Babe, is that you?"

"If you mean the man you're married to, then yes." Croy pulls back the curtain revealing a head and beard full of shampoo foam. "Were you looking for me, or that other guy?"

"I was looking for you." I laugh, watching the suds drip from his beard. "Do we have enough time for coffee or are you taking it with you?" I haven't seen the time, but it's early enough to still be more dark than light.

"My workout ran over a bit because I had company, but for you, my love, I'll make the time."

"What do you mean, company? Did the women here finally figure out they have to be dressed and ready to go before the sun if they want to watch the three of you work out? I'm sure the Real Housewives of Vermilion have missed seeing you half-naked since the pool closed for the season."

"Ha! Very funny. But no. Kelly was awake when I was leaving and asked to go with me. That's why I didn't wake you.

Guess he figured we could do some male bonding and whatnot. I get the feeling you might have suggested he win me over while he's here." Croy turns off the water and pulls back the curtain.

Okay, so remember before when I said I didn't fall in love with Croy because of his muscles? Well, seeing him stand in front of me wet and naked pretty much just broke my brain. I'm not sure I can remember my name at this point, let alone how to make coffee. No matter how many times I see him, I'll never fully accept the idea he's mine.

"Why are you staring at me like that?" He wraps the towel around his waist and steps forward to join me in the doorway. "That look reminds me of when we were in the hospital and I changed into your extra sweatpants. I'll never forget; you had the exact same expression on your face. It was like you were seeing a shirtless man for the first time and went into shock. Five months later, and it's just as cute as ever." He takes my face in his hand and kisses me.

My fingers slowly slip from his shoulders to his waist, stopping when they reach the white cotton towel. "Better get used to it, my dear, because I don't think I ever will."

Twelve

TODAY IS one of those inviting October days where the soul aches to be outside, soaking in the remaining autumn warmth because deep down you know winter is peeking around the corner. I sit on the patio, watching as a sailboat skims across the tranquil waters, contemplating the day ahead. There's currently an exceedingly handsome dark-haired man asleep on the couch in my living room and he's going to expect me to have a plan when he wakes up.

Between the fall air, the picturesque scene, and the company I intend to keep, I'm deep in thought, mapping out what I hope will be an interesting mini-adventure around town when the sound of an incoming text startles me and I nearly drop my coffee.

Croy: I need to run something by you but the final decision is yours. No pressure.

: Spit it out so I can tell you NO and you can convince me to do it anyway. LoL.

Croy: Is that what I normally do? Damn, what a jerk you're married to. Hahahaha. This time if you say no, I'll leave it at that. My sister has been texting me all morning and she's demanding to meet you. I told her you had a friend visiting, but she's being an insistent little pest. Seriously, she's annoying the shit out of me and I can't work with my phone going off every three minutes.

: Two questions. Are you making these plans for tonight? And is this going to be a repeat of what happened with your parents? I know you and your sister are close, but that doesn't seem to fall in my favor.

Croy: Yes to the first and no to the second. Astrid is a lot like me, so you'll love her. I think she wants to come over tonight because of what happened with our parents. She feels like she needs to make amends and give you a proper welcome into the family. I guess Mom called her to tell her what happened, and Astrid hung up mid-conversation.

: Great, now I get to feel bad about that too. Does it have to be tonight?

Croy: I get the feeling she's trying to do damage control before I write off everyone in the family, including her.

Croy might be willing to stand in opposition against his mother because they weren't close to begin with, but his sister is a different story. The way he talks about Astrid, I know her opinion matters, so if I fail to leave a good impression my marriage is doomed. So much for *no pressure*.

: Are we meeting her at the house or is she coming here? I should probably clean. What time is all of this happening?

Croy: Could you be at the house around 3:00? I can head that way when I get out. I figured you might be planning to take Kelly over there.

: Yeah, that'll work. I'm nervous, but also excited to finally meet her.

Croy: You're the best! Thanks for doing this, hun. I know I'm asking a lot, and I appreciate you. I'll probably work through lunch so I can sneak out early. I love you.

: There's nothing I wouldn't do for you. I love you more.

Croy ends our conversation by sending a gif of Mother Gothel with the caption "I Love You Most." It makes me laugh out loud. I love when he does cute stuff like that because I know that side of him is reserved only for me.

I wonder what his sister has to say about him. I'd imagine if anyone's got the inside scoop on some juicy secrets, it's her. Hopefully, we'll get an opportunity to talk. Things didn't exactly work out that way with his parents.

As adorable as Kelly looks sleeping on the couch, I need him to wake up and join the living. There are places I want to take him and things I'd like to see before heading over to the house, and now I have to convince him to hang out with Croy *and* his sister.

I move the blanket and take a seat on the couch next to him. Kelly is wearing a pair of shorts and nothing else. The sight of him half naked, here in my living room, causes my pulse to quicken as my breath catches in my throat. Before I can say anything, he reaches out and pulls me beside him.

Being stretched out on the couch like this with Croy in the evening is one of my favorite ways to unwind. He knows exactly how to hold me so I feel comfortable and protected. With Kelly, it feels nice, but different, like I can't fully relax. I love Kelly, but if I'm being honest, I don't fully trust him.

"Why are you so tense? Just lay with me for a few minutes. I want to make the most of what time I have with you, unless you think I can convince you to run away with me." He locks me into place against him, with one arm across my chest and the other on my leg.

If the hand that's currently rubbing my leg moves anywhere near my stomach, he's going to find out exactly why I'm so tense. Kelly doesn't know I'm pregnant, because I've been too scared to tell him. I hide it well, under the extra weight I was already carrying, unless I'm lying on my side, precisely as I am right now.

"I figured you might want to shower. Then, we can get coffee in town and take a walk to the lighthouse. There's plenty of shops and places to eat and even a small art museum." I briefly considered retreating to the patio, but my resistance would only tighten his embrace. Best to relax, and ride it out.

"If Croy gets to keep you for the rest of your life, let me hold on to this moment a little longer." His hand squeezes my thigh as he presses himself into me. "I won't ask you to do anything you don't want to."

I close my eyes and breathe him in, allowing the heat from his body to melt away my tension. "Okay." There's a lot of comfort to be found in his arms, a fact time has yet to change. As we lay together, Kelly tells me about his time at the gym with Croy, and slowly my defenses crumble. I don't long for his touch the way I used to, but I have missed it. Once I stop fighting against my feelings, I drift off to sleep, and the minutes pass without my notice.

When I open my eyes, Kelly's arms are still around me, but his muscles are no longer flexed. I get the feeling he's fallen asleep as well. It's been over an hour since I joined him on the couch and if we don't get a move on, we might as well forget about leaving the condo altogether. I flip onto my other side so I'm facing him and lightly kiss his lips.

In hindsight, not the best move on my part. What starts as a friendly kiss quickly evolves into us making out and rubbing against each other for another twenty minutes. My conscience, while late to the party, eventually arrives, reminding me that I'm a happily married woman. Croy might be okay with certain things happening in his company, but I doubt he would feel the same if he found out it occurred behind his back.

"Kelly, I can't do this."

"Yes, you can. Pack a bag and come home with me." Something about his tone is pleading. "Move into my place. There's a job at the police department that would be perfect. It's administrative, and a lot of the cops there already know you. We could get a second chance and you could have your life back. I can protect you."

"Don't you get it, Kelly? I'm the one trying to protect you."

He kisses me again with the full fire of his passion, the way someone kisses you when they're trying to turn you on. "Tell me you love me like I love you."

"I do love you, but I can't have sex with you and I can't run away." This moment is heartbreaking in a way I know it shouldn't be.

"You're right. I'm sorry. I shouldn't have kissed you like that. If you'll excuse me, I'll be taking a cold shower and trying to forget how badly I want you." He kisses my forehead and climbs over top of me, leaving me on the couch alone.

When I hear the water from the shower, I locate my phone and send Croy a message.

> : My friend mentioned you made him look like a little bitch this morning in the gym. Do you feel better now?

Croy: Hahaha. Babe, you have to give me something. If I'm not allowed to hit the guy, at least let me emasculate him a little. I need a win.

: You got the girl, wasn't that a win?

Croy: Point taken. But what was I supposed to do? He lifts as much as you.

: Did you go out of your way to max out the machines?

Croy: Maybe. =)

: What am I going to do with you? So much for male bonding.

Croy: Everyone was nice to him and it was kinda fun. He'll be sore for a few days, but I promise he'll survive. Don't be mad at me. I can't help that your boyfriend is weak.

: He's still NOT my boyfriend.

A good old-fashioned bar crawl is off the table, since I'm not able to drink, so we opt to keep our afternoon sober. Hand in hand, we walk around downtown, stopping in all of the little shops, before taking a stroll along the beach. Hardly a moment passes in silence, and our dialog is reminiscent of conversations shared during perimeter checks and lunch breaks at the jail. Kelly insists I choose the lunch destination but refuses to let me pay the tab. According to him, I'm still entitled to a birthday lunch, even though it was four months ago. It's an interesting feeling, being out with him like this.

Today feels like the first date we never had.

Thirteen

THESE MUCH-NEEDED hours with Kelly have renewed my sense of self, and I wish he still lived three miles away, instead of three hours away. It's going to be hard for me to let him go and watch him leave, so I need to make the most of the days we have. If I could go back in time and change anything, I would've made an effort to hang out more during those months when we worked together. My days in Oak Falls could have been a lot less lonely had Kelly and I been *that* kind of friends. That being said, I'm happy to have him now, and since I can't change the past, there's no point in dwelling on it.

As Kelly and I walk hand in hand, discussing the past, present, and future, I lose track of the time. It's a small town, but there's a lot to see. Unfortunately, it's a *very* small town, so chances are good Croy might wind up receiving a phone call from a concerned citizen about his cheating wife.

In truth, I'm not overly concerned about the outcome of hypothetical phone calls because I know my husband. He'd most likely play along, pretending to be shocked by the horror of it all, and then laugh about it later as he recalled the confession in vivid detail. As worried as we might be about losing one another, that fear isn't limited to infidelity.

I *want* Kelly in my life, but it's nothing compared to how much I *need* Croy by my side.

It's already a quarter to three when I finally glance at my watch. "Oh shit, we've got to go." I've been intentionally secretive with Kelly over the last few months because I wanted everything at the house to be a surprise. Part of me held out hope that I could convince him to come for a visit, and now here we are.

As we turn into the driveway, I spot two cars parked by the house. I wanted to be first to arrive and ended up being last, which seems to be on brand for my life as of late. Croy is standing in the driveway, pointing toward the back of the property, and next to him is a tall, thin blonde I'm hoping is his sister. Even from this distance, I can feel how excited he is to be showing off the reality of our dream. Out of habit, I smile and let slip a small laugh.

Up close, Astrid is even more impressive than she was from a hundred feet away. Kelly seems to have noticed as well because he hopped out of the car while it was still rolling to a stop, leaving me to sit here on my own as I rally the nerve to join them. Surveying the three of them standing together, I'm starting to feel like the ugly friend. A song from my childhood begins playing in my head. *One of these things is not like the others. One of these things does not belong.* That's me. I'm the thing that doesn't belong.

After an extended minute Croy jogs over, opening my driver's side door. "Is everything alright? Do you not want to do this?" There's concern laced through his questions, feeding my guilt.

"I'm fine. I just needed a moment. I think I'm getting a headache." This is my go-to excuse since most days it's true. Only this time, it's a panic attack I'm fighting off, not a headache.

"Hang on a second." Croy retrieves the lunch box from his car and a bottle of pills he keeps in the glove box. "Take as much time as you need. I'll start the tour and you can find us when you're ready. Okay? I love you." He ducks his head into the car and kisses me.

"I promise I'll be quick." I open the bottle of ibuprofen and shake two pills into my palm. Sitting here, getting myself worked up over nothing, my head is starting to hurt. I watch as Croy walks away, wondering how I got so lucky.

One would think by twenty-nine years old I would be able to ingest pills like an adult, but they would be wrong. I take a small bite of Croy's untouched lunch, chew, and stuff the pills inside before swallowing. The bite of food goes down, but the lump in my throat remains.

"Come on, you have nothing to worry about." I try to psych myself up, but it doesn't help. "You can do this. She isn't her parents. She's just the gorgeous supermodel sister with the great job, who's making you look like a fat little leach by comparison. Dammit! I can't do this."

Astrid takes a long glance in my direction before following her brother and Kelly around the back of the house. Looks like the tour is starting at the pool. I close my eyes and breathe in deeply, holding the air for a moment. Counting to ten, I exhale to the point of emptiness, before filling my lungs with clean air. I continue this pattern of controlled breathing before opening my eyes. "There's nothing to fear. Croy isn't going to let anything bad happen again, and you have Kelly with you for backup. You have to suck it up and get through it."

When I finally reach the group, Croy is in the middle of showing off his new gym. As I walk through the door, I hear him saying, "Come on Matt, you ready for round two?"

Matt?

Since when does Croy call him Matt, as if they're old pals? I'll never forget the time he told me Kelly's first name. I thought for sure he was joking around, trying to be funny. Turns out, Croy was friends with someone who lived down the hall from Kelly's apartment. That name, Matt, still sounds as fake to me today as it did back then.

"I can barely lift my arms after this morning." The look on Kelly's face is playful and charming. 1 remember how it felt the first time he looked at me that way. I nearly melted into a puddle like a snowman in summer. Even now, I can feel the room getting warmer.

"Fair enough." Croy turns his attention to the doorway where I'm lingering. "Ahhh, and here she is. Sis, I would like to formally introduce you to my incredibly amazing, beautiful, and talented wife, without whom none of this would be possible." He gestures towards me, and in one synchronized motion, both Kelly and Astrid turn to look at me.

"That was quite the introduction." I feel my cheeks flush with embarrassment. Wife might be the only one of those words that accurately describes me, and even then, I'm not sure I deserve the title.

"Oh my god, I'm dying! You have no idea how badly I've been wanting to meet you. I don't understand why my jerk of a brother has been hiding you away. You're lovely. I can't believe I have a sister! And if that's not exciting enough, I heard you're making me an aunt in a few months! You two certainly didn't waste any time and I love that! Everyone dreams of finding their other half and you guys did it. It's so exciting!" Her words cause my heart to stop, but I try not to react. Slowly, I shift my gaze, trying to gauge Kelly's reaction, but he refuses to meet my eyes.

"Yeah, I'm not sure anymore why we decided to keep things so hush-hush, but it seems the cat's out of the bag." I want to melt into the rubber floor and disappear forever. That panic attack is starting to feel a little more like a warning bell. Maybe I need to start listening.

Croy gets a good sense of what just happened and attempts to move the tour outside. "Should we head back towards the orchard or into the house? What would you like to see while you're here?"

"Are you kidding me? I want to see it all. Show off. Brag. Be the annoyingly perfect older brother, per usual. This is your moment." Astrid's voice floats through the air like a song. It must be something that runs in the family because I've frequently found the melodic quality of Croy's voice incredibly pleasing.

As the tour continues, Kelly still refuses to look at me directly, even as he brushes past me on his way out the door. Everything about this moment feels like the end. And why shouldn't it be? I've been lying to him for months, and there's no changing that. I wanted to tell him the truth, so many times, but I was too afraid of the consequences.

The other day, Croy laid out, in black and white, his feelings as they pertain to my continued actions and poor choices, and now I'm being exposed yet again. Guess I'm not as good of a person as I thought. Maybe it's me who is irredeemable.

I drag my shell along the rest of the tour, going through all the motions expected of me. Mirroring Croy's emotional cues, I smile and laugh in all the right places, and do my best to hide the fact that I'm dead inside.

When we circle back in the driveway, Croy pulls the keys from my pocket and tosses them to Kelly. "Would you mind driving Heather's car? I'd feel better if she rode home with me. Plus, I haven't seen her all day." He wraps his arm around me, propping me up. "Sis, are you good to follow me or do you want the address?"

"I'm certain I can keep up, and if not, I'm sure Matt won't go out of his way to lose me." Astrid shoots Croy a playful scowl, drenched in sibling rivalry.

What am I doing? This was supposed to be a friendly interaction with his sister, who is evidently a very nice person, and I'm over here ruining it. I take a deep breath and straighten my spine, pulling back my shoulders and lifting my head.

I wave as our guests depart, leaving Croy and me in the driveway. I'm certain I owe him an apology, but before I can speak, he kisses me and says, "I swear to you, I never told my sister about you being pregnant. It slipped out while I was screaming at my mom the other day. I wasn't thinking and I'm sorry. I'm sure that's where she heard it. This situation is all my fault. I really screwed up this time, didn't I? Do you hate me?"

I'm only half listening as I watch the cars turn onto the road at the end of the driveway, heading towards the condo. Hopefully, Kelly is smart enough to realize he has my key, so they don't hang out in the parking lot, waiting for us.

"I think I'll reserve being pissed at you for when you actually do something wrong," I say, trying to lighten the moment. "In all seriousness, it's fine. Maybe it's better this way. Now that everyone knows, we don't have to keep dancing around conversations. And you're not the one who screwed up. I'm the one who's been lying to Kelly. I messed up the visit with your parents and now I made myself look like an asshole to your sister. I keep getting stuck in my head, worried about a hundred different things, and none of that is your fault. I need to be the one apologizing to you." I give his waist a squeeze and angle my head upwards. "I'm sorry I haven't been myself lately. Do you think we could blame it on pregnancy hormones?"

"I think that's brilliant! I mean, come on. What better reason is there? Not that we even need to make excuses. Honestly, babe, you weren't that bad. You were quiet, but you weren't an asshole." Croy's calm demeanor washes over me. "Are you worried about Matt being pissed off?"

"Oh my god, stop! You cannot start calling him Matt. It's too weird." I attempt to shake the name out of my head. "As for him being mad at me, it is what it is. He was going to find out eventually. So, now we wait and see what he says." I'm not sure if I'm going home to get yelled at, or if he'll take off and never speak to me again.

Croy steps forward and touches my arm. "No matter what happens moving forward, I'm on your side, but I need you to be honest with me. Now that he knows, are you going to tell him the rest?"

How am I supposed to answer that? I've been torn in two on

this issue since we found out it was a possibility, and I've yet to fully weigh the burden of my guilt against the heft of vast uncertainty. Secrets are like poison, and this one has been slowly killing me for months. "If he asks me, I have to tell him. Babe, I can't keep lying about this. It's too important."

"I know you feel like you have to do the right thing, and as much as I admire that, it also scares the shit out of me." Croy's words and fears carry additional weight that hangs heavy upon me, like Jacob Marley's chains. "If this baby daddy coin flip doesn't fall in my favor, I'm going to lose everything. My wife, my daughter, my will to live..."

"Please don't say that. I swear to you, I'm not that good of a person. No matter what, you'll have your family. I promise you. I know I was quick to forgive him and I've struggled to let him go, but he's not my person. You are! I never should have prioritized Kelly and put him before you. As soon as we got released from the hospital, I should've stayed with you, but I was too worried about how it might look if we walked into the jail together and I was afraid of losing my job or getting into trouble. I'm sorry I didn't do the right thing." I wish I could go back in time and make different choices so I wouldn't have to carry a lifetime of regret.

"You don't need to be sorry. I understood why we had to part ways in he parking lot. There was no way you could've left with me, I know that. I don't care about any of that, babe. All that matters is that the three of us are a family. You, me, and our baby girl whose name is still being debated because her parents can't make any more decisions right now." Croy lets out a small laugh. "I still think it should be Juniper Jepsen because it sounds like a superhero's name!"

"I like Juniper, but not with your last name." I run through the list of possible baby names in my head, pulling out my favorites and moving them to the top.

"You mean to say, 'our last name' or is your delay more than being too busy? Do you not want to change your name?" Croy's eyebrows pull together at the center, as he questions my motives. "I offered to change *mine* if you'd rather. Croy Belk does have a certain ring to it."

"No. I'll make an effort to get it done, as soon as Kelly leaves. Switching everything to Heather Jepsen will be my top priority. Then we'll have the baby's last name locked in." I take his hand and pull him toward me. We should probably continue this conversation in the car, but first I need to hug.

I swear, Croy has a real knack for getting my mind off track, while simultaneously setting things right.

During the drive, we continue to discuss potential names. Croy's top picks are Tinsley, Harlow, and Wren. All three names, while lovely, sound like characters from a vampire movie set in some fancy private school. I can't help but laugh, picturing a teenage Croy in a school uniform, tattoos and all. He'd be every girl's not-so-secret crush, kind of like he is now.

As for me, my top three names are Hayden, Blair, and Verlaine. I'm not sure why, but I enjoy a good unisex name. Maybe because 'Heather' is so girly, and I never quite felt like I could live up to the expectation. No matter which way we go, it's clear our daughter will be unique.

Fourteen

BACK AT THE CONDO, Kelly and Astrid have made themselves comfortable in our absence. Although, maybe a little too much for my liking. When Croy and I walk into the living room, I spot the pair of them on the back patio, laughing, and sharing a bottle of wine I recognize.

"Well shit, they seem to be getting along." It's a bit unnerving to see my ex with another woman, even though we were only together for a minute. I keep saying I want him to meet someone, but I never intended to sit in the front row and watch it happen. Thankfully, he's not from around here, and most women aren't interested in long-distance relationships, so maybe it's nothing. We did sort of bail on them. Perhaps they're simply two people making the most of being stuck together, like talking to a stranger seated next to you on a long flight.

"Guess we'd better get out there and join them before I end up with a new brother." Croy laughs at his own joke and takes my hand.

"That's not funny." There's a feeling inside of me, scraping below the surface, I'm not ready to acknowledge. At first, I thought it was fear. My relationship with Kelly, while confusing at times, is essential. Sure, we started as acquaintances and sexual partners, but over the last few months, our relationship has become so much more. Losing him as a friend would be detrimental.

At the sight of Kelly with someone else, my anxiety begins to twist and turn itself into jealousy. Which is stupid, I know. Losing him was only a matter of time, especially after the conversation Croy and I had in the driveway. I knew I couldn't keep him forever, but that doesn't mean I've mentally prepared myself for things to change. Doesn't Kelly know how much I need him? Doesn't he care?

I wish I could stop time so I could talk to him alone, to find out where we stand. "Babe, do you think you could take your sister for a walk? Show her the pool or the beach or something. But make sure Kelly's not invited."

On the patio, Croy tries to get Astrid to join him for a walk, but she's not having it. According to her, she came out here to spend time with me and that is exactly what she's going to do. The second I move a chair and make myself comfortable, she bombards me with questions and requests for stories, and I do my best to answer. Occasionally, Croy or Kelly jump in, adding color where it's missing and filling in the blanks that still plague my memory.

When she asks about *Matt* and how we met, he's quick to jump in. Kelly omits any mention of us having a fling or the subsequent breakdown of our relationship, and according to him, we're friends who used to work together. Period. Not best friends who talk every day and certainly not anyone he knows intimately. Funny, that's not what it felt like a few hours ago on the couch, but fine. As heartbreaking as his recollection is, I'm happy to go along with his version of events, since the alternative paints me in a bad light.

"Heather, I'll be brutally honest, I'm shocked my brother *allows* this friendship to exist. He must genuinely trust you." Astrid's nonchalant statement sends my mind reeling.

What is she talking about? Does she know more about me

than she's letting on? Kelly has been going out of his way to hide the fact we hooked up, so I doubt he mentioned it before we got here, and I've never known Croy to be the jealous type. He hates Kelly, and yet he accommodates my unusual friendship without complaint, for the most part. In fact, Croy's easygoing about pretty much everything, which is one of the reasons we work so well together. He likes everything to be calm, and has a way of getting me to match his energy. Why would my friendship with Kelly be shocking?

"I don't know what you mean by that. Were his previous girl-friends not allowed to have friends?" How much am I willing to believe, and does her answer even matter? Let's say Croy was the jealous type in the past. That doesn't have any bearing on the person he is today. After all, people grow, they change with age and experience. I'm nothing like the person I used to be ten years ago and I wouldn't appreciate the character flaws I maintained a decade ago being held against me today.

Before Astrid can respond, Croy wedges himself into the conversation. "Do *not* paint me to be some controlling asshole, especially when you're talking to my wife. You know damn well what was going on back then, and I *allowed* plenty. It's not my fault you chose the wrong side. How long was I supposed to go to work and not care that my girlfriend was off vacationing on a beach somewhere with another guy?" It's clear his sister's comment struck a chord he didn't want played.

I place my hand on his leg in hopes of redirecting his atten-tion. "The only man I want to be vacationing on the beach with is you."

Croy lifts my hand to his lips and places a kiss against my skin. "Let's go for a walk." I can see he needs a moment away, and I'm happy to accommodate his request.

Maybe it's because we both move quickly, but when he takes my hand again, I'm zapped by static electricity.

"Goddamnit babe! I swear, you need to get your wiring checked out." I feel the current running the length of my arm, and I'm reminded of the first time it happened. We were in the ambulance together and I touched his arm so he wouldn't feel alone. Then again in the hospital when I cried my eyes out as he was sleeping, confessing my guilt and questioning his reasons for saving me. He's constantly zapping me with static electricity and I swear, one of these days, he's going to give me a heart attack.

"I thought you were the one shocking me. I even thought about hiding dryer sheets in your pockets." Croy regains his playful nature, and the previous tension of the moment is released.

"Are you alright here without us? I feel like I'm making a terrible first impression." I feel bad for leaving, but neither of them seems to mind.

Kelly turns his face towards the lake, still ignoring me. Maybe he's thinking about the same things I am. A few hours ago, we were snuggled next to each other at the beach downtown, sitting on a fallen tree, drinking coffee, looking out at the lake, and talking about all the things that could've been. And now, we're nothing more than two people who used to work together.

"Are you kidding me? I'm having a great time. Who could be mad at this view, or the company?" Astrid smiles and waves us away. "We'll be fine. Go have more of your secret conversations."

Croy and I are through the condo and out the door, with barely enough time for me to stop and slip on my sandals. He seems to require distance from the situation. I get it, siblings can be annoying because they know exactly which buttons to push, and no one enjoys that. Personally, I thought her comment was tame, but this isn't about what I think, it's about how Croy feels.

Once we make it to the beach, he turns around and bear-hugs me. I get the feeling, all those emotions he keeps below the surface are threatening to spill out on the sand, and I'm not sure if I'm supposed to hold him together, or catch him when he falls.

"I need to be alone with you. Is that alright?" After I nod in agreement, we take a seat on two large rocks, facing one another. This is one of my favorite places to sit when we come here together, so I'm glad he chose this spot.

"Can I say one thing?" It's important that he hears me, so I make sure to establish a physical connection first, leaning forward to place my hand atop his leg. "I'm sorry your ex didn't appreciate what she had. That was a flaw in her character, not yours. She might not have known what kind of man you are, but I do. I'm not sure what point your sister was trying to make, but no one could change my opinion of you."

Croy lifts my hand and gently pulls me forward until our lips meet in the middle. The combination of his touch and his kiss makes my body tingle. I try to control my physical reaction, but my brain is swirling in desire. I need to get a grip. This is not the right time or place for these feelings. If I want to be an active listener and a better wife, I need to focus, and not allow my mind to venture off into some sexual fantasy land.

"I know that, love. Astrid just hit a nerve that's still pretty raw after the fight with my parents. It's hard to explain, and it might sound stupid, but bear with me for a moment." Croy releases my hand, stands, and begins to pace back and forth in front of me. He's beginning to wear a path into the sand as he starts his story.

"When I was around nine, my cousin Emma and I were playing in the backyard. She was pretty much my best friend back then because she lived next door and we were the same age, and truth be told she was a bit of a tomboy. She'd throw handfuls of mud at my head and chase me around with worms trying to taunt me into eating one. Anyways, one day, we were messing around and she shoved me in the back. I went flying face-first into the grass and busted my lip open. She apologized and tried to help me stop the bleeding, but I was upset and embarrassed. I let my anger determine my reaction and I shoved her. Not hard enough to make her fall or anything, but still…

My dad was watching us out the window and saw what I

did. He came storming out of the house, screaming at me, and I'll never forget what he said. 'Does that make you feel good about yourself, hitting a girl? Are you going to be the type of guy who beats his wife?' It might seem like such a small thing, but those two sentences destroyed me.

By the time I was thirteen, I was taller than my dad, and like most teenagers, I was angry at the world for one reason or another. But unlike other teens, I wasn't allowed to be mad or upset or disappointed. I wasn't allowed to feel anything, because I was bigger than the other kids, and guys who can't control their emotions grow up to beat their wives.

My dad constantly reminded me that I had to keep my emotions in check because I could hurt someone.

In high school, I found an outlet for some of those teenage emotions by playing football and working out, but the damage was already done." Croy continues to pace and I continue to listen. This is the first time I've heard any of this from him, and it's both fascinating and sad.

"I mean, it wasn't something he said one or two times, it was a sentiment he repeated over and over again. That I could *hurt* someone if I felt emotions. What do you think that does to a person? Because you know what, I can tell you. I buried my feelings and tried to never react, which resulted in people calling me an unemotional robot.

My girlfriends would say I was weak because I didn't want to argue with them. They said I didn't care enough to fight. Every girl I dated ended up cheating on me, but I wasn't allowed to get upset or angry about it. Nope, I had to take it on the chin and keep my mouth shut. So, that's what I did. I let my ex-girlfriends treat me like shit until they broke things off and moved on.

Everyone thinks because you're this big guy you can't be hurt, but I'm a just regular person underneath all of that.

When I was nineteen, I came home from college over the break and wound up getting into an argument with my parents. My mom freaked out and called the cops on me. That was the first time I got put in handcuffs and the last time I slept under their roof. The only reason I visit for holidays is to see my sister." Croy stops walking and sits on the rock in front of me.

I don't know what to say, but I can't sit still while he's hurting. Sliding myself down the smooth side of the rock, I stand in front of him, looping my arms around his waist. As I press my cheek to his chest, his arms come around me, pulling me in. I wish I knew what to do or say to absorb all of these years of hurt. I'm so used to feeling pain, I'm almost numb to it. Being able to endure this discomfort and suffer in his place, would be a pleasure.

"So, I started working out more and getting tattoos. I figured, if everyone was going to treat me like the bad guy, then I might as well give them something to be afraid of. But that stuff was on the outside, which is all most people see.

It took twenty-nine years for someone to come along and look past all of that. You saw a huge tattooed guy in prison scrubs, covered in blood, who had been dragged out of the middle of a melee, and said, 'He seems like a nice guy. Let me sneak into his hospital room and have a little cry on his arm while unburdening my soul.' And from that point on, I knew no matter where you went, I would follow."

The memory of that time frame never ceases to bring tears to my eyes. We had such different vantage points for our first few introductions. "No, babe. I took one look at the flawless man who saved my life, who was everything I had ever dreamt of, and more, and I thought, *even if it takes me the rest of my life, I will prove to him that I'm worth holding onto.* And then I broke down and cried all over your arm because I thought you were unconscious, and because I realized I would never be good enough or pretty enough for you to love me as much as I knew I was going to love you."

Croy looks at me and rolls his eyes while letting out an exasperated huff. "I wish you didn't see yourself that way, especially because you're stunning and amazing and by far the best thing that's ever happened to me. Not good enough or pretty enough? I don't even understand how you can think that. I guarantee Kelly over there, has never dated an unattractive girl in his life. The guy's as shallow as a kiddie pool, and he's obsessed with you." Croy's joke, while ridiculous, does ease the gravity of our shared mood. I can't help but laugh and it feels good when he joins me.

"I don't think he's obsessed with me anymore. Not after hearing the news about us having a kid together. Judging by his reaction, I might even go so far as to say he hates me, but I don't care about any of that. Right now, all I care about is you, and us, and our life together." I give Croy a final squeeze before allowing my arms to fall away.

"That being said, we should probably think about getting back, before those two have sex in our bed." As my small laugh evaporates, it leaves behind a slight tightening in my chest. Initially, I was joking, but now that the words have escaped my mouth, my brain begins to panic. I do a quick scan of the building, locating the patio where Astrid and Kelly remain. They're still sitting together, talking, right where we left them.

On the short walk home, I think about everything Croy said on the beach and I worry he's giving me too much credit. Aren't I as guilty as the others? Don't I treat him like some big, strong unemotional robot? Haven't I contributed to his pain by not giving him the space to express how he feels?

The one time he got angry, I recoiled in fear out of habit, but that was a lingering response from my past, left there by men who had no trouble showing their disdain for me. I remember how hurt Croy was by my reaction. He thought I was scared of him and maybe for a second I was, but I've met guys who beat their wives, in fact, one of them tried to kill me, and that's not Croy.

My husband may be a beast, but he's not a villain.

Fifteen

AS SOON AS we get back to the condo, I get started on dinner. Croy offered to order food, but I'm certain I can throw together something equally delicious and just as quick as take-out. I'm embarrassed to admit, but I've been a terrible host all afternoon, and this might be my last chance to sway Astrid's first impression. Luckily, I'm a wiz in the kitchen, which is one of my few redeeming qualities.

I have everything I need to make homemade guacamole and chicken quesadillas. Add to that a pouch of 90 second spanish rice, some veggies, sour cream, and a can of refried black beans, and we have ourselves a dinner.

Certainly not my finest culinary venture, but if Astrid is anything like her brother, she'll appreciate the effort. As for Kelly, he lives on a steady diet of jail food, frozen pizza, and takeout, so I know he'll eat pretty much anything.

During dinner, we take turns starting random conversations, each one trailing off from the last, and by the end of the meal, we've joked around so much I get a cramp in my side and my facial muscles get sore from smiling. I hold up my hand and beg, "Please stop, it hurts. I can't take anymore." Which further encourages everyone to crack up laughing, tightening the stitch in my side.

As Croy starts cleaning the kitchen, Astrid begins saying her goodbyes. "Heather, it was so lovely to meet you. Call or text me anytime. Then we can talk without my brother's commentary. I want to make plans to come out again, especially once the new house is finished. After my niece comes, we'll leave her home with Dad, and you and I can have a girl's night out."

Kelly mentions he's leaving as well. Something about not wanting to overstay his welcome and needing to give us our privacy. Bullshit lies that make for a convenient exit. He's been avoiding me since 3:05 and it has nothing to do with wearing out his welcome on the couch. I had hoped he would stay and we'd get an opportunity to talk, but I can see that isn't going to happen, and I don't want to be too transparent in front of Astrid.

We walk with them to the parking lot, share a hug and a pair of goodbyes, and then head back inside to enjoy our now quiet living space. I help finish the kitchen cleaning so we can sit together on the couch.

"So, there's a thing I want to mention, in order to get it off my chest, you know, but feel free to take what I say and throw it away afterward, okay?" My stomach hurts thinking about having this conversation, but maybe I should swallow my feelings rather than let them out.

"You can talk to me about anything. I don't need a disclaimer. If there's something on your mind, I'd like to know." Croy's fingers lace into mine, signaling his full intent to listen.

"Well, I'm fairly confident you love me, and I try my best to believe you when you say you're attracted to me..." I allow my statement to trail off with a shaky voice, and I feel sick. "But there's this internal dialog playing on repeat in my head that tries to convince me otherwise. You know one of my biggest insecurities is feeling like I'm a secret. Like I'm not good enough to be claimed, or I'm an embarrassment to be seen with."

Croy's expression is a mix of confusion and hurt. "I don't

understand. Are you talking about the comment I made on the beach, about Kelly not dating unattractive girls? Babe, I didn't mean to imply anything negatively, and I'm so sorry if it came across that way. Or am I the one making you feel that way? Like I'm embarrassed to claim you?"

I should stop, and yet I continue. "Look, I understand why we didn't invite people to the wedding and why we haven't told people about the baby. I know, I was in on all of those conversations and it was a decision we made together. I'm not blaming you or anything. You're amazing and I love you. But I want to be good enough for you. That's all. I want you to be proud to call me your wife. And it makes me sad to see you out there killin' it, while I'm chillin' over here in the leach bed." I don't want to cry, and I'm not looking for pity, but the tears come and I despise their presence.

Croy lets out a laugh but quickly reins in his response. "Babe, you know a leach bed isn't a tiny bed where a leach sleeps, right?"

"Yes, I know that. It was the only 'leach' thing I could think of, but that's beside the point." Now I'm picturing a fat little leach tucked into bed for the night, with its little leach head on a tiny leach pillow. I rub my face with my hands, trying to regain my composure even though laughter makes the heavy conversations feel less weighted.

"You're the main reason I'm able to leave the house every morning and give work my undivided focus. I'm only 'killin' it' because you're such an incredible wife. You take care of everything here and at the other house. If you think I could have built this life without you, you're wrong. Since the wedding, I've noticed something upsetting you, but I never put two and two together. You've mentioned all of this before, about the guys in your past making you feel like an option for their convenience, and I should have considered your words more carefully. I'm sorry. I should have asked you what was wrong instead of assuming. I thought you regretted getting married to me, and I didn't want to say anything because I was afraid you would ask for a divorce."

"If we ever get divorced it'll be because you don't want me, not the other way around. Saying *yes* to a lifetime with you was the easiest question I've ever had to answer, and I have no regrets about that." Wherever he is, that's where I want to be.

"Good, so we're in full agreement. We're never getting divorced! I'm glad that's settled." He sounds relieved, as if our failed marriage was a genuine concern.

The more we talk, the more I'm starting to realize I need to take accountability for the parts I've played. If I want to spend more time with my husband and feel less like a secret, then I need to make an effort to leave the condo with him. It's not like he doesn't ask.

Neither of us is necessarily the problem, or maybe I am, who knows? Either way, we both have an opportunity to be the solution.

Sixteen

WHEN BOTH ALARMS begin buzzing and singing, it's only 5:00 am. Croy is quick to silence his phone, but mine continues to sound. I'm exhausted from yesterday, so it takes my body a few extra seconds to react. Still in the fog of sleep, I almost forget my plan to be the change I want to see by putting forth an honest effort.

"Babe, why is your phone so loud? That ringer about gave me a damn heart attack. I thought it was the smoke detector going off." Croy pulls a sleeveless t-shirt on after tightening the drawstring of his shorts. If I don't get moving quickly, I'll be walking to the gym alone.

"I didn't want to miss working out with you. Can't have this fit, gorgeous husband, and be some fat, dumpy wife." I know how much he hates when I disparage myself and my appearance, but that's how I feel most of the time.

"You're not fat! And I don't want to hear those words come out of your mouth again. If anything, I think you're thinner now than when we met, and I swear to you, if I find out you're starving yourself and our daughter because you're worried about losing me, or some other craziness, I will take you to the hospital and have them stick a feeding tube in you. I'm not kidding. So, you had better be joking around." His tone is stern, and I know he's serious.

"Save all that anger for the gym, mister. I know you worry but I promise I'm not starving myself and the morning sickness stage has officially passed. Turns out cooking at home is healthier than jail food and I've lost some weight. It's not a big deal. Everything with the baby is fine and I'm fine. I had an appointment last week, and we're good." I laid out my clothes last night before bed since I had a feeling it might be a slow start. Thankfully, this conversation has bought me enough time to catch up and get ready to go.

"When's your next appointment? Maybe your doctor can alleviate some of my concerns, so I don't have to get mad over nothing. Plus, I haven't been to an ultrasound in months, and the last time I saw her, she was an adorable little speck." Croy takes my hand and kisses my forehead. "I apologize for raising my voice."

"If you don't trust me, you can go with me to the next appointment. I'll check my calendar and let you know when it is, okay? Now, let's get to the gym so I can show you up in front of your friends."

"Ha! If you wanted to show someone up, you needed to be there yesterday." Croy laughs, and I imagine he's remembering Kelly's attempts to keep up with his crew.

The walk to the gym is dark and quiet, setting my warning senses to alert. Too many dreams have left me weary, even though the scariest guy in a hundred-mile radius is most likely the one holding my hand. In hindsight, sometimes I wonder if I should have declined to watch the security footage from the jail. Maybe ignorance could have preserved my sense of safety. Then again, seeing Croy batter the first three assholes who hoped to kill me was quite the aphrodisiac.

Brian and Nate are already mid-workout when we arrive, and per usual, Croy steers me away from the weights. He never allows me to lift anything heavier than a book, so I get on the rowing machine and begin to pull. But even *that* turns out to be too much for the little pregnant wife, and he walks over to slide the resistance from 10 to 2. I swear, if I didn't know he meant well, I might assume he was controlling. But I do know him, and he's told me more than once he's yet to figure out how to protect me from myself, so it isn't a need to control that drives his actions, it's concern.

As I'm rowing, my mind has plenty of opportunity to wander, and more than enough material to use. Brian and Nate are relatively attractive guys, but both are happily married to women I've become friendly with. So I notice them, but not really.

Croy on the other hand, I very much notice. He's organized a circuit, and my eyes follow him from one exercise to the next. Each machine or free weight causes a different muscle group to flex, and before long he's glistening with a layer of sweat.

I'm adrift mid-fantasy when I hear him next to me. "Babe, how the hell are you doing that?" The proximity of his voice snaps my mind back to the present.

"Huh? What do you mean?" For a moment I'm afraid I might have said something while daydreaming.

"You've been on that machine since we got here, almost an hour ago. I can't do ten minutes on that thing without feeling like I might die." Croy looks at the timer on the machine. "It's been 57 minutes. I think you've sufficiently shown me up for today."

"We both know you suck at cardio. And it's not all that impressive since someone set the machine at a two." My noncha-lant tone, as I deliver the information, causes his mouth to drop open. "It's all about pacing yourself. I normally do between thirty minutes to an hour on the rower."

"Normally when? How did I not know this?" Croy offers me his hand and helps me back to my feet. Seems like our workout time has concluded since he still has to shower and eat before leaving for work.

"You're so restrictive when we work out together, so I sneak back while you're at work. And that's what happens when you marry someone after only knowing them for three months. Lots to learn." It's silly to admit, but I've been too intimidated to work out the way I'm used to, while he's here. He's so good at everything, and I'm a novice, at best. Usually, I walk here after we talk at lunch and work out with all the retired folks. The 80+ crowd is a little more my speed.

"Oh, really? Well, I hope you know that's going to be a conversation." He shakes his head and I nod in response.

As soon as I open the door and step outside, the cold air smacks me in the face and a shiver runs the length of my spine. So much for the indian summer we've been having. The lake breeze has a bite, and I swear, it feels like it's dropped ten degrees since we walked over an hour ago.

Croy pulls off his hoodie and slides it on over my head before pulling me into a hug. The cotton sweatshirt is the same temperature as his body and smells like him. I love that he still wears the hoodie I gave him in the hospital. It will forever make me think of our first date, when he asked me to join him for dinner.

"Aren't you going to be cold?" I already know what he's going to say, but I ask the question anyway. Croy values my needs over his own, one hundred percent of the time, especially since finding out I was pregnant. His reaction to that specific news has been a lot different than my own. I've been in a near constant state of panic since seeing a plus sign on the at-home test, while he's drifting away on cloud nine.

There's a small part of me that wants to voice my many concerns about this impending motherhood, but I can't. Don't get me wrong. I love my husband. He's tolerant and understanding and kind. I trust him with my secrets and my life, but there have been times when my honesty has taken a toll on him. For the most part, I try to be forthcoming, even though it might not seem that way as of late, with so many secrets bubbling to the surface.

Croy looks at me and laughs, tossing his arm over my shoulder to further protect me from the crisp fall breeze. "I'll be fine. It's not that cold. Plus, you're the one that matters. I would do anything for you. You know that. I would die protecting you, if the occasion should ever present itself, again."

His statement stops me dead in my tracks. "Don't say that. I can't forgive you for putting yourself in harm's way the first time. If you die, I die. So, you will have accomplished nothing. Plus, that doesn't even make sense. Out of the two of us, you're far more important. I'll never be able to provide a life for our daughter like you can. So, if it's ever a choice between the two of us, it has to be you who stays. I'm expendable."

"If you're trying to hurt me, I'd rather you punch me in the face or kick me in the balls, instead of verbally stabbing me in the chest. The last thing I want to think about all day, while I'm stuck at work, is you sacrificing yourself for me because you think you're *expendable*. I can't do it, babe. I can't. If I start thinking about something happening to you, I'll fall apart. You know you're my weakness, and my strength." Croy brings both arms around me and kisses the top of my head.

I've grown to understand the deeper meaning of this embrace. So often, people have deceived me with their words, and had I been paying attention to their actions, I might not have been led astray. Croy is unlike anyone I've dealt with in the past. His words and actions consistently align, he seems to have my best interest at heart, and even in silence, he reassures me. But his touch is also a reminder that some things are too much to handle, even for Croy Jepsen.

I accept his hand when it's offered, and we speed walk back to the condo. Thankfully, the heat has kicked on, and it's warmer inside than it was out.

Croy gets in the shower and I grab my phone, making my way to the couch. I've yet to hear from Kelly, and his absence is weighing on me. Now that I'm finally ready to bare my soul and share the truth, he's stepped away. My last message is sitting there, seen, and yet neglected. I read it over before crafting a new message.

> : I appreciate you for coming here to check on me. You have no idea how much I needed that visit. I'm glad we had the chance to get lunch together and that you were able to see the new house, but I wish we could've had more time alone. There were things I wanted to say, in person, and I missed my opportunity. Let me know when you make it home, otherwise you know I'll worry. I miss you already.

> : Please talk to me. You can yell at me if you want. I deserve it. I'm sorry I didn't tell you about being pregnant. I wanted to. I should have. I hate when you're mad at me. Kelly, please don't disappear. I need you.

Yet again, my text is delivered and read, but I fail to warrant a response. I suppose that's my answer. Looks like Croy is finally getting his wish, and there's no more Matt Kelly in our lives.

The realization makes my throat burn all the way to my stomach, like I've swallowed hot coals. Probably acid reflux from the stress, or an ulcer. Croy said I was playing with fire, trying to stay friends with Kelly, and I spent so much time trying to convince him otherwise. But now that I'm eating my words they're red-hot and agonizing.

When Croy leaves for work, I'll be alone. Truly alone. Alone with my regrets. Alone with my nightmares. Alone with all my self-doubt and my racing thoughts. Alone with my concerns and my loathing. Alone, without a friend in the world. It'll only be me, and my failure.

I can feel myself falling into a death spiral of depression but Croy is out of the shower so I do my best to go through the usual motions.

"Hey, I have something for you." I send the playlist I made

last night to his phone. "You can listen to it on the way into work, and think of me."

"All I do is think about you, my love, but I enjoy having a custom soundtrack." As Croy kisses me goodbye at the door, he pauses to look deeper. He knows something is wrong. I didn't hide it well enough. But there's no time for discussion. He leaves me with one final kiss and a promise.

"I've loved you since before I met you, and nothing could change my feelings for you."

Seventeen

I GRAB my earbuds from the table by the door and push them into my ears. If I time it right, it'll almost be like Croy and I are listening to our latest playlist together. Each one of these songs reminds me of a moment in our relationship. The time he saved me. The first time I had to say goodbye. The exact second I let myself fall in love. Being away on my birthday. When I thought I might lose him. The day we got married. Finding out I was pregnant. Waking up alone. Being the reason his parents fought with him. Knowing I couldn't live without him.

> Croy: Why would you do that to me? My eyes are red from crying for the last 25 minutes straight, and now I have to go into work and tell everyone my dog died or something. That was the saddest playlist I've ever heard. I mean, message received. Goddamn! Are you trying to kill me?

Something about my husband's over dramatic reaction makes me chuckle, even though I should probably feel bad.

: Well shit, I was feeling a little emotional when I
made the list but I didn't think it was that sad.
LoL. I wasn't trying to push you off a cliff or
anything. My bad. I thought it would be sweet. I
was thinking about how we used to stay awake
all night, listening to music together.

Croy: It was a very sweet and meaningful
gesture. One I greatly appreciate. I just wasn't
prepared for that level of emotion to be
dropped in my lap at 6:30 in the morning. Now
that I know what's on it, I'll listen to it again on
the drive home and absorb what's there.
Maybe I can make you a sappy playlist while
I'm stuck in my afternoon meeting.

: Sounds good. Sorry I made you cry, tough
guy. I think I might make the crew lunch and
head to the house in a few hours. The
countertops and island are getting installed
today and I want to sneak a peek. There isn't a
whole lot left. Might see if I can get a move-in
date confirmed. Fingers Crossed!

Croy: Be careful while you're there. It is still a
construction site. Call me at lunch. I want to
hear what they have to say. And babe, I'm sorry
I gave you a hard time about your playlist. It
really was good. A little more heartbreaking
than I was expecting, but if that's how you've
been feeling, I need to acknowledge that. I love
you. I can't wait to come home and see you.

Croy walking through the front door is the best part of my
day, even though he doesn't stick around.

: Don't you have boxing or some shit tonight?

Croy: Nope. I told the guys I needed to cut back. I'm sorting out my priorities and making sure it's clear you're at the top of the list. No more classes, and no more gym on the weekends or in the evenings. I assumed you heard me talking about it with the guys this morning.

: I was so distracted by how sexy you looked that my mind was lost in full-blown sexual fantasy mode. And let me state for the record, you were fantastic. LoL.

I bite my lip, recalling a few of the spicier moments.

Croy: Why don't you tell me these things when I'm home?

: Because we never have the time to act on it.

Croy: Wonderful. Now I'm sad and horny. Hahaha. You got me all over the place this morning. What should I do with you?

: Hopefully, anything you want.

I'm determined to keep my mind busy and refuse to obsessively check my phone every five seconds, looking for a text from Kelly. In the kitchen, I begin collecting the ingredients for lunch. Today I'm fixing lasagna rolls and garlic bread, which is pretty straight forward. I wish I had chosen something more complex because it doesn't take me long to get everything together and into the oven. While that's cooking, I make a list of all the places I need to call and online sites I have to visit in order to change my last name. Croy acts like it's all easy peasy lemon squeezy, but it's a little more complicated than that.

After the food comes out of the oven, I take a shower and begrudgingly dress myself in real clothes. The air outside is getting colder by the minute, so I make sure to select an outfit with several layers. I catch sight of myself in the mirror and smile in recognition of a job well done.

I've managed to get through the last couple of hours without looking at my phone.

Now all I have to do is locate the keys so I can get my marriage license out of the safe and then I'll be ready to venture into the next part of my day. Croy insists on keeping certain documents in the locked metal box so they're protected from fire, on the off chance the building burns to the ground. As if we couldn't get another copy. Though, I suppose this one has senti-mental value. In addition to the marriage license, the safe also contains our passports, birth certificates, social security cards, some random paperwork in a sealed envelope, a stack of photos, quite a bit of cash, a box of bullets, and a handgun. If we ever had to leave town in a hurry, I imagine this is what we're packing.

I wasn't keen on the idea of having a gun in the house, but after several debates, I let him keep it. Croy thinks my concern is for our child, that she might accidentally find it someday, and while that is a legitimate fear of mine, that's not why I need him to get rid of it. The real danger is that I'll be the one to go looking for it when I'm not in control of my decision-making, and the other Heather who's too excluded to continue will do something irreversible.

I take my passport, birth certificate, and social security card, in addition to the marriage license, and set them on the floor beside me. I'm sure I'll need some combination of these at some point during the name change process so it's best to have them all at the ready.

For one brief moment, I allow my mind to wander. I think about all the things I would write in my final letter as the tip of each finger brushes across the cold metal of Croy's handgun. Then I close the safe, lock it up tight, and proceed with my day.

As a teenager, I was frequently consumed by thoughts of

suicide. I would obsessively think through and plan every detail, write letters, and imagine the after-effects. In the end, it wasn't the idea of death that stopped me, it was the mess left behind. I hated the thought of traumatizing whoever was unlucky enough to find me. That part of my escape never felt fair.

Now that I'm older, things have changed. The thoughts still come, but I'm able to process them faster and tuck them away. Depression is unrelenting, but I've found ways to cope. Until recently, I was doing alright. My job at the jail had offered me a much-needed sense of purpose and I felt like I'd found my place. But, fate had other plans and most days I feel like I'm still falling. I'm not sure if it's the hormones or what, but pregnancy is tripping me up.

On paper, my life is amazing. I have everything I could have ever dreamt of and more, and yet I'm incapable of being happy. Logically, I know what I should feel, but I can't seem to get there. Sexual desire has become the closest thing I have to a positive human emotion, so thankfully I've got that in spades.

When everything I need is packed and ready to go, I'm out the door. My first stop is the house. I drop off lunch for the guys and ask about a possible move-in date. Everything's coming together and what they have done inside looks incredible. I love how bright the house feels, with all of its natural lighting. As I walk around, I try to picture our furniture in each space.

We've bought exactly nothing for the baby's room. Croy keeps assuring me we'll have plenty of time to get it set up before she arrives, but I'm beginning to have my doubts. He keeps saying it's silly to buy stuff only to pack it into boxes, so I've refrained, but now that the move-in date is approaching, I'm starting to get the itch to go shopping. He might need to increase the credit limit because my patience is going to cost him.

When the text alert on my phone goes off, it makes my heart beat against my ribs.

Croy: Would you like to join me for lunch?

Not who I was expecting to hear from, but I'm certainly not disappointed.

> : I'm at the house dropping off food, but I was going to head that way after. I need to stop at the Social Security office and the BMV, but I can do that after I see you. Where should we meet?

Croy: Do my girls feel up to thai food, or does that make the little one angry? I can't remember.

> : Thai sounds good. It was the italian restaurant we went to that didn't agree with me. Remember? That place in Cleveland. You had to stop like three times so I could puke on the side of the road. Hahaha. Memories.

Croy: Oh my god, that's right. I kept trying to convince you to throw up on my floor mats because I was afraid you were going to get hit by a semi-truck. If that's not love, I don't know what is.

Considering Croy's SUV probably cost more than every car I've ever owned combined, I'd say his offer was most definitely a symbol of his love.

> : Well, we have a few months left, so it could still happen. But enough about that. I need to finish here and then I'll meet you at the restaurant.

Croy: Can't wait to see you. Love you.

Eighteen

WHEN I WAS A TEENAGER, I moved to California for a couple of months to stay with family members I had previously never met. I left a few weeks after my high school graduation with a train ticket, a bit of cash, and a duffle bag full of clothes. After three long days on the train with no shower and very little food, I arrived at my destination. I remember it was my eighteenth birthday, and my uncle had a chocolate cake in his hands when he picked me up from the station. If he didn't look so much like my dad, I would have never recognized him.

There I was, an overweight teenage girl from a small town in Ohio, off to explore the big city on her own. My aunt worked in San Francisco at the time so I could hitch a ride into the city if I woke up early enough. Otherwise, I could take the tram downtown. California felt like a different world.

During the two months I stayed with my aunt and uncle, I developed a fondness and appreciation for several "new" things. The first was avocados. It's funny to admit this now, but prior to visiting the West Coast, I had never even seen an avocado, let alone tasted one. Now, a decade later, I eat avocado on toast with cheddar cheese and two fried egg whites nearly every day. It's my go-to meal when I'm cooking for myself.

The second thing I fell in love with during my time in California was art museums. Since that time, I've visited dozens of museums within the States and in other countries. It can be easy to forget the world is a big place, especially if you've never left home. Something about being in a museum, with its high ceilings and vast echoing chambers, each filled with culture and visual stimulation, makes you feel small, yet significant. A feeling that's become all too familiar.

The next new thing was initially a harder pill to swallow. It happened when my aunt offered to take me to a spa. As I was only eighteen, I had never experienced anything close to what this spa had to offer, so my level of excitement was high. She told me there would be mud baths, a sauna, and massages, among other things, and this was sure to be the highlight of my trip.

Words fail me when trying to adequately describe the location. It was truly remarkable. When I say spa, I'm not talking about your average, run-of-the-mill, Ohio strip mall massage studios. This place was like a palace.

As we checked in at the front desk, we were handed a crisp white sheet and directed to the locker room. Up until this point, my only locker room experience was getting changed before and after gym class, where girls learn how to get dressed and undressed while never removing their shirts. It's a real art form.

But anyway, this California spa locker room was nothing like the ones back home. My aunt stripped down to nothing, without a care in the world, and casually draped the sheet over her shoulder. I, on the other hand, was terrified. Luckily, I had trained for such occasions. I wrapped the bed sheet around myself and undressed within the privacy it afforded me. I was ready for every experience this spa had to offer. Or so I thought.

We made our way from the locker room, down an elegant hallway, to a glass door labeled *Ladies. Ooooo, so fancy* I thought. This is where I would learn to love my third new thing. As the frosted glass door closed behind us, a clothed lady with an outstretched hand, was there to collect our sheets. Panic and shock, embarrassment and horror, shame and self-doubt threatened to light me up like a neon sign. Lacking options, I handed the lady my sheet and shot toward the nearest mud bath. Surely, I could hide there, right?

Wrong. I tried getting into the mud but it was too thick. My aunt took the bath next to me, lying atop the mud. I mimicked her action, figuring she knew better than I how to submerge one's self. That's when a lovely four-foot-tall, hundred-year-old lady came over to help me. Starting at my feet, she began scooping the mud with her hands and slowly covering my body. Eventually, she made it to my torso, but by then I was nearly half-dead from the overwhelming embarrassment of being naked in front of a room full of strangers. Once my chest and arms were covered, I could relax.

However, what goes in, must come out, including me, and it was time for me to endure the horror of having a little old lady wipe mud from my naked body with her bare hands. I wanted to die. From there it was into the showers, open for all to see. Then a short stroll to a mineral bath, before melting in the sauna. My lovely white bed sheet was nowhere to be seen.

Eventually, while soaking in the tub drinking cucumber water with fresh mint, I realized that no one was looking at me. Not one person had judged me with their eyes or criticized my bloated form. There were no disgusted faces or dismissive sound effects as I walked from station to station. No one was interested in negatively scrutinizing my body, so why was I so hell-bent on doing it to myself?

And there it was, the third new thing, a newfound level of acceptance for my naked form. Once I made it to my massage, I was putty in their hands.

I can't say I've often loved myself, but after that day, I stopped being disgusted, and that was truly a victory.

The fourth thing I came to love was wine. All it took was a day in Sonoma, hopping from winery to winery, and I was hooked. Which brings me to my fifth and final new thing. While in California, visiting my aunt, uncle, and cousin, the four of us would frequently go out for Thai food. One bite into my shrimp pad thai and I was obsessed. Never had I tasted something so complex. It was from that point forward I would open myself up to new flavors and new cultures.

Without that trip to California, I'm not sure who I would be, but she would most likely be someone who ate city chicken and mashed potatoes for dinner once a week and avoided mirrors after exiting the shower.

Nineteen

I MANAGE to pull into the restaurant parking lot with time to spare, and inside I find a table for two that's open along the wall. As I wait, I sit and study the menu before pulling out my phone. Still no messages from Kelly, but I pretend like it doesn't bother me. I scroll through my contacts and locate a name, stopping before I get to K.

: I'm glad we finally got to meet. Your brother talks about you all the time. All good things. And I wanted to thank you for making the trip out. I promise next time I'll be less nervous and more engaging. This is Heather, by the way.

Astrid: You're perfect. No worries. I fully expected you to be guarded after what happened with my parents, and I would have fully understood had you not spoken a word to me. But you were welcoming and polite and funny and can see why my brother gushes about you constantly.

: He does?

Astrid: He messaged me a day or two after he met you and told me he found the love of his life and that he was going to marry you. Then a few days later he called to tell me you guys got engaged and I swear I've never heard him more excited. I knew I was going to love you based on his stories, but then I saw photos of the two of you and that was it. I was sold. I could see how perfectly you fit together. It's like a modern-day fairy tale. That being said, I still think he's lying to me about how the two of you met.

: How did he say we met?

Astrid: In the hospital. He said he saw you walk past his room and knew you were the one, so he asked if you'd join him for dinner, and your first date was disgusting hospital food. According to him, you've been inseparable ever since.

: There's a little more to it than that, but for the most part, that's all true. Maybe, down the road, I can tell you the rest of the story.

Astrid: I knew he was hiding something. Promise you'll tell me someday. I'm dying to know.

: Let me talk to him about it, and then I'll let you know.

Astrid: I'm going get it out of one of you, eventually.

: Fair enough.

Astrid: Oh lord, you even sound like him. You two truly are a matched set.

There's a bell hanging above the door, and with each jingle, my head shoots up. The first three rings welcomed random patrons retrieving to-go orders. On the fourth jingle, Croy comes walking through the door and I feel the smile spread across my face. With each step he takes in my direction, the butterflies multiply.

He slides into the small booth, laying both arms across the top of the table in my direction. I bring my hands to meet his and allow our fingers to lace together. Croy does this every time we go out to eat, and we'll remain this way until the food comes. If, for some reason, I need to look at a menu, he's willing to release one hand back to me, but only one.

There's an immense level of comfort to be found within the confines of certainty. I know exactly what I'll get with him and I appreciate that.

Croy orders a diet coke, spring rolls, and pad thai, while I settle on ice water and chicken satay with an extra cucumber salad.

"Did you already eat?" His tone remains friendly, but his question is a clear sign of his dissatisfaction.

"No. Why do you ask?" I exhale deeply and force a smile.

"You know what I'm about to say. Chicken satay is not a meal, it's an appetizer. You don't eat enough. I'm willing to do anything at this point, up to and including begging. What is it going to take? Name it and it's yours. Seriously, I'll pay off your credit card if you eat half of my lunch. I'll buy you a new car if you promise to eat a real meal twice a day until the baby comes." Croy keeps our hands heaped together at the center of the table, like a ball of frustration.

"You don't have to do anything, and I don't want any more of your money being spent on me. I have an interview on Monday, so hopefully I can sort my shit out. I still feel bad enough about the phone." I attempt to free my hands, but he's expecting that.

"Wait, what? First off, I didn't even buy you a new phone, because you won't let me. I gave you my old one that was sitting in a drawer collecting dust, so stop feeling bad over nothing. Secondly, it is *my* job to take care of you financially, that's why I work so much. And third, what interview? This is news to me. Why am I only just now hearing about this?"

"I applied for a couple of random jobs the other day, and I received an email back this morning. This is me telling you." Ever since the *leach* comment, I've had my mind set on going back to work. My husband's reaction was one expected, so I neglected to mention anything sooner. Plus, I wasn't sure I would hear back from anyone about an interview, and I didn't want to generate a fuss over another hypothetical situation.

"So, what's the job?" Croy's hands slide up my arms as he leans across the table, moving closer to me.

There's already an intensity in his eyes, and I know my answer is going to send him over the top. I suck in a breath and steel my nerves. "The interview is for a position as a corrections officer… at the state prison in Grafton."

"Oh, hell no! Absolutely fucking not!"

"Babe, please." I don't wish to discount his feelings or reinforce the need for robotic reactions. I truly value his opinion, and I want him to open up, but I'm also not a fan of public scrutiny and I'm not looking to be part of a scene.

"You can call and cancel because you're not going." His words sound like the end of a conversation as if there is nothing left to discuss.

The waitress arrives with drinks, spring rolls, and my meal, but Croy still refuses to release me. She positions the plates and glasses around our outstretched arms and retreats to the kitchen.

"Babe, please let go and we can talk. I love you, but I need my hands back if you want me to eat." I smile, attempting to temper the growing tension.

"As soon as I get to my office, I'm going to call Oak Falls Correctional Facility and I'm going to ask Grant to send me the video from the night we met because evidently, you've forgotten what happened there." Croy unbuttons each sleeve of his dress shirt and cuffs them to his elbows. "Heather, please don't do this to me."

"I'm not doing anything to you. I'm getting a job so I can pay bills and contribute to the household. A lot of women have kids and careers. You can't keep me in a bubble, trying to protect me from the world. I'm not that fragile." I wish he would trust me on this, but he won't. "What happened last time isn't going to happen again."

"It's like you have zero regard for your personal safety, and you're trying to get yourself killed! Help me understand why you would put our daughter at risk over a paycheck when I make more than enough to support all of us. Why can't you let me take care of you? Christ! I love you so much, but this shit needs to stop. If you don't care enough about yourself, that sucks, but I can't keep fighting you on that. I'm asking you to care about me and that little girl. I mean it. If you love me at all, you will start eating, stop sneaking over to the gym while I'm at work, get your iron tested, talk to someone about your depression, cancel this interview, and let me pay your one stupid credit card bill!"

The waitress approaches with Croy's meal and we've yet to touch the starters or our drinks. I take a deep breath and blow it out, attempting to combat my urge to cry. This wasn't the lunch date with my husband I was hoping for, but I can appreciate where he's coming from. The nice thing about Croy is he doesn't get angry and rude, he speaks in an incredibly direct manner and then allows me the space to receive the information as I choose. I've had my share of exes who would start fights anywhere and everywhere, which was embarrassing. I hate any kind of public display that draws attention.

"I'll think about it, okay? But if I don't do everything on your list, does that mean I don't love you?" This conversation is giving me a lot to think about on my drive home. The BMV and social security office are going to have to wait for another day when I'm feeling less drained.

"I shouldn't have said it that way. That was more like my wish list of things that would make me happy. I would feel better and I would worry a lot less, but they're not requirements for me to feel loved by you."

"Eat more, no gym, iron test, unemployed, and be wholly dependent on you. Got it!" There's one I left out intentionally because it's not currently available for discussion.

"When you say it that way, it sounds like I'm being a controlling asshole, which is not at all what I want. So, do whatever makes you happy, and I'll keep my mouth shut. After the baby comes, we can work opposite shifts and never see each other." This is the last thing he says on the matter.

The rest of the meal is silent.

Once we're in the parking lot, Croy presses me against the side of my car and kisses me. He moves over to my neck, pausing to whisper in my ear. "I love you." His kiss feels like an apology and forgiveness all wrapped into one. It also feels like a trap.

He's being a tease and he knows it. This shit drives me wild. He'll turn me on and send me home to suffer. I have to wait four hours until I can have him, and it's cruel. Croy is planning to use sexual torture to break me and get his way because he knows I'll cave. He'll get everything on that list and then some. I can't say no to him as it is, and once I'm turned on it's impossible.

"I have to get back to work, but I plan on picking this up where we left off once I get home. Unless you don't want to." Croy releases me and opens my car door.

"I want to. Of course, I want to." He knows that.

One last kiss before we part ways. Of all his many kisses, this is by far my least favorite. I hate saying goodbye to him. It hurts my heart, every time.

Twenty

THERE ARE TWO PLACES, I've found, that offer the best opportunity for clear thought. Driving in the car alone and taking a shower. Oddly enough, those are also the best locations for singing, though I don't believe there's any correlation. This particular drive home affords me the time to think about my husband's happiness and his list of non-demands.

Is there anything I am unwilling to do for him? That's the question. I suppose I'd have some serious reservations about committing crimes or hurting others in his name unless it was an act of self-defense, but those aren't demands he would ever ask of me. Best to keep this in the realm of actual requests, since my drive is only twenty minutes.

I try to remember the list he gave me at lunch. Maybe I should have written it down. My brain is in a fog and, at the moment, I'm only recalling the first request. Eat more. On the surface, this is simple enough. Croy thinks being pregnant equates to eating for two, and according to him, I'm barely eating enough for one.

Like most issues, this one has several layers, with a chewy core soaked in self-hatred. Long story short, I was a skinny kid until puberty hit. No matter what I tried, diets, exercise, appetite suppressants, or playing sports, nothing stopped my weight from increasing. And then, the bullying started, and it was all downhill from there.

By twenty, I was away from my daily tormentors, but still couldn't locate the path to permanent weight loss. At that point, I was heavy enough to qualify for gastric bypass. I had nothing to lose, except the ever-increasing weight of my demons. So, two days before Thanksgiving, I went under the knife. After that, it was two weeks of sipping on chicken broth, followed by two weeks of pudding with protein powder mixed in. The first year I lost 110 lbs., which I've kept off to this day.

But everything comes at a cost. While I could eat more than what I do currently, I can't eat much more. Not all at one time. Bread, pasta, and meats usually collect in my esophagus. When I can no longer swallow my own spit, I know it's time to excuse myself from the table. There's a quick-release valve in the back of the throat, and if you wiggle it just right with your finger, every-thing will come spilling out. In my case, throwing up is not a weight loss tool, but an unfortunate side effect, and over the years I've gotten good at hiding it. Normally, I can keep food down for a little while, but it's painful. Let's just say, spaghetti and meatballs, an hour from home, was a pretty piss poor idea. Thankfully, the few times Croy has noticed, I've been able to blame my nausea on being pregnant. After all, everyone's heard of morning sickness.

Besides the physical limitations, there are several mental hurdles Croy is unknowingly requesting I jump over. My weight has become a memory marker. I can tell you exactly what I weighed on graduation from high school and college, the number on the scale associated with each guy I dated, and every pound Croy caught in his arms. Honestly, I messed up when I married a man who looked like he should be on the cover of Men's Health. He thinks I'm miserable now, wait until I start gaining weight and can't get it off. My anxiety will be through the roof.

Another unintended consequence of my weight loss surgery was that my stomach no longer absorbed iron from the food I ate. It took eight years, but when that one finally caught up with me it was like getting hit by a truck. My iron deficiency anemia is what caused me to blackout in the jail, and nearly cost me my life. It makes me lightheaded and eating a bag of ice a day resulted in a few broken molars that had to be repaired.

Which reminds me of another item from Croy's wish list. I need to get my iron level tested. That one is easy enough, although I already know it's low. With everything that's been going on at the house, I haven't had time to commit to sitting at the infusion center. Maybe after the move, I'll schedule something. I have a six-month appointment scheduled in a few weeks, and I can have them check it then. So, that'll be one item I can check off the list.

What else was there? Eat more, iron check, depression, and...

There are few things in life I hate more than talking to doctors about my depression, but for Croy, I'd be willing to mention it at my next visit, along with the iron.

As I'm driving, I pass a billboard for one of those chain fitness centers, which reminds me of another item on Croy's request list. No more sneaking off to the gym.

If I'm being honest, this issue goes hand in hand with the first item on his list. I haven't been eating as much and I've been working out more because I feel an intense pressure to look better. You would think, of all people, Croy would understand. He works out more than anyone I've ever met, and that includes my ex from two years ago, who was a personal trainer.

Eat more. Iron check. Mention depression. Stop working out.

Alright, fine. These four items are potentially doable if Croy's happiness is at stake. Maybe we could negotiate, and he'd let me work out in the mornings if I agreed to drink one of those peanut butter, banana, protein shakes he makes afterward.

Jesus. When did we become *that* couple? I can't help but laugh at the images running through my head. Our faces, superimposed on random muscular men and fit women, doing fitness challenges for likes on the internet.

I pull into the parking lot behind the condo and turn into my assigned spot. For whatever reason, I can't remember what else Croy asked me to do. It's like I took stupid pills this morning instead of my vitamins.

: Hey babe, what were the last two things on your list? Food. Gym. Iron. Depression... and then what? I can't remember what you said.

Croy: Don't go back to work, and let me take care of you.

Croy: Am I being a complete asshole not wanting you to work? I don't want our daughter raised by other people. I know having a job gives you a sense of purpose, but does it have to be working at the state prison? I can't keep getting arrested, and the last thing I need is another Kelly texting you. LoL.

There will never be another Kelly, and it seems I've lost the one I had. As for the job, I already forgot about the interview, so it must not have been that important to me.

Is there a cure for pregnancy brain? It seems to be getting worse, and by February, I'll be lucky if I can remember my name. As I get to the top of the stairs, I notice something placed in front of our door. It's a bouquet of brightly colored flowers, professionally arranged in a clear glass vase.

Who the hell are these from, and who are they meant for? Do women send flowers to men? I swear to god, if some random chick sent my husband flowers, I'm going to be the one getting sent to prison.

Poking out from between the flowers, is a small white envelope, held in place by a clear plastic floral pick. As I lift the vase from the welcome mat, I see the name written on the front of the envelope is my own.

Looks like Croy's off the hook.

The anticipation builds as I unlock the front door and get myself situated at the kitchen counter. Could these be from Kelly? Something along the lines of, "I'm sorry for leaving in a rush, can we talk?" He still hasn't responded to either of my messages, so that seems unlikely.

They could be from Astrid. That's possible. Maybe a *nice to meet you and welcome to the family* sort of gesture. She does seem like the type of person who would send flowers. I picked up a caring, thoughtful, friendly vibe from her, even if she did piss Croy off by mentioning the past.

Perhaps I have a secret admirer, someone who lives around here, who's seen me alone at the gym. Ha! Wouldn't that be something? I could imagine Croy's reaction. He would probably take them downstairs and set them gently on the sidewalk with a little folded note card that said FREE.

I take the bouquet with me as I move to the couch, setting the vase on the coffee table. There are sunflowers, orange and yellow roses, maroon daisies, something that looks like wheat, and beautiful rust-colored chrysanthemums. This is the perfect fall arrangement. Whoever sent these flowers had good taste, and didn't mind spending a hundred dollars.

All this speculation and they'll probably turn out to be from my mom.

Moment of truth, let's find out who thought enough to send me these, shall we? I pluck the small envelope from its bed of flowers and open the flap on the back. Removing the card slowly from its protective sleeve, letting the tension build. I flip the card and read its inscription.

My love for you grows deeper by the day.

And there's my answer. In twenty-nine years, there has only ever been one person who would say something like that to me. He's charming and thoughtful, loving and intelligent, handsome and kind, and without him, I would cease to exist.

> : Thank you for the flowers, they're gorgeous. I love them. And I love you.

> Croy: I love you too. I realized the other day I hadn't given you flowers since we got engaged. That bouquet jumped out at me straight away when I saw it. Like it was made for you. I'm glad it got delivered today. And I'm sorry about what I said during lunch. You don't need me telling you what to do or making you feel guilty. Can you forgive me?

> : There's nothing to forgive. You have my best interest at heart, I know that. I thought about what you said and I'll try to make the necessary adjustments. I want to make you happy, more than anything.

In the past, I frequently catered to the fleeting wants of boys who only cared for themselves. I poured the best parts of myself into those relationships because I thought that was the sacrifice love required. No one bothered with what I needed because they viewed me as temporary. I was never a priority, not even to myself, and that's a sad realization to come to terms with.

> Croy: Your happiness is my happiness.

Twenty-One

THE STEAM of the shower does nothing to remove the chill in my bones and for a moment, I think of Kelly. There's a fire that burns within him. The heat would roll off his body in waves like a furnace, and for a time that warmth was comforting. But when I considered what a future with him might look like, even in my mind, Kelly and I never made it past six months. I knew we'd burn hot and fast, and eventually, I would end up alone.

Friendship was never going to be enough for him, but I could no longer offer more. I suppose, missing Kelly is better than never having him at all, but it still hurts like hell.

Had I known yesterday's hug goodbye would be our last, I would've held on a little tighter for a little longer. I would have filled my lungs with him, one more time, and carried that part of him with me. Instead, I'm left with only my memories and my regrets.

When my head begins to spin, I know it's time to turn the water off and get out. I'm clean-shaven and ready for whatever the evening holds. Croy hinted at the possibility of some sexy time, and I'm not trying to rub against my husband with cactus legs. But that's for later when he gets home. For now, I need to get myself dressed and in the kitchen, or we're going to be ordering takeout for dinner. I wrap the towel across my chest, click off the bathroom light, and step into the bedroom.

It takes my eyes a moment to adjust. The room is darker than it usually is at this time of day, and when I look to my left, I can see that a blanket has been hung across the window, over top of the closed mini blinds. For a second it reminds me of the butterscotch curtains that used to blackout the sun at my old apartment, allowing me to sleep during the peak of daylight hours.

The room is dim, but not dark. There are two candles lit, one on each bedside table, casting a hazy orange glow onto the walls and ceiling. The flames dance, as do the shadows, drawing my attention to the movement.

I take two measured steps towards Croy, who is sitting at the foot of the bed. Even in this muted lighting, I can see the grin playing at the corners of his lips, and I know he's up to something. The space between us disappears, as he stands and kisses me. His hands cup my face as his caress intensifies. The tips of his fingers brush my neck and across my shoulders before coming back across my collarbones and down my chest, stopping when they reach the damp cotton. His fingers play at the tucked corner of my towel, loosening its hold, and allowing it to fall away to the floor.

"I want you to lay on the bed, face down, and close your eyes." His bedroom voice is impossible to disobey, so I do as I'm told.

I press my cheek against the bed sheet and allow my eyes to close. My heart races as the anticipation builds. Not entirely sure where this is headed, I lie still and await further instructions.

"You look so good right now. This is going to be harder than I thought." His suggestive confession causes me to bite my lip.

With my eyes closed and my face angled away, I have no idea what's coming. All I know is that I can trust him, and that's enough to keep any concerns tucked safely away.

Croy drapes something over me, covering my waist and thighs. It feels like a tiny blanket, but not heavy enough to be a towel. I get lost in thought trying to guess what he's covered me with when the mattress shifts, announcing his arrival next to me on the bed.

"Are you ready?" The heaviness of his exhaled breath in combination with his question, quickens my already racing heart.

One word is all it takes. "Yes." I'm practically begging for his touch.

Starting at my shoulders, Croy begins rubbing lotion into my skin. He takes his time, massaging the muscles, working through the knots he comes across. Quite a bit of time is spent on my neck and shoulders before moving further down my back. He skips over the covered area, and massages my thighs, calves, and feet.

Croy knows exactly how to touch me, on any occasion, so his attention to detail comes as no surprise, but I can't remember the last time I felt this calm. Had I known he was capable of giving a massage this good, I would have asked for one a long time ago.

"Does your lower back hurt, or is it mostly your neck that's been bothering you?"

I feel so good, it's hard to remember ever feeling pain, but I'm not ready for him to stop. "My lower back has been bothering me quite a bit."

He adds more lotion and begins working his way up the back of my thighs. "I know just the thing for that."

Croy gently pulls the small cover away, leaving me exposed. For a moment, I mistakenly assumed my massage was ending, but I couldn't have been more wrong. He kneads the thick layer of muscle and fat over my sciatic nerve and every concern I've carried with me through life melts away beneath his touch.

If you've never had your butt massaged by a man who lives to please you, you're missing out.

"Now turn over so I can do the front."

I do as I'm told and flip onto my back, and finally, I get to see him. As his hand slides toward my chest, I place my hand atop his. "I thought about what you said earlier."

"You're supposed to be relaxing, my love. We can talk about that later, after I make you dinner." He bends to kiss me, then continues the massage.

"No. I want to talk about it now." I need to get my feelings out while I have them neatly arranged at the front of my mind, otherwise I'm likely to forget. "I thought about what you said. About the job and the dangers. I know you think it's your husbandly duty to provide for us, and I think that's an admirable trait, but what happens if someday you aren't there to take care of everything? I have to be able to maintain this life for our daughter, in your absence." As my words stop, so do Croy's hands.

"And where exactly have I gone, in this hypothetical future? Are you worried about me leaving you? Or in this scenario am I dead?" His hands rest on my stomach and I wonder if he can feel anyone in there.

"My hope is that we grow old together. You know that. But sometimes unexpected things happen, and we lose people before we're ready. I worry about you dying, and me losing everything because I can't afford all the bills left behind. I mean, come on, let's be honest and face the facts, you make way more money than I ever will."

I don't like this conversation because it forces me to consider a day when Croy is no longer around. However, I'm hoping this clears up any confusion as to why I feel so compelled to go back to work.

"Is that really your reasoning? Because if it is, I'm an idiot. This whole time I've been getting upset over nothing. I assumed you thought I was incapable of taking care of our family, or that you wanted to go back to work so you could leave me. If your concern is about paying bills after I die, that's something we can sit down and go over. You don't have to worry. I have no intention of leaving my girls to fend for themselves."

When he bends forward to kiss me again, I link my arms around his neck, locking his body in place. "Can you please lay with me, and grab a blanket. I'm freezing to death." I laugh and release my arms.

Croy removes his shirt and hands it to me. A blanket would've been nice, but this is better. I sit up, slipping the shirt over my head, and allow the heated fabric to fall around me. It's warm and smells every bit as good as he does. When he removes his pants and positions himself above me, I have a pretty good idea about which direction we're headed.

"I can warm things up, if you still want me to." His whispered breath tickles my neck, making my body shake uncontrollably.

"You're all I've ever wanted," I whisper back.

This isn't merely a line said in the heat of the moment. It's a fact. Throughout the day, my mind tends to wander in various directions, but not during moments like these. Not since Croy came into my life. There is no place I want to be, other than right here with him. Mind, body, and soul.

All of me belongs with all of him.

Twenty~Two

AS WE FINISH PREPARING DINNER, I allow my mind to ramble into the future. In an effort to have a child who's willing to eat more than chicken nuggets and buttered noodles, I've been consciously consuming a wide variety of foods, especially vegetables, while she's taking up residence in my belly. I'm not sure if my diet will influence hers, but it's worth a shot. For dinner, we're making baked chicken with a mix of vegetables and smashed golden potatoes.

While I'm at the stove making sure we don't burn anything, Croy is sitting on the counter reviewing the minutiae of our finances. According to my husband, we made enough money selling the old house to pay for the pool, hot tub, stamped concrete, pond, landscaping, outbuilding, and down payment. The land was paid for in cash. So, we only have a loan for the cost of building the house. All of the figures are neatly organized on his spreadsheet, which he printed off at work and brought home to show me. Our monthly payment for the new house is equal to one week of his current salary, so I see that he can handle it, but I still feel guilty.

"Pretty soon, we'll be done paying rent for this place, and I want to get you a new car. So, start thinking about what you want." He says it like the idea has already been discussed and decided.

Finally seeing all the dollar amounts on paper, and doing some quick adding in my head, makes me feel like his mom might have had a point. Maybe I am some kind of financial succubus. Croy is acting like it's all no big deal, but he and I live in two very different realities when it comes to money.

"Um. No. I don't need a car payment, and there's nothing wrong with the vehicle I have. It gets me from point A to B and that's all I need, so you can put the extra money back into your savings." My tone is cordial but defiant.

Being married, it can be easy to forget we've only been together for five months and we're still learning about one another. Getting a glimpse into how organized he is does ease my mind a bit. I can see now when he says he's got it under control, he does, but I still want to contribute. I crave the sort of autonomy and security that comes from financial independence.

"You've had that car since you graduated high school. It doesn't even have a backup camera. Please let me get you something safe and reliable."

"When my car stops running or I start working, we can revisit this conversation. Until that time, I'm good." I'm doing my best to keep my annoyance in check, but it's right there, itching for a fight.

"What kind of car do you think you would want, when the time comes?"

I'm on to his tricks and I know how his mind works. He'd sooner beg for forgiveness than ask for permission because he knows I can't stay mad, but his not-so-subtle fishing expedition will yield little results.

"I'm not even going to answer that because I know you. I'll wake up one morning and the thing will be sitting in the driveway with a goddamn giant bow on it, like some kind of holiday auto ad on TV. So, drop it." I feel like I'm making myself clear, but he isn't taking me seriously. When will Croy understand that needing him doesn't mean needing him to do every-thing for me?

Our conversation continues as I mash the potatoes and by the time the yellow spuds are smashed and seasoned, I'm willing to compromise. "If I agree to send an email canceling my interview, can we table the new car discussion?"

I need to stop being so reactionary. When Croy's mom called me a leach, the first thing I did was start looking for jobs. Well, okay, maybe not the first thing, but close to it. And not because I wanted to work or because I thought I should work, but because I didn't like the way she thought of me. In the end, it isn't her opinion that matters and I can't allow others outside of my marriage to influence the decisions I'm making for my family.

Why should some woman who doesn't know me dictate what path I take or assign a value to my worth? Since when is being a stay-at-home mom a negative thing? It's important to Croy that our child be raised by the pair of us, which is some-thing we talked about before I even knew I was pregnant. Being a mom and maintaining the home is a full-time job, and I'm not sure why I insist on downplaying its importance. Maybe because I continue to question my qualifications for the position.

If I keep telling myself not to feel worthless, will it eventually sink in?

I arrange our dinner on a pair of plates as Croy continues going over investment portfolio details, life insurance policies, and other things I'm not even sure I understand. He wants to put my mind at ease and show me I never have to worry, but all that stuff means nothing to me without him. Don't get me wrong, it's great he's been saving his whole life specifically for this moment, but I didn't marry him for the money.

In point of fact, I fell in love with a guy who had no money, no cell phone, no clothes, no possessions at all. Sometimes I miss that person; the inmate in the hospital who was pretending to be asleep. The guy who made me laugh until I stopped crying. Who made me smile until my face hurt. Who held me together when I fell apart. Who waited for me even though I kept walking away. I miss being with a man I felt equal to.

We're halfway through eating dinner when I blurt out, "If one of us dies much sooner than the other, fingers crossed it's me. Our daughter would fare far better with you."

Croy's fork clangs and clatters against his plate as it drops from his hand. A look of shock and disbelief spreads across his face. "Why do you insist on saying stupid shit like that when you know it hurts me? Do you not love me?"

"That's ridiculous. I love you more than anything. But if something happens to me, what do I leave behind? What changes? Nothing. You could meet someone else and, you know, carry on..." I allow my words to trail off. The hurt and anger are evident in Croy's demeanor, and I know I've said something stupid.

"Carry on? Is that what you think we would do? carry on like you never existed. I have a job, so it wouldn't matter that my wife died and my whole world fell apart. Everything's fine because I can go to work and make more money." Croy pushes his chair back but doesn't stand. Instead, he looks at me and shakes his head. "I should walk away because I don't want to get angry and scare you, but part of me thinks you want to see me flip out. That's why you keep saying this shit, so I'll react. You think, because I hold it together in front of you, that I don't care."

I didn't realize that was something I was doing, but now that he's pointing it out, I know he's right. I'm trying to force the emotion out of him because, without it, I question whether his feelings match my own. I'm sitting here doing the same thing his exes did, right before they cheated on him. I'm treating him like an unemotional automaton, instead of a person with feelings.

Pushing my chair back, I move to his lap and drape my arms over his shoulders. "I'm sorry. I wasn't trying to upset you. The financial stuff makes me feel worthless, but that's my own hang-up and not because of anything you're doing wrong."

"Well, I'd like to make myself abundantly clear while we're

on the topic and I hope for once that you hear me. I have no interest in meeting someone else and I have no intention of *carrying on* without you. If something happened to you, I would drag myself through the rest of this life for the sake of our daughter, but I would miss you every second of every day. There's no end to my love for you." Croy takes my face in his hand and kisses me.

I wish I could've come into our marriage less damaged. It's sad that I need to be yelled at and disrespected in order to feel something, as if that were love. Croy deserves better, but this is the version of me he found, so, this shattered shell of a human is what he's stuck with. Who knows, maybe over time I can rebuild. Maybe his love could make me whole again.

Croy kisses my forehead and starts for the kitchen with our plates as I move to the couch. I scroll through the channels looking for a show to watch before bed. We slip into our nightly routine without skipping a beat and I appreciate his insistence on maintaining healthy dialogue, despite my efforts to poke the bear.

Laying on the couch together, I feel myself drifting off, and I'm pretty sure Croy already fell asleep behind me. Being in his arms feels good enough that I hate the idea of moving, but I know we'll both sleep better in bed.

As I'm brushing my teeth, he joins me in the bathroom and slowly pushes me away from the sink, pretending to hog the water, like he used to when we first met. I laugh as I use my hip to push him back. Croy is a lot harder to move than I am, but he plays along and lets me win.

When we get into bed, he holds me like he did on the couch, with one arm under my pillow and the other resting atop the length of my body. His fingers trace circular patterns onto my thigh as I fall asleep. It turns out, Croy is still the same man he was five months ago. He's still the man in my dreams.

For some reason, I'm the one who changed.

Twenty~Three

IT'S JUST before noon when we get to the park and the sky is a brilliant blue. The clouds are the big fluffy kind, like pillows you want to fall into, suspended from the ceiling by invisible strings. When I look out ahead of us, it reminds me of the sort of scene one might find painted on a nursery wall. The image calls to mind a decision that remains undecided.

As Croy and I walk hand in hand, we discuss possible baby name combinations. I feel like I'm all but settled on Verlaine for the first name, and Jepsen for the last, leaving the middle a question mark. Croy likes Harlow, and I agree it has a nice ring to it. Verlaine Harlow Jepsen. Sounds like someone I can't wait to meet.

I didn't notice, at first, the man approaching. He seems to come out of nowhere and when he speaks it startles me. "Are you the type of people who enjoy adventure?"

Croy turns to look at me, a cheshire grin spreading across his handsome face. I already know what he's going to say, and I know I will follow him anywhere he goes. Croy takes my hand and we follow the stranger to a tent I hadn't seen before. But how could I have missed it?

"Come on babe, we're going on an adventure." Croy's as

excited as a kid on Christmas, and it's been a while since I've seen him like this. His overwhelming joy gives me courage and I step through the opening of the canvas wall.

The inside of the tent looks like a sporting goods store, which is not at all what I was expecting. To the right, there are rows of clothing racks, all holding full-body spandex suits in every color imaginable. To the left, there are couches, a kitchen, and a wall full of jumbo flat-screen televisions.

The stranger hands us each a black spandex suit and points straight ahead. "Go get changed, and then the real fun can begin."

Croy gives me a reassuring smile, and I do my best to smile back before pushing open the dressing room door. What the hell has he gotten us into? I've never known Croy to be this trusting around strangers, especially when it involves me. He's friendly, engaging, funny, and charming, but he remains vigilant when I'm within arm's reach.

When I finally look into the mirror, I can't contain my laughter. The skin-tight black spandex suit is ridiculous, but it does smooth the imperfections nicely. The only parts of me still exposed are my feet, hands, and head. For the life of me, I can't even begin to guess what we need these for, but I'm going to trust my husband and his instincts.

As soon as I open the dressing room door, I explode into another fit of laughter. Croy's outfit seems even tighter than mine, if that's even possible, and he might as well be naked.

Although, now that I'm over my initial reaction, seeing him like this is starting to give me a tingly feeling. The way the material molds itself to his muscular frame, I can't help but reach out and touch him. I allow my hands to glide over his shoulders and down his arms. He mirrors my every action, compelling me to continue. I start back at his shoulders, only this time I move slower, allowing my hands to slide over his chest and along the sides of his waist.

I look at his face and read the desire written there. The way my body aches for him, it's almost painful, and I wonder if he feels the same way when he looks at me. It's as though I'm frozen in place. My hands remain at Croy's waist while he continues to explore the curves of my body. For a moment, I fear my legs might buckle under the weight of our shared devotion, but in true Croy Jepsen fashion, he's prepared to catch me before I fall.

His hands grip onto the spot where my legs intersect with my butt, and without the slightest hint of strain, I'm lifted off my feet. My body's reaction to this move has become an involuntary function. Without thinking, my legs wrap around his waist and my arms rest atop his shoulders. I lean in and kiss him, the way I should have the first time he picked me up like this. If I could go back in time, I would redo that moment, and make it look a lot more like this one.

"If you two are about ready, we can get you on your way." The stranger's voice comes from somewhere close behind me. "Unless *this* was the kind of adventure you were needing, in which case, I can give you some privacy."

I swear, kissing Croy causes temporary amnesia. I had already forgotten about the stranger and the tent and the mystery adventure awaiting us. Before releasing my hold on him, I look deep into Croy's eyes and ask the one question I already know the answer to. "Can I trust you to keep me safe?"

"Always." Croy seals his promise with a kiss and lowers me back to my feet.

The two of us walk hand in hand towards the entrance, where the canvas tent flaps have been replaced by sliding glass doors. As we pass the clothing racks, I notice the spandex suits are gone, and in their place, new suits have been hung. It's a material I don't recognize and there are metal cuffs at the ankles, wrist, and neck.

My anxiety begins to bubble and I wish we could rewind back to our previous moment and stay there. I don't like the thought of metal cuffs around my wrists and ankles. It reminds me of being inside the jail and the way we'd shackle inmates who had to leave for court or the hospital. I'm glad they didn't chain Croy on our way to the ambulance. I would have fought for his freedom like I did in the blocks when Grant tried to hand-cuff him. Even then, I knew I could trust Croy like I know I can trust him now.

I find the will to steady my breath and continue forward, borrowing my husband's strength. Once we step through the glass doors and into the sun, I realize we're already wearing the new suits over top of our other ones. How did that happen? I don't remember agreeing to this and I certainly didn't stop to put it on.

"Alright friends, the time for adventure is upon us. All you have to do is press the button on your neck." The stranger bows his head, waves goodbye, and disappears, taking the tent with him.

"Do you want me to go first, so you don't have to be scared?" Croy's voice is calm, but his cheshire grin is wider than ever and his eyes keep changing colors.

"No! Wait! We don't even know what this does. How do we know pressing this button isn't going to kill us? Why are we doing this?" I'm trying not to panic, but fail miserably.

"I'll press the button on my suit, and if something bad happens, then you'll know not to press yours. Okay? Then you can leave me and get help." His tone is measured, but his words don't make sense.

"What?" I try finding Croy somewhere inside the man standing next to me, but he's lost behind kaleidoscope eyes. "Just wait one second and let me think."

I take his hand and lift it to my lips, planting a kiss there against his skin like my Croy does to me. Then I press his palm to my cheek and allow it to linger there. He doesn't speak, not yet, but his eyes have finally settled on a brilliant blue, and I have a pretty good idea of what has to be done if I want him back.

"We have to do this together. We're on the same team, remember? Wherever you go, I go. So, we press our buttons at the same time, and we see what happens. Okay?" I'm not convinced this is a smart idea, but it's better than the alternative. Watching Croy die in front of me and being left here alone is unacceptable. Better to follow him into the nothing, where I know we can find each other again.

"Alright, my love. We do it together." With his words, the plan is set.

Croy leans his head towards me and I come up to meet his lips there in the center. There is no space left between us, no room for self-doubt or fear or hesitation. Those emotions have all disappeared with the stranger. Now, what remains is the pair of us, and our unshakable love for one another.

"One. Two. Three..."

I press the button on my neck half expecting my head to explode, but it doesn't. Instead, my suit begins to fill with some sort of gas. It's cold, and it doesn't feel like regular air.

I look at my hands and wiggle my fingers. Nothing strange there. But something catches my eye, something I didn't notice before. Inscribed on the cuff encircling my left wrist, are the numbers 09102022 and the words Zeppelin Suit.

"Babe, I think these suits are filled with helium." The words no sooner leave my lips, as my feet begin to lift off the ground. In a sudden burst of renewed panic, I shout, "Don't let me go!"

"I would never dream of letting you go. You can trust me." Croy remains as calm and reassuring as ever while my heart threatens to beat clean out of my chest. He pulls at a strap attached to his suit and I float straight into his open arms. "I've got you."

Our feet say goodbye to the grass, together this time, as we begin drifting along a few inches off the ground. Floating is such an odd feeling. I imagine this is what it's like when you're a ghost, and the only thing keeping you here is your inability to let go. I know if something unexpected ever happened, I would haunt Croy until the day he joined me. If for no other reason than to scare off the line of women waiting to take my place.

After a few minutes, I get used to the new weightless sensation and allow myself to relax. My eyes close and I take a deep breath in, before exhaling slowly. I feel us getting further from the ground, but I refuse to look down. Adventures are meant to be experienced and enjoyed, and that's exactly what I'm going to do.

True to his word, Croy never lets go of my hand.

Twenty-Four

THE 5:00 am alarm bounces between the bedroom walls, grounding my flight. What a strange dream to have. I wonder what it meant. Croy will be happy to hear he made it out alive for a change. I'm going to have to replay it in my head while I get dressed, so I can remember it long enough to accurately recall the details.

When I was a kid, I used to dream about flying, only back then, I never made it very far from the ground. Looking back now, perhaps I needed a partner to give me the courage I lacked on my own.

"I wish the other wives would start coming to the gym in the morning, then you'd have someone to talk to." Croy's out-of-the-blue statement snaps me back to the present, and I grab the first shirt my hand touches in the drawer.

Now that I'm dressed and focused, I can respond. "Yeah, that would be fun. But I'm fine with listening to music and staring at you. Also, don't let me forget to tell you about the dream I had."

"Did I finally save you?" There's a twinge of aspiration in his voice. I can tell this is important to him. I think my nightmares were making him feel like a failure, or at the very least making him feel weak. Two words I would never use to describe Croy in real life.

"We sort of saved each other, and finally agreed on a name." I turn to face him and smile. As I exhale, a subtle laugh comes with it.

"Well, don't leave me in suspense. What name did we finally agree on?" Croy catches me at the door and holds it open as I stride through.

As we walk to the gym, I play back my dream in as much detail as possible, including the potential name. I describe the stranger and the tent, the skin-tight suits and the perfect kiss, the buttons on our neck, and his kaleidoscope eyes. I try to explain the different feelings and emotions, but my words hardly do them justice, and before I can finish talking, we're at the door to the gym, as if we floated over on a stiff breeze.

"Evidently, Verlaine has chosen her name, and she whispers it to you as you sleep. You've had a dozen dreams where one of us calls her that. Seems pretty set in stone at this point." His voice is a mix of relief and disappointment.

"They're only dreams. We can still talk about the name and choose one together, when we're awake." I reach for the handle of the door, but he catches my hand and pulls me into a hug. The last thing I want is to choose a name he hates.

"I love the name, so let's leave it as is and call the matter settled." He kisses the top of my head and opens the door for me. "Is a Zeppelin suit a real thing? Because if not, they need to be."

I walk into the building laughing, imagining us in those black spandex skin suits. This might need to happen in real life, as a private joke. Or foreplay. I'm nearly a hundred percent certain I could find full length adult bodysuits for sale online.

It's a shame I've slept through so many alarms and missed out on coming to the gym with Croy during the week. By being on opposite sleep schedules, I passed up several opportunities to take in the best view in Vermilion.

I spend the next hour walking on the treadmill, listening to the music I was obsessed with in college, and fantasizing about the guy working out across from me. Here in the confines of my mind, we're both super kinky, and neither of us walks away unfulfilled.

If I had the option to hang out with anyone, living or dead, and Tom Hardy was busy that day, I would choose my husband. Not simply because of the way he looks, but because of the way he makes me feel. I wonder if I asked him, who his answer would be.

"Are you ready to go? I don't want you to slip in a puddle of drool." Stopping my treadmill, Croy laughs and tosses his sweatshirt at me. "I hope to god you were thinking about me, and not the other two guys over there. It would be a shame for me to have to kill my workout friends."

"I mean, you were there too. Does that count?" I slip into his hoodie and make my way to the door, determined to get there first.

"Tell me you're joking." His arm comes across my chest and I'm dragged backward. "Say you're joking or I will hold you down and tickle you to death, right here and now."

As Croy's fingers scribble across my skin frantically searching for the places that make me squirm, his one arm continues to lock me in place against his chest. There's no such thing as a fair fight when your opponent is a foot taller and twice your weight, but I don't mind. His kiss against my neck sends a shiver up my spine and down my arms. I am trapped in the pleasure of his embrace and I will happily remain here for as long as he'll have me. To make sure I know he means business, he whispers in my ear. "I have no intention of sharing you with anyone, ever again."

Nate and Brian each make a joking comment on their way out the door. "Heather, are you good? Is this guy bothering you?" "Yeah, why don't you walk with us? We'll make sure you get home safe."

I worry the guys might have accidentally chosen the wrong topic to joke around about. My concern is validated the second I hear Croy's voice and the manner in which he replies.

"She's good. I know how to take care of her." Croy has me locked in with both arms as he steps away from the door, carrying me with him. His tone is direct and mildly aggressive.

I look up and see a flash of genuine concern on Nate's face. "Bro, it was a joke. What's your problem? Lighten up and let her go."

I feel the muscles around me tighten, and I know if I don't speak now, it's going to be too late. Someone is going to end up in the hospital or jail. "It's all good, Nate. We'll see you tomorrow. Okay?"

I watch as the door closes, leaving the pair of us alone. Croy's arms relax and I'm free to walk away, if I choose to, but where would I go? I don't even understand what happened. One minute we're joking around and the next he's about to knock out his best friend. How did everything go left so quickly?

"What in the actual fuck? I can't even play around with my wife without some guy thinking I'm what? Abusing you? He's gonna step in and defend you, against me of all people? Some friend." Croy places a hand lightly on my shoulder. "Are you alright? I didn't hurt you, did I?"

"I'm fine. Please don't make this into a thing. Nate misread the situation, that's all. Drop it and let's go home." I lace my fingers into his and start for the door.

"I know you're right, but that's a lot for me to forgive and forget."

"I understand, and I'm sorry he said what he said, but you have to get ready for work and I have a question to ask you." I pull him toward the door and attempt to change the subject. "If you could hang out with anyone, living or dead, who would it be?"

"Um, I don't know. I guess probably Neil Fallon, the lead singer of Clutch. He seems like he'd be interesting to talk to." He opens the door ahead of me and we're back in the cool morning air. Croy's answer throws me for a loop. One, I don't know who he's talking about. And two, I sort of thought he would choose me.

"Oh, that's cool." I hide my scowl by shaking my head.

"You'll always be my first choice. I thought you were looking for a less obvious answer, but maybe I over-thought the question and should've gone with my real number one. What about you? Who's on your hang out wish list?"

"Well, shit, my answer would have been you, but then you had to go and pick some random ass dude to hang out with instead of your wife." I laugh and squeeze his hand. "So, I guess I'll say Marcus Sjofjord."

"Okay, now who's the one throwing out random ass names? If I look this dude up online, he better be ugly."

It feels good to laugh together. I only wish it was the weekend so he didn't have to leave. Once Croy gets showered and dressed, it's going to be time for him to say goodbye. We might not even have enough time for coffee this morning. I click on the coffee maker and drag myself into the bedroom to lie down while I wait.

"What the hell, babe? Is this him? He could be my younger brother." Croy comes out of the bathroom with only a towel around his waist, holding his phone in front of him. "If I die, you could ask this guy to be my stand-in for the family Christmas card photo."

I can't help but laugh.

"You definitely have a type, that's for sure. How the hell are you into guys who look like this, but dated Kelly?"

Twenty-Five

THE DAYS of the week begin to blur together as Croy and I settle into our updated routine. I keep my 5:00 am alarm and our dates to the gym, thankful for the moments we share. A few days after the incident between Nate and Croy, the guys were able to settle their mini beef, and remain friends. All it took was a good old-fashioned weightlifting competition in front of the wives, and a round of apologies.

We still make time for 6:30 coffee before exchanging a long kiss goodbye. We meet for lunch at noon or talk on the phone for an hour. And each day he's home by 5:00, giving us plenty of time to relax. We eat dinner, exchange ideas about the day and plans for the near future, and then watch an hour of TV before heading off to bed. Anymore, we're both asleep by 9:30.

Married life has become wonderfully boring, and I couldn't be happier.

The last two weeks, we started watching strongman competitions pretty much every night. At this point, we each have a list of favorites that we root for, and I get the feeling Croy dreams of building a few of the event stations in our yard after we move.

On the weekends, we go on dates, trying to make the most of our child-free time while we have it, both aware everything's going to change in three months. I don't know how to be prepared for that. Croy, on the other hand, is ready to have the baby here today, so we can get started on the next one. I shake my head and laugh each time he talks about growing our family. The last thing I want to do is quell his excitement. After all, I want as much help as I can get changing diapers and making bottles.

As for myself, I've been doing more self-reflection. It didn't take me long to realize married life, without Matt Kelly, was a lot smoother. Looking back, Croy was way too gracious about my friendship for far too long. I wish he would've put his foot down straight away, instead of trying so hard to accommodate my wishes, but I probably would've fought back. My track record with men, prior to falling in Croy's arms, was pretty much shit, and Kelly was no exception.

I'm not sure if it was the truth finally coming to the surface, or the fact Croy and I finally adjusted to the same sleep schedule, but I haven't had a nightmare in weeks. My mood has improved and so have my eating habits, which has eliminated the need for any further discussion on the matter. Croy is still planning to meet with me later today at my doctor's appointment, so fingers crossed that all goes well. Otherwise, he's going to have a new wish list of complaints for me.

As for the original list, it took some time, but my last name has officially changed, and I've stopped applying for random jobs. Croy paid off my credit card and started giving me an allowance. Well, he doesn't call it that, but that's what it is. He transfers money into my account every Friday, mostly because he likes it when I drive to see him for lunch. For a little while, I stopped going because I couldn't afford the gas, and now, I have no excuse.

Overall, things have been good the last few weeks. Croy's mom even attempted to apologize by sending a text. She claims she never would have said what she did, had she known we were married and expecting a child. I decided to accept what was offered since a semi-apology was better than nothing, but I'm happy to maintain my distance.

I don't have time to stress and worry about people outside of my home. Croy and I are getting the keys to the new house this weekend, earlier than expected, and I have to mentally prepare myself to move again. My goal is to have the pods unpacked and hauled away by Thanksgiving, which is in two weeks.

As fantastic as all of this is, it's also overwhelming. The speed at which my life is moving is enough to make my head spin, and I wonder if things will slow down once we're settled into the new house. I certainly hope so.

Otherwise, I'm afraid I might blink and my baby girl will be heading off to college.

Twenty-Six

MY CURRENT STRESS level is through the roof ahead of today's appointment, which is causing my mind to run off in several directions at once. Will Croy be angry if I haven't gained weight? Will the doctor order iron infusions straight away, or will I be able to put it off until after the holidays? Is our baby healthy and growing, or have I messed everything up? Could Croy forgive me if I'm the reason there's an issue? What are the odds my child will inherit my depression? Will I end up being a horrible mother? Are they both better off without me? I don't want to get pregnant again! Will Croy understand or be disappointed? We built a two-bedroom house. Where would we even put a second kid? What if we have a boy? We can't expect them to share a bedroom forever.

My thoughts continue on a crash course while I shower. It's only 11:00, and my appointment isn't until 3:00, so I have plenty of time to kill. All I have to do is choose my murder weapon. What are my options? Binging a documentary. Meeting Croy for lunch. Going over to check on the house. Walking to my parents' house and watering the plants. Watching videos online. Walking to the mailbox to get the mail. Prepping for dinner. Texting Croy and bothering him at work. Reading more of the baby book. Or unlocking the safe and ending it all.

Okay, maybe not the last one.

> Croy: Are you coming to see me for lunch today
> or are we meeting later? If you want, I can leave
> at noon and come home, instead of waiting
> until 2. It's up to you. I don't want to be in your
> way if you have other plans.

> : Good timing. I was sitting here planning to
> make a plan but had yet to come to a decision.
> If you can leave for the day at lunchtime, do it.
> Then we only have to take one car to the
> appointment, and it will give us a chance to
> talk.

> Croy: Is there something on your mind? Things
> here are going smoothly for a change, so I'm
> without distraction and at your disposal.

Croy does his best to respond to my messages during work hours, but I've come to expect delays. He seems to be permanently scheduled for one meeting or another, so I try not to be needy.

> : It's nothing. I'm feeling momentarily
> overwhelmed by life, but I'll be fine.

> Croy: Is there anything I can do to relieve some
> of the stress? You can make me a list and I'll
> take care of it, okay? This is an exciting time,
> my love, and I want you to be able to enjoy it.

> : I'll be okay. It's the final push, of sorts, and
> then we'll be settled in the new house. I'm
> feeling drained, but I promise I'll relax after we
> unpack.

Croy: You always promise me you'll relax, but you keep pushing back the start date.

: Fair enough. LoL. This time I mean it.

I grab the mailbox key and slip my feet into my shoes. My head feels like it's filled with fog, and I'm hoping some fresh air will help. As I walk to the mailboxes, I think about the order I want to move things and how I want to decorate the new house.

Two pieces of junk mail and my brand-new social security card. That was certainly worth the trip over here. It's weird seeing Heather Jepsen printed above my social security number. Maybe it'll sink in after I receive my updated driver's license, credit card, and debit card. Or, maybe it'll be weird forever, and eventually, I'll grow numb and forget I'm lost.

I return the mail key to its home on the hook, grab my key ring from the table, and head into the bedroom closet. Best to lock my new card in the safe with the old ones, so I don't lose it while packing. I locate the safe key on my ring, slide it into the opening, and twist.

: What's in this little black box?

Croy: Do NOT open that. Why are you in there?

: My new SS card came in the mail and I was packing it away so I wouldn't misplace it. What's in the box? Is it something for your other girlfriend?

Croy: Please don't look.

: I'm sure she'll love it.

Croy: I don't have a girlfriend and you're not funny. I need to submit this report and then I'm heading out. I can stop and buy lunch on the way home. Do you have a taste for anything in particular, or do you want me to surprise you?

: Whatever.

Croy: Don't be like that. It's a Christmas present. For you! I need to find a better place to hide things.

I run a finger over the smooth top of the unopened jewelry box before closing the safe, curious about its contents, but unwilling to succumb to temptation.

: Stop spending money on me. I'd be happy with a new pair of sweatpants.

Croy: Noted. Be home soon. Love you.

I take a hoodie from the hook on the closet door, grab my pillow from the bed, and make my way to the living room couch. It's not that I'm tired, but I can feel a headache coming on and I'd like to cut it off at the pass. The hoodie I chose is drenched in Croy's scent, so it makes for the perfect blanket. I inhale deeply, filling my lungs with him, and allow the calm to wash over me.

Once I close my eyes, I'm already asleep.

Twenty-Seven

I BRING my arms up over my head and allow the stretch to extend down my back. What I wouldn't give for a massage. It's crazy to me that there are women out there who enjoy being pregnant. Thankfully, the morning sickness has subsided, but it's been replaced by pain in my lower back and migraines. Once was enough for me, and after this experience, I'm strongly considering donating my ovaries to science.

When I finally open my eyes, I notice Croy standing in the bedroom doorway, watching me. He's changed out of his work clothes, and into a pair of shorts. That's it. A pair of shorts and nothing else. My breath catches in my throat at the sight of him standing there, and it takes me a second to locate my voice.

"I didn't hear you come in." I sound as though I'm still half asleep and I start to wonder if this is another one of those vivid dreams. Pregnancy is messing with my mind, and I don't even know what's real anymore.

"You looked so peaceful. I made sure to be quiet so I wouldn't wake you." Croy moves from the doorway, takes a seat on the couch, and places my feet on his lap. "Are you feeling alright?"

"Yeah, I'm fine." Oddly enough, I feel exhausted from the

mental marathon I've been running all morning, even though my body has mostly remained still. If only overthinking burned calories, I'd never have to work out again.

We go back and forth, exchanging the typical banter, while Croy rubs my feet. This type of conversation never holds my attention for long. There are only so many times I can hear about the guys at work and random airplane parts, so I entertain myself by trying to guess what he's brought home for lunch. The smell is muted and difficult to discern. The disinterest must be written all over my face because Croy stands and holds his hand out to me. Time to move this conversation to the table so we can eat.

Sitting forward, I slip the hoodie on over my head. I'm so cold all the time. Probably another weird pregnancy thing I'll have to remember to look up in the book. I swear, if it's not one thing, it's another.

I accept Croy's outstretched hand and find my footing. How is it possible he's half naked and warm to the touch, while I'm in sweats and a hoodie and my hands are like ice? Whatever the reason, I want more. I crave his touch. When we're apart, I think about how badly I want him next to me, and when he's next to me I need him even more. I hope this honeymoon phase never ends.

Lunch is laid out on the table, but Croy walks past without pausing as he guides me into the bedroom. He releases my hand before sitting on the bed facing me, his intentions remaining somewhat unclear. Even though he's half-naked, I'm not getting a sex vibe for our current interaction. The moment feels heavier. I stand there, examining his face for clues, waiting for him to make the first move.

"Do you remember our first kiss?" Croy's question catches me off guard. Not because I don't remember, but because I wasn't expecting him to ask me about something that happened when we lived down south. Normally, he avoids talking about that particular time frame.

Taking a couple of steps forward, I position myself between his knees. "I remember it being something like this." My hands gravitate towards his, placing them on my hips, like I did that night. Then, I lean in and kiss him.

Our first kiss was such a pivotal moment in my life, and it's not something I intend to forget. We had spent hours in the hospital together, talking and flirting, laughing and bonding. Then, he held me in his arms and told me he would spend the rest of his life protecting me. Everything was perfect until I ruined it.

At the time, I still had one foot in my old life as a corrections officer, while the rest of me was cautiously preparing to dive into this new reality. As soon as I said the word *inappropriate*, the mood shifted and the moment was lost. It was as though I could feel Croy's heart breaking as he accepted we would never be together.

I had to do something to reassure him, to eliminate any question or doubt about where I stood. So, I kissed him. That night I spent hours cuddled in his arms, and then, the next morning, I said goodbye, and went home with another man.

Looking back at it now, through a lens framed by wedding bands, every choice I made the next morning was wrong. I knew my heart was with Croy, but I was too afraid of the negative consequences. I walked away from the love of my life, like a goddamn idiot, and it only got worse from there.

"Do you remember the first time we had sex?" He supports my body with his arms and falls back, pulling me onto the bed with him. Thankfully, it's a controlled fall, so I land softly on the comforter instead of crashing into his chest. Finally, we're getting to the good stuff. I was wondering if having a half-naked hottie in the bedroom would lead to a little afternoon sexy time, but I was beginning to lose hope.

"As if I could forget. That's when you got me pregnant." I say with a wink. "Fingers crossed."

I'm missing something, that much is clear, because for the life of me, I cannot figure out where Croy is going with this. Not that I mind the trip down memory lane, but these events occurred less than six months ago. Why is he questioning my memory as if these moments aren't permanently inked into the fabric of my being? Does he doubt my feelings for him? Or has he become skeptical of his feelings for me?

Croy pulls me in and whispers in my ear, "Do you remember the first time we said *I love you*?" His tone is as soft as rose petals, but all I'm feeling is the thorns.

"We were on the back patio at your house after Kelly slapped me." I move to get up and he makes no attempt to stop me, so I continue. None of this makes sense. "I think I'm going to go eat before everything gets cold."

I'm halfway to the door when he says, "Do you remember the night I proposed?"

What is he playing at? I feel the irritation rise within me and hesitate to turn around for fear I might say something I don't mean. He's acting strangely and this entire interaction feels off. This isn't the man I know and love.

In an attempt to calm myself, I take a deep breath and close my eyes. "I remember I got stuck in my head and I walked away. I have a lot of memories like that with you in them, and I'm sorry. I'm not sure why you didn't give up on me. I'll probably never understand it, even if you explain it slowly and use small words. You came looking for me, like you always do, and found me surrounded by darkness. Then you asked me to marry you."

Is that what this is about? Me making shit choices and almost ending things before they had a real chance to begin, leaving with Kelly, having unprotected sex, being weak, and walking out of the restaurant. What else would he like me to feel guilty about? Would he like me to recall the time he got stabbed and had to have surgery because he was protecting me? Or the time I kissed my ex right in front of him, then talked him into having a threesome? Maybe we can reminisce about the time I pissed off his entire family by merely existing. That should be a real hoot.

"What's your point, Croy? Just tell me I'm a piece of shit and be done with it."

I spin on my heels to face him and find him a step behind me.

"Your mind goes to some weird places, my love. Clearly, this isn't going as planned and I've annoyed you." He holds out his hand to me, and I take it. The moment we touch, my agitation dissipates and I'm left feeling embarrassed. "Now I'm afraid to ask you my last question."

"I didn't think you were afraid of anything," I say, with a sheepish half smile. "I'm sorry I ruined this too. Feel free to add it to the list."

"I was wondering if you would marry me?"

"Yeah, we did that already. Do you remember our wedding day?" My tone is mocking and I'm being an asshole, so I shake my head and regroup before speaking again. "I'm sorry, I didn't mean to say it like that."

"It's fine. But I would like an answer, please."

"You're asking me if I would marry you? Like if I had it to do all over again, would I still say yes?" Why does he think my answer would have changed? I thought things between us had finally fallen into a nice rhythm. Where is this coming from? "I would marry you over and over again if it's what you wanted. Would you still want to marry me?"

"I do want to marry you. That's why I'm asking. So, is your answer *yes*?"

"You know I can't do any of this life stuff without you. Can you please kiss me and tell me what's going on?"

I'm not sure why I'm so irritable. He's given me no real reason to doubt him, and yet, I continue to look for grounds to question his intentions. Croy isn't the same as my exes, but he seems destined to pay for their mistakes. I wonder how long it's going to take for me to stop being this unpleasant version of myself. It seems I was wrong, yet again, and the right thing to do is acknowledge it and apologize.

Croy brings his hand up to meet my cheek. His thumb

brushes slowly across my lips and comes back to rest at the center, before gliding down my chin, along my neck, and over my collarbone. This slow-motion teasing is torture, and he knows it.

My legs go numb as a tingling sensation spreads throughout my body and an immeasurable yearning overtakes me. It is a desperate need and I am lost to it. All I can do is wait for Croy to pardon me, and end my suffering, but he is unwilling to relent.

While I'm trapped in this purgatory of desire, the nanoseconds tick by like hours. My pleading eyes beg for relief until eventually it comes. Croy lifts me off my feet and presses my back against the bedroom wall. His kiss begins at my lips but doesn't linger for nearly long enough. I need more, but he's already moved on. My head tilts to the side as his lips plant a garden of kisses along the outstretched side of my neck, working their way upwards.

"My life begins and ends with you. Don't you know that? You're my everything." His words are fuel to the fire, and if I don't find my voice now, I may lose the ability to speak.

"I need you." I don't know a better way to say it. Croy is essential to my existence. Everything makes sense in the moments driven by passion. Why can't I find the same reassurance in the other aspects of our life? This is one of my major fundamental flaws, and I don't know how to reset my programming.

After a decade of covert interactions with the opposite sex, I've accepted that my only value as a person is sexual. There is comfort to be found in these moments of desire, where I know I have something to offer him. After all, everything comes at a cost, even love, and women like me are accustomed to paying in flesh.

Croy carries me to the bed and pulls the comforter over us. "Tell me you love me. And don't just say it so I'll have sex with you. I want you to mean it."

"Okay." I wiggle out of my hoodie and shirt, tossing them

over the side of the bed. Between the thickness of the blanket, the heat of Croy's body, and the weight of the moment, I'm having difficulty breathing.

His fingertips trace circular patterns into my exposed skin and I struggle to regain my thoughts. When my voice does come out, it's soaked in desperate pleading. "I remember the weight of your body pressed into mine. Your voice leading me out of the darkness. The way it felt the first time your hand touched mine. I remember needing to know you were okay, and not caring how many rules I had to break to find out. I would listen to the chatter in the hallways, hoping someone would say your name. I remember crying on your arm, asking you why you saved me. Talking to you for hours. Laughing with you. Seeing you. Finding comfort in your arms. And falling deeply in love with you. I remember desperately needing to kiss you and wishing we didn't have to stop. When you came into my room and joked about locking the door and having sex, I was ready. I wanted you so badly. I was in love with you before I said it, but I remember when and where I finally told you. It was the first time I had ever meant those words as they slipped past my lips. And no matter how many years pass, I'll always remember the night you proposed and the day we got married. I remember all the conversations we've had about hypothetical futures and the effort you've put into making our dreams a reality. I appreciate you and the lengths you go to in order to make sure I feel protected and loved. You're more than I deserve and everything I have searched for, so, to answer all of your questions and set your mind at ease, my answer is yes. I remember every moment we've spent together. I cherish those memories."

My chest presses into his as I eliminate any distance between us. What else is there left to say? "I love you, every second of every day."

Croy's hand comes to my heart as his lips pull up into a smile. "I want to marry you again, in front of our family and friends, but before you panic, it doesn't have to be right now. I was thinking we could do it next year, on our anniversary, or some other date of your choosing. I don't care about that part. What I want is for everyone to see how important you are to me. I love you so much."

"Is this because of what I said, about feeling like a secret?" Part of me loves the idea of having a wedding with guests and marrying him all over again, but the other part of me hates the thought of spending money on something we already did in order to prove to people what we already know. "That's what all of this has been about? The walk down memory lane was so you could propose?"

"Yeah. In my head, I thought it would be more romantic. Sorry about that. But hey, I'm happy you said yes. Do you want to eat lunch now, or should we have sex first?" He's offering sex in a way that makes it sound like a trip to the store to buy toothpaste.

"I mean, we're already in bed, so, might as well get it over with."

Twenty-Eight

THE DRIVE to the doctor's office is quiet. I have a lot on my mind, but nothing I want to share. Normally, I'm the one driving our conversations, so when my lips are buttoned shut, things tend to remain on mute. I have to give Croy credit though, because he's a fantastic active listener. Maybe that's the secret to our relationship's success, one person who never runs out of things to say and one who never gets tired of hearing her voice. They do say healthy communication is the key to a happy marriage.

"How was work this morning?" I decide to ask a question, remembering I have a love/hate relationship with silence.

"You hate when I talk about work. Every time I mention the shop, your eyes glaze over, and the little hamster who runs your brain jumps off his wheel and hides in his little peanut house."

I take a moment to color in the picture he's presented and laugh. "Two things: How do you even come up with this stuff? And why is the hamster in my head a boy?"

"Why are you asking me? It's your hamster." Croy squeezes my leg as we pull into the parking lot of the doctor's office. "Are you ready to get in there and see what they have to say?"

"Not really, but it's probably best to get it over with." I've been dreading this appointment since Croy informed me he wanted to come with me. It's not that I don't want him here, I do. I love how excited he is, even if it stands in glaring contrast to my questionable terror. Everything's better when he's with me, normally. And that's just it. I know he's here to critique my efforts, and I'm not looking forward to receiving his evaluation on the way home.

"We're early as hell, so if you want to sit out here and talk, we can. Are you running through your worst-case scenario playlist, or is it something else? Because everything's going to be fine." He lifts my hand to his lips and lingers there. This kiss feels like a promise. No matter what comes next, I'll never again be left to handle the perils and pitfalls of life on my own.

If I could dive into the depths of Croy's ocean-blue eyes and drown there, I would. Sometimes I wonder what it would be like to wander around inside his head, getting lost in thought. He seems so steady and long-term, like a lighthouse. Croy has saved my life so many times, in so many ways, and I forget he doesn't know.

"I don't want you to be mad at me." I weighed myself this morning on the scale at home, so I already know what's coming. I run through the list of small items in the car, anything heavy I can stuff into my pocket without getting caught. Maybe If I leave my shoes on and keep my wallet and phone on me, it'll offset.

"Okay. Well, I have no reason to be mad at you. Unless you're having an affair with your doctor or something? Short of that, I think we're good. Have I turned into a complete asshole and I'm not aware of it? Because if so, you need to tell me." Croy turns to face me, as much as one can in the driver's seat, and continues to hold onto my hand. "If you feel like I'm mistreating you, say something so I can change my tone, behavior, mindset, whatever it is. You should never have to worry about me being mad. I don't want that."

"No. That's not what I meant. You're not mistreating me, and

I don't feel that way." I release an exasperated huff and pull my hand back. "Forget it. Let's just go in."

"Are you having an affair with your doctor?" Croy's eyebrows pull together as he examines my face, and I can't tell if this is a serious question.

"No. What? Can you sober up and be genuine for a moment?"

He's got to be joking. He's being his usual Croy self, and trying to lighten the mood. Which would be fine, if I weren't slightly freaking out.

"Wouldn't want to get DUI for driving under the influence of human emotions."

I step out of the car and slam the door behind me. Whether he's trying to be funny or an asshole, I don't care. I'm done with whatever this is, and I need to walk away and regroup.

I'm nearly to the entrance when Croy catches up to me. He loops his fingers around the silver handle and swings the door open, holding it back as I pass through. It doesn't take him more than a step or two for him to fall in line beside me. Damn him and his long legs.

I push the arrow next to the elevator and watch as the green light illuminates. For some reason, it reminds me of the button in Kelly's apartment building and my mind starts to wander. I should've told him the truth from the start and settled for him being an enemy, instead of a friend. Now, he won't talk to me, and the biggest secret has yet to be shared.

Croy's fingers tangle into mine as we wait for the doors ahead of us to slide open.

Twenty-Nine

WHAT IS it about waiting rooms? I sit, scanning the rows, secretly passing judgment on the other patients and their partners. I fill the time by creating little backstories and hypothetical futures based on whatever clues are at hand, and then I wonder if they're doing the same thing I am, looking from me to Croy and back again. They probably assume we've been together for years and I must have been prettier when I was younger. Poor guy.

The electric lock clicks before the door to the back opens and the nurse says, "Heather."

I begin to stand, but notice the girl across from me mirrors my movement. We exchange an acknowledging glance, before turning our attention towards the nurse.

"Heather Belk." She amends her call after looking at the paperwork in her hand.

Well, shit. I'm not even to the scale yet and I've already got one strike against me. This is the first time I've been here since the official name change and I forgot to mention it. When I checked in, I said my first name, the time of my appointment, and the name of the doctor. When the receptionist asked if the address and phone number were the same, I said yes, taking that to be the end of our exchange.

Croy doesn't say anything, but I know him. He's keeping a mental checklist and this will be in the **Items to Discuss Later** column.

We make our way through the door and right there, straight ahead down the shortened hallway, is the scale. It's as though I'm being dragged forward, toward my impending doom, though from the outside it merely looks like walking.

"I'll hold your wallet and your phone for you," Croy says, holding out his hand. Damn hive mind. He always seems to know exactly what I'm thinking.

"Oh, and could you take off your shoes, please?" The nurse interjects, openly conspiring with my husband. Maybe they're the ones having an affair.

I kick my shoes off and laugh quietly. This little inside joke is my spoonful of sugar, and now it's time for the medicine. Stepping on the scale, I watch as the digital numbers adjust and settle. My fortune has been read and my fate decided, nothing more can be done here.

"131. Alright, if you'll follow me, you're in room three today." She motions with her hand, and I mentally prepare myself for the next round of judgment. I can't help but wonder what the fair market value is for a wife who doesn't listen and a mother who is unsure of all that lies ahead.

Once we're inside the room, I take a seat next to Croy in a pair of wooden chairs located in the corner. I avoid sitting on the exam table, if and when possible. The sound of crinkling paper makes my skin crawl and I don't enjoy being the center of attention. For the time being, I can draw comfort from the weight of my husband's hand on my leg as I run through my answers to the standard questions.

The nurse enters the last of my information into the computer and exits the room, leaving me to marinate in the deafening silence of all that goes unsaid. Having been here enough times, I know it'll be fifteen minutes until the doctor comes in. Plenty of time to iron out any tension, should I find the nerve to speak.

Croy gently squeezes my thigh and shifts his position so he's looking at me instead of towards the door. "Do you want me to leave? You seem uncomfortable."

"It's not you, I just don't like being here." In my head, it's not only Croy judging me, it's everyone. The nurses, the doctors, the other patients, and their partners. Even the ladies working the reception desk seem to be eyeing me suspiciously. Everyone can see I'm unequipped. Inappropriate. Ill-suited. Clueless.

"Come here." He opens his arms and I allow myself to fall into his embrace. "We'll go straight home after this, change into comfy clothes, and watch a movie."

It's cute he thinks my discomfort can be eased by changing out of my jeans. If only. My issues run so much deeper than the contents of a dresser drawer, but I can't tell him. What kind of mother could I possibly be? I don't even like kids. Even as a child, I found it easier to talk to adults than my peers. I have no experience with babies and I seem to lack maternal instinct.

This kid is going to hate me.

The door opens and two new people join us in the room. I take my seat on the exam table and lie back when I'm told. It's reassuring to hear the doctor say, "Everything looks great, and from what I can see, your baby looks perfect." Croy and I simultaneously exhale a sigh of relief.

I'm not sure why I get myself worked up before these appointments. I take vitamins, I eat whole foods, I don't drink, or smoke, and I haven't been in the company of drugs since high school. Even then, it wasn't anything crazy. From the outside, Croy and I look hardcore, but the reality is, those days are behind us. Now we're two people low-key obsessed with watching strongman competitions, walking around the outdoor farmers market, and hanging out with each other.

Even though the appointment yielded fantastic results, I still feel tense being back in the quiet of the car. On the trip home, the silence persists, broken only by the annoying sound of Croy's thumb nervously tapping on the steering wheel as he drives. Something about repetitive sounds makes me want to burn the world to the ground and lie still with the ashes that remain. Thankfully, he stops, momentarily.

It's a good thing Croy isn't a poker player because his tells are as easy to read as a neon sign hanging overhead. I wish he would yell at me already and be done with it. I hate waiting for shoes to drop. Best to get it over with. "If you have something to say, just say it."

"I was thinking about the ultrasound and how crazy detailed all those pictures are. There's an entire tiny person in your belly and she's perfect. She has your cute little nose and everything." Croy moves his hand, going from his usual place on my leg over to my stomach. "Thank you for letting me go with you. I didn't realize how much I needed all of that, to be there with you, to see her, and to hear what the doctor had to say. It's given me a lot to think about but it's also taken a lot off my mind, if that makes sense."

"So, you're not mad at me?" I'm better at navigating through hostile waters. Peace still feels like foreign territory and I've yet to get my bearings.

"You mean about the fifteen pounds? I was never mad at you, I was concerned. There's a difference. Your doctor says everything looks good, and I'm going to assume he knows what he's talking about." His tone is calm and his words are measured.

"It's not fifteen pounds." It is, but he can't know that, so I bluff. I'm not sure why I feel the need to downplay it, since he doesn't even seem to care anymore. If I were smart, I would let it go. But this is me we're talking about.

"Just stop. You were 146 when we went to the infusion center for your first IV treatment. I remember, because the nurse made you get on the scale in order to double-check the dosage, and you were concerned about what my reaction would be. I thought it was adorable. And now you're 131. I told you I'm not mad, but if you start talking to me like I'm an idiot who can't do basic math, I'm not going to be happy."

"You know, you're not supposed to retain information like that. If you *ever* hear a girl's weight, you're meant to scrub the detail from your memory, post haste." I love that Croy pays attention, but come on, this is too much. "Anyways, can we talk about something else?"

"We can talk about the wedding. What kind of car you want. When we want to move everything to the new house. If we're going to my sister's place for Thanksgiving. Anything you want." Croy's list is overwhelming.

I'm going to need him to take the reins and start making some of these decisions for us.

Thirty

I MAKE my retreat to the darkened bedroom, where I strip out of my clothes and crawl into bed. Jumping mental hurdles all afternoon has been exhausting. Maybe if I close my eyes, I can wake up a better person. My family deserves that much, if not more, and I desperately want to deliver.

I've been honest with Croy about my depression. It never felt right to keep it from him, and I knew I couldn't hide it forever. Since we were talking about getting married, and I wanted him to make a fully informed decision, I opted for an early truth. But the truth has many layers, and I probably wasn't as honest as I could have been.

My past has taught me some things are better left unsaid. People will hold onto your most vulnerable information so they can use it against you at a later date. A good old fashion low blow; the individually specific insult that cuts like an ax to the chest. I'm sure we've all been on the receiving end or maybe thrown a few during a particularly nasty fight. Well, I've been hit with my fair share of low blows over the years, mostly about my weight, sexuality, or depression. Those attacks caused me to lock away the parts of myself that made me an easy target.

I lost my faith in people but never stopped looking for love.

When I met Croy, I knew he was different. I felt like he already knew me, as though we were the two halves destined to make each other whole. But I wanted him to like me, so I did my best to keep it cute, even though he could see my life falling apart. I wasn't going to spill my guts and make myself look worse.

As time passes, we learn more about one another, and our bond strengthens. Croy is incredibly thoughtful and understanding, which he proves on a daily basis. Yet another reason why he isn't the problem, I am. Some things are beyond explanation, and even if I could find the words, why would I want to? Honesty is a risk. Would he still look at me the same way? Could he love someone so broken?

How do you tell the man you love you don't want to leave, but the thought of escape is always on your mind?

Thirty-One

I FEEL the warmth of his body as the bed shifts and he crawls in behind me. Croy never disappoints me, even when I give him reason to. "How'd you know I needed you?" I ask, but my question goes unanswered.

Instead of telling me why he's here, he uses his hands to show me. I bite my lip and squeeze my eyes shut tight, as the tips of his fingers brush along the curve of my neck and over the exposed section of my shoulder. The heat of his skin, where it makes contact with mine, lingers long after he's moved on. I press my back into his chest and sink deeply into his embrace as his arm locks me into place.

Without warning, he playfully bites into my shoulder, causing my back to arch away. Unsurprisingly, he's expecting this reaction and holds on tightly. The man knows my every thought. He's explored my body in detail, mapping out the various pathways to my pleasure. It's clear he intends for this to be a slow torture, and we're only at the beginning.

I want to tell him I'm sorry, for everything, but it's not the right time. My fingers lace into his, and I open my eyes.

The room is cast in shadow, but light enough for me to see

the arm across my chest is absent of tattoos. Whoever this person is, he's not my husband.

Time stops.

Where's Croy and who's behind me? Panic freezes me in place as I attempt to make sense of my current predicament. Where am I and how did I get here? If I play along, can I escape?

With one arm locked across my chest and his other hand on my hip, he wastes little time, grinding himself against me and showing me he's ready. I try to breathe, but my heart is pounding and my head is spinning. I don't understand how this happened, and while I'm struggling to sort through the details, the scene plays on without me.

"Tell me you want me, and I'll give you everything." His voice and these words are familiar, but I'm too scared to think straight.

I attempt to roll over onto my back, but he refuses to loosen his grip. This isn't going to be easy, no matter what choice I make next. In the hypothetical version of this situation, I would fight to the death before letting a man force himself on me, but locked in the moment, submission seems easier and faster.

"I want you… to kiss me first." The words come out on their own, and I realize I'm no longer in control. What happens next is already written, because there is no changing the past. This moment is a memory, from the life I left behind.

The text alert on my phone sounds, pulling me to the surface.

Kells: I need to talk to you about something.

: Now you want to talk? After taking off and ignoring me for three weeks.

Kells: Go to hell, Belk, you're so selfish! I've thought about you every day. You have no idea how much I miss you.

: Yeah, I guess I wouldn't know because you never responded to my messages. Why are you even texting me?

Kells: I told you. I need to talk to you about something.

: Okay. Well, I don't know if it's your baby or not, so I guess you'll have to wait and find out with the rest of us.

After a few minutes of nothing, I realize what I've done. That wasn't the conversation Kelly was expecting. He hadn't even considered the possibility until now.

I need to talk to Croy. He'll know what to do.

It doesn't take me long to search the condo and realize Croy isn't home and his car is missing from its usual parking spot. I've only been asleep for a couple of hours, so he couldn't have gone far.

: Babe, are you at the gym or something? I need to talk to you.

Croy: Is everything alright? What happened? I'm at the house with the builder, doing the final walk-thru, but I'll leave now and be home in ten minutes.

: No. Stop.

: You went to the house for the final walk-thru without me?

Croy: He called and I didn't want to wake you. I'm sorry. I'll come home.

: No. Don't worry about it. I'm good. Stay there and finish what you're doing. I'm good.

Croy: When you say "I'm good" I know you
aren't, and you said it twice, so I know I
messed up. I'll be home in a few minutes.

: I don't want you here!

It's all too much, the feelings crashing in around me from all sides, and I can't do it anymore. I'll never be happy, things will never get better, and I'm so tired of pretending. I want to scream. I want to break things. I want to disappear to a place where no one will ever find me. I want to burn there, devoured by my grief, so Croy can carry on without me.

Croy: You know what, that's fine. You had a
rough day and looked so peaceful sleeping. I
thought I could handle this on my own, but I
made a mistake. Let me know when I'm
allowed to come home.

: Don't bother. Maybe you should move into the
new house and I should stay here until the
lease is up.

Croy: Okay. We can talk about it face-to-face if
that's what you want. Can I take you to dinner
tonight?

: Take your other girlfriend. I'm not hungry.

Croy: Alright. Can I call you to discuss the
details of our separation, or would you prefer to
have this conversation in text, so everything's in
writing? I'd like to come to some sort of
amicable agreement without involving the
courts.

: No courts needed. I'll sign whatever you want.
Everything's yours.

Croy: We can discuss it and come up with
something fair for both parties. I told you I
would take care of you and I intend to honor
my vow.

: So, you're finally giving up on me?

Croy: Absolutely not. I was just stalling for time.

As I read the last message, Croy walks through the front door and makes a beeline for the couch where I'm sitting. I want to be angry, but there's no room for anything besides my heartbreak.

For a moment, I thought he was okay with losing me. Accepting his detachment, I could feel myself shatter and drift away. Even as he sits here, holding me together.

Tears spill from my eyes and absorb into the cotton polyester blend of his hooded sweatshirt. The cool Autumn air still clinging to the fabric prickles my skin as I'm cloaked in his presence. I can't handle the thought of losing him, so why do I keep trying to push him away?

I know my reasons for loving Croy, their abundance would take me centuries to list. And once I got to the end, I would require another hundred years to note the discoveries I'd made along the way. Every day since we've met, I've learned more about my better half and I've fallen deeper into the embrace of his love. Croy is my certainty.

Prior to meeting my husband, I dated a fair amount. I mean, how else are you supposed to find someone unless you're willing to put yourself out there? I was never sure what to look for, so I made a point to cast a wide net. I dated a few guys who were totally average, and a couple of guys who were out of my league. I got into a relationship with a window cleaner who lived in one-bedroom apartments and blew all his money on drugs. I lived with an IT tech, a cabinet maker, a machinist, a personal trainer, and a loss prevention officer.

When I wasn't in a committed relationship, I would go on

two or more first dates a week, and not because I needed someone to buy me a meal. I was driven by human need; the desire that lives within all of us, compelling us toward potential mates. I would pluck and prune, shower and shave, adorn myself in pleasing fragrances and understated accoutrement. I would consider the hobbies, education, and employment of my date, and tailor my conversational interests accordingly. I would smile and laugh, and be always the best version of myself, to no avail. No matter how hard I tried to be perfect, I still ended up alone.

With Croy, everything is different because of how we met. He had already seen me at my weakest, most vulnerable state, so there was no point in pretending to be strong. I knew he was my person, but I didn't initially think being together was ever going to be an option, so I allowed myself to be fully revealed and brutally honest. And because of that, I'm at a loss, unsure of how to navigate our future. I have no experience, in this lifetime, with the sort of partnership I've committed to, and I fear I'm fooling myself even though I know better.

"How can you love someone so broken, when you deserve so much better?" My question sounds as pathetic as I feel. Here I am, yet again, fishing for reassurances. Offering him an out and praying he doesn't take it.

"I don't know what *better* than you looks like, and I'm not as good at expressing myself as you are, so I'm trying to think of how to describe my feelings for you." Croy's exhaled breath passes over the top of my head like a summer breeze, or the sun, at the center of my universe.

"Do you remember the first time we hung out with Megan and Brian, and she asked you about how we met? You changed the location, but it was the way you described the feeling. You said it was like electricity being passed back and forth between us, and everything in the background disappeared, and all you could focus on was me. Hearing you tell the story, it was like you watched it from my eyes and were expressing my innermost thoughts. That was exactly how I felt, and the sensation continued in the hospital when we talked, in the parking lot when we parted, on the couch at my house listening to music, in the pool, while hiking trails, and at the restaurant when we got engaged. It's never stopped feeling that way. You're all I care about, and all I think about. My attention is laser-focused on you and your happiness. I knew the second I met you my future was directly tied to yours, and so when I fought for you, that was me fighting for us. Better than you, doesn't exist in my world, and you aren't broken. You just don't give yourself enough credit." I sit silently, absorbing his words and their intention.

Croy isn't wrong. I have trouble giving myself credit for the things I've accomplished and what I bring to the table. I tend to measure value in monetary contributions, not in regard to others, but certainly myself.

"I love you." I wiggle in closer, rubbing my face against his chest. Finally, the temperature of his sweatshirt has risen to match his body, melting away my insecurities.

"I know you do, which is why I left and came home as soon as you messaged me." Croy's words spark a memory from a time that felt like a dream. "Speaking of, what did you need to talk to me about?"

I pull the phone from my pocket and sit back against the couch. If I'm able to see his face while he's reading the conversation I had with Kelly, then I'll know what he's thinking before he has a chance to soften the message he relays back to me.

"Okay, so he thinks about you every day, and misses you like crazy, but ignores your efforts to communicate? Why? What is it that he needs to talk to you about? Everything with Kelly is some bullshit manipulation and I don't like it." Croy hands the phone back to me without commenting on the most crucial section of the conversation.

"And? What about the part I said?" I need to know if Croy's still on my team. He's been against me telling Kelly since the very beginning, and I doubt that's changed.

"I worry about him making things difficult for us, but I don't think there's much Kelly can do that we can't handle. He might not even want to be involved since winning you back is off the table. I don't know, babe. We'll have to wait and see what he says, okay?" Croy is as calm as expected.

He's my voice of reason, the logical side that balances my emotions. This, right here, is exactly why I needed to talk to him straight away.

"And what if he doesn't say anything?" Something about Kelly's silence is terrifying. He's smart, calculated, and manipulative. I know this. And Croy's right, if Kelly wants to make our life difficult, he'll exploit this situation for all its worth. He'll use this leverage to drive a wedge into the center of my marriage, and I handed him the tools to do it.

"By February, Verlaine will be here and we can put any unanswered questions to rest, once and for all. No matter what, we'll sort it out. Believe it or not, I do know a good lawyer, despite my reluctance to use one in the past. And if that's not enough, my parents can send in their legal team. They aren't exactly going to let their first grand-kid get taken three hours away." Croy says the last part like it's a joke, but I'm not laughing.

"I don't want your parents or their money involved in any of this. Are we clear?" It'll be over my dead body his mother has a say in our daughter's future. The Leach and Her Illegitimate Child, will not be the name of my autobiography.

Thirty-Two

PER USUAL, Croy's stomach is calling the shots, so it looks like we're going out for dinner after all. He tells me it's a celebration, and I should get dressed nicely, but our destination remains a mystery. I hope there isn't another marriage proposal on the horizon. After all, how many times can a girl say *yes*? I suppose in this case, this girl could say yes as many times as this guy felt the need to ask the question, but let's hope that isn't the point of our meal.

I disguise myself with makeup and curl the hair that's gotten unbelievably thick since getting pregnant. Whatever combination of hormones stops your period, grows your hair, and makes your skin glow, science needs to find a way to mass produce. I can't think of a woman out there who would be unhappy with these results.

"Let me see what you're wearing," I call out to the living room before selecting my outfit. Croy comes into the bedroom and I momentarily forget how to breathe. "How do you always look so good?" I can't possibly match the level he's on, glowing skin or not. His outfit is coordinated runway perfection, and on my best day, I'm a middle-aged trip to the grocery store.

"How about the dress you're saving for Thanksgiving dinner

at my sister's house?" There's a certain twinkle in Croy's eye when he mentions the new dress I bought, so I know what I'm wearing.

"Alright, but that means no pictures from tonight. I'm trying to make a good impression on your very fashionable sister next week, and the whole effect is lost if she sees me in it before-hand." I put a lot of effort into this look, even going so far as to enlist the help of a girl I knew in college.

"My sister doesn't care what you wear to her holiday party, and she's already impressed by you. I've talked to her more in the last few months than I have in the three years prior and she's always asking about you."

I take the dress from the hanger and pull the corresponding undergarments from my dresser. "Alright, you can go now. I'll be out in a minute."

At my dismissal, I assume Croy will turn on his heels and retreat to the couch in the living room, but he doesn't move. Rather, he holds his position in the open doorway and smiles. "I'm good."

Who knew my husband was such a voyeur? Now, instead of getting dressed like a normal person, I have to attempt to be seductive. For me, this is easier said than done. I'm not naturally sexy like some girls are. I have to work at it, and even then, I'm better in the dark.

All I can do is my best, and thankfully he doesn't seem disap-pointed. By the time I have the dress on, Croy looks like he's ready to rip it off of me. Slowly I approach and spin around. "Would you mind helping me with the zipper, sir?"

I could probably get the dress zipped myself, but asking for assistance seems like the oldest trick in the book. I've seen it done a million times in the movies, so there must be something to it. The painfully slow way in which he zips the dress confirms he's enjoying himself.

Catching me off guard, Croy twirls me around and pins me against the wall. There is a reason I call him a beast and it's not only his bench press. When he kisses my neck, I nearly lose my ability to stand and what he whispers into my ear gives me goosebumps.

I know what he's hoping for, so I decide to tease him. "When we get home, I want you to take your time," I whisper back, before biting my lip. I'm so turned on, I'm not sure if I can wait, so I know he can't either.

"Dammit. I was afraid you were going to say that. Okay, fine. But I'm tying you to bed when we get home, and I'm going make beg for me to stop, so be prepared."

I swallow the lump in my throat as my eyes plead for mercy. He will break me, in the way every woman dreams of, and I will be helpless to stop him. This night just got a whole lot better.

It takes me a second to compose myself and another minute to get my legs working again, but eventually, I'm ready to proceed with the evening. If I had my choice, we'd stay home, eat dinner on the couch, and celebrate in the bedroom, but tonight Croy's calling the shots.

It didn't take long for me to notice his odd affinity for expensive restaurants, and even though I grumble about the cost, when it comes to food Croy loves to overindulge in decadence. So, based on our clothing and my prior experiences, I'm not the least bit surprised when he parks in front of Vermilion's most upscale dining location.

The restaurant has a dress code, if that's any indication, and personally, I don't care for it, but again, it's not my show. I'm willing to be a good sport, so long as he makes good on his after-dinner promise. One step in the door and I remember why I don't like coming here. Croy and I look out of place, like dirty little kids, dressed up in their parents' clothes, pretending to be fancy. Oddly enough, I think that's exactly why he enjoys coming here.

Croy doesn't subscribe to the idea of not belonging. He feels like our tattoos don't define the caliber of our character, and I agree, for the most part. However, I'd take a burger at the bar and a draft cider on tap over just about any of the upscale places we've been.

Maybe because I know how to cook, I perceive eating out as an insult. If my husband wants a healthy delicious meal, I'd rather be the one to make it. So, when we do go out, I want food that tastes of guilt. I want to feel like I cheated on my diet, and I'm going to have to beg for forgiveness in the gym. I want salt and fat and flavor. And I want my salad dressing to come in a little plastic cup, off to the side, without anyone feeling the need to make an issue out of my request.

Thankfully, it's Thursday night and the restaurant is relatively quiet. One might even go so far as to say it feels romantic. Croy lays his arm across the top of the table, and I respond by giving him my hand. It's better when he's not wearing a suit jacket, but those are the rules. I wonder if he'll still hold my hand like this when we're older. I can picture us withered and wrinkled, long past our prime. Knowing my luck, Croy will age like fine wine and end up a silver fox while I turn into one of those frogs that resemble an avocado.

"What are you thinking about?" Croy asks, rubbing his thumb across the back of my hand. "Your face lit up like a Christmas tree, and then it disappeared so quickly I nearly missed it."

"I was imagining our future." I smile, and he smiles, and I'm reminded our connection is so much more than the physical. Croy didn't fall in love with me on the surface. He walked through hell and reached out his hand, leaving me with a debt I have yet to repay.

When the waiter arrives with our drinks, Croy orders steak for both of us, one rare and the other medium rare. At this point, I don't care what we eat. My mind is currently gallivanting through fantasy land with the gray-haired version of my spouse, and I'm in no rush to relocate reality.

"You're always beautiful, but goddamn you look good right now. I'm not sure I'll make it through Thanksgiving dinner if you're next to me in this dress. Seriously, all I can think about is how badly I want to rip it off of you." His voice is hushed, but I'm certain someone could overhear if they had a mind to.

"Buy me a new outfit this weekend, and I'll let you tear this one to ribbons tonight." My playful statement is topped off with a wink. Flirtatious banter isn't meant to be a binding verbal contract, but it is fun.

The meal is delicious, the atmosphere is intimate, and the conversation is as engaging as ever, but this isn't where I want to be. My mind and soul are at home, still pressed against the bedroom wall, while my empty shell occupies this seat, doing its best impression of an entire person. Don't get me wrong, every moment with my husband is a moment I want to be involved in. There is no other company I would rather keep, but I'm horny, and eating steak isn't going to scratch that itch, no matter how well it's seasoned.

And then there is the other guy who still leases real estate in my head space. Occasionally, when it's quiet, I miss having a friend. Specifically, I miss Kelly and the bond we formed over time. Why did I have to ruin things by allowing it to get physical? Then again, I wonder if we would have had the relationship we ultimately did, had we never taken it to that level.

With Croy, our connection was instant. I always say we felt like lovers from a past life, reuniting in the next. With Kelly, there was a spark that raged into an inferno, burning out the oxygen in the room and taking my life with it.

Not always, but now and then, for a minute or two, I miss the fire and all the ways it engulfed me. Why am I drawn to things I know are bad for me? Why do I walk to danger instead of running toward freedom? I worry I might be addicted to the pain of being mistreated.

"Where are you right now? You haven't heard a word I said." Croy's arm is across the table, holding my hand, and I'm surprised to see our dinner plates have been cleared away. "Are you thinking about Kelly?"

Too often I forget Croy can read my mind and now I'm caught. I'm meant to be out on a date celebrating the completion of our housing project, and I'm sitting here thinking about my fake ex. Seriously, what's wrong with me?

"I'm sorry, babe. What were you saying?" Now I feel bad. It's rude to let my attention drift away. "Did you want something sweet?"

"I'll have my dessert at home," Croy says with a wink. I'm glad my wandering thoughts haven't derailed the best part of the evening.

Holding my free hand in the air, I motion toward no one in particular.

"Check Please."

Thirty-Three

BEFORE LEAVING THE RESTAURANT, I excuse myself to the restroom in case this is my last opportunity. Croy has given me fair warning about what lies ahead, so I take a moment to run through my pre-sex checklist. After draining my bladder of fluids, I wash my hands, check my teeth for food, and wrangle any stray hairs back onto their side of the part. Whoever this lady is in the mirror looking back at me, she does look pretty this evening. It's unfortunate her cute little dress is about to get put through the shredder.

On the short drive home, there's a lot on my mind. In a way that's difficult to describe, I would say I'm nervous. It's not that I'm scared of what Croy might do, merely concerned about what he might think. It was only two hours ago I was standing naked in front of him getting dressed for our date, so it's not as though he'll be surprised, but the thought of being tied to the bed, without clothes, unable to hide my flaws, is stoking my anxiety. God forbid he leaves the light on, I'm going to have a full-blown panic attack.

According to Croy's mother, his exes have all been attractive, and I'm a hideous soul-sucking leach. And as much as he likes to tease me about my GQ model ex and how shallow he is, my husband clearly gravitates toward a similar caliber of woman, and that's never going to be me. This realization concerns me daily. Is he with me out of pity or obligation? Was I simply a situationship that turned into a trap?

The first time Kelly told me he loved me, I knew he never meant it, and that was okay because it made sense. There was no hiding the fact he was out of my league and everyone could see that. Croy, on the other hand, goes to great lengths to prove his love and commitment, and I haven't been able to square that circle. He's perfect and I'm not. The math doesn't add up.

"Make it make sense," I say, without realizing the words escaped my head to come spilling out of my mouth.

"What's that, babe?" Croy pulls into his designated parking spot and kills the engine.

"You know I'm not good enough for you, don't you? How can you not see that?" I'm not sure how I got to this place, or why I frequently feel the need to visit, but perhaps it's time to cancel my membership.

"Nope, not happening. Not tonight. Your crushing self-doubt and crippling depression are not going to save you from what's coming, so save it for tomorrow. Right now, we are going into the condo, and I am going to tease you until you beg me to stop, and then I'm going to fuck you." Croy is dead serious, and it's sexy as hell.

"Well, alright." I would have to be a damn fool to argue with that logic. Plus, he isn't wrong. I'm in my head and being ridiculous. Of course, he loves me. He proposed long before finding out I was pregnant. And it's clear he's attracted to me. The man has to be touching me every moment we spend together. A guy like Croy doesn't give up his whole life to move three hours away in order to be with a girl out of pity. I was never a situationship.

I'm his soulmate, goddamnit, and it's time I wake up to the reality of my life.

Thirty-Four

THE MORNING ALARM wails its usual sob story, but something feels wrong. It's already 6:00 am. For some reason, the gym alarms didn't go off as scheduled, and Croy seems unfazed. I know last night was exhausting, but it isn't like him to miss a workout. "Are you feeling alright?"

He laughs and launches his body toward the bed. Upon impact, I nearly bounce off the edge onto the floor, the sight of which makes him laugh harder. "I feel great. Why do you ask?"

"The alarm never goes off this late during the week." I'm still so tired. I might close my eyes after he leaves and catch a few more hours of rest before heading over to the house to clean. The plan is to have Croy and the guys start moving things out of the pods tomorrow since it's the weekend and all three guys work Monday through Friday. If I clean today, I won't have to sweep around the furniture.

"I know, but I thought we could use a break after last night." He sounds like he's been awake for hours and I'm wondering if he was able to sneak away and come back without me knowing.

Memories of last night's sexual activities race through my mind like the New York City Marathon, sweaty and unrelenting. True to his word, Croy did not let me off easy. He was determined to make me beg, and I was forced to oblige. Something about that painfully slow teasing torture gets me every time, and he knows it.

I have a love/hate relationship with foreplay. On one hand, it's the best part of sex because it sets the tone and gets everyone ready to go, which is important. But on the flip side, foreplay or sex without the release is a fate worse than death. Guys seem to think they've done you some kind of favor simply by showing up when in reality they've left you worse off than they found you.

Thankfully, my husband is good about making sure I get to where I need to be, and I appreciate him for that, but last night was excessive and I'm going to be tender for the rest of the day. My abdominal muscles are sore from convulsing three times in a row, my jaw hurts, my neck and shoulders are laced with knots, and I'm not entirely sure I'll be able to sit. I suppose I'll need to accept the consequences of my actions, endure, and press on.

Our days here are numbered and I have a list of items requiring my attention. There's a plan for the current day, a weekend checklist, and a Thanksgiving Day self-imposed deadline I need to address. I'm not worried about clearing out the condo this week, but I want those damn moving pods off my new lawn, pronto.

While Croy is in the shower getting ready for work, I set my alarm for 8:00 am and close my eyes. Our usual schedule would have me up, making coffee, and chatting with him about the day ahead, but my battery is only at fifty percent and I can't do the whole loving wife routine right now. He'll understand. He always does.

Without even realizing it, I drift off into a dreamless sleep.

Thirty-Five

I SPRING upright in bed as the text alert on my phone signals an incoming message. It's probably Croy checking on me. I was fast asleep before he finished his shower, so I missed my opportunity to say goodbye before he left for work. I retrieve the phone with a smile, excited to know he's thinking about me.

When I look at the screen, I'm surprised to find it's not Croy who's thinking of me, it's his sister.

> Astrid: Good morning, lovely. I was wondering if I could ask you for a favor.

> : Sure. What did you have in mind?

It's too early in the morning for favors and texting, but any sister of Croys is a sister-in-law of mine, and anyway, I want her to like me. Astrid and I haven't spent much time together, but if I'm able to help her out in some way, I'm happy to do it. I rub my eyes, crack my neck, and give my back a quick stretch as I await her response.

Astrid: I'm not sure if you remember or not, but when I was at your place, I had some red wine that was to die for, and I was wondering if you could tell me what it was so I could get some for Thursday.

: That's not much of a favor. I thought you were going to ask for help collecting on a debt or dumping a body in the lake or something.

Astrid: Normally I go to my brother for help with that kind of stuff, but he does lack a certain subtlety. Hahaha.

: Men usually do. As for the wine you're looking for, it isn't available in stores. I can swing by the winery when they open and buy a few bottles if you'd like. Let me know how many you need. The red you had was blueberry, but they also have a pear (white wine) that's equally addicting.

Astrid: I feel bad asking you to bring the alcohol. Can you drink a glass of wine when you're pregnant? I don't even know.

: I'm not entirely sure, to be honest, but I'll be sticking with water. You might not know this, but your brother is a bit on the overprotective side. How many people are you having for dinner?

Astrid: For better or worse, Croy is only like that with you. Must be a soulmate thing. As for dinner, I think there's going to be six of us. I invited our brother, but I don't think he's coming.

Wait what? Croy has never mentioned having additional siblings, which is weird because I remember us speaking at length about my hodgepodge of full, half, and step brothers and sisters. That seems like it would have been the perfect opportunity for him to chime in and mention something.

: Hey hun, out of curiosity, do you have a brother I don't know about?

Croy: Why do you ask? He's not sitting on our couch right now, is he?

: I take it you two don't get along?

Croy: What's going on? If he's there you need to tell me.

: There's nobody here. I don't even know who he is. You're being weird. Forget it. Keep your secrets.

Croy: Where is this coming from?

What the hell is going on here? Yet another huge, deeply rooted story, and I'm the blissfully ignorant little wife kicking rocks on the surface. Croy claims to be honest until I ask him about something he doesn't feel up to sharing. I read over the messages again, trying to sort out if he's the one overreacting or if it's me. I have been known to do that.

Astrid: Would you be willing to bring two bottles of the red and two of the white? I can send you the money now if you'd like.

: Don't be silly. Croy and I can go later when he gets home from work. Let me know if you need us to bring anything else. We'll be unpacking all week, so I'm looking forward to a nice home-cooked meal.

Astrid: Hahaha. I'm guessing my brother didn't
tell you. I don't cook. The meal is going to be
delicious, but I'm leaving it in the hands of
professionals.

: Okay. I'm officially jealous. I want your life.

Astrid: If that were true, all you'd have to do is
say the word.

Talk about some fancy-pants holiday party planning. I can't even imagine having the kind of money where you could afford to hire someone to do all the tasks you didn't feel like learning. Growing up, my parents were committed to all things do-it-yourself, and I was right there in the mix, helping out. I could build you a deck, tile your bathroom, wallpaper your bedroom, or design and install a kitchen remodel, simply point me in the direction of your project and give me a moment to collect the appropriate tools.

Astrid can't even be bothered to watch a video online and learn how to cook a turkey. Come to think of it, I take back what I said, I don't want her life.

I add a trip to the winery to my mental checklist, get myself out of bed, and stumble into the shower on wobbly legs. This day has to start eventually, and the house isn't going to clean itself. I suppose I could wait and shower later, but oh well, too late now. My brain is a little like a train, once the wheels are in motion, it's best to let it go along its merry way. Sudden stops or deviations from the set course can derail everything, and that tends to be messy.

To-go coffee, phone, earbuds, keys. Check. Shoes on, hood up. Check. A Text for the hubby to let him know I'm leaving the house. Might as well, even if I am annoyed by his omissions.

My message is delivered, but unread. No worries. He'll get back to me eventually, he always does. I wish I had a career. Croy was so much smarter than I was after college, focusing on himself, investing in his future, and growing his brand. I squandered my 20s chasing after boys who didn't want to be seen with me and mourning the loss of relationships that should've never existed. Lessons learned the hard way. At what point do we graduate and move on to an enjoyable life? I'm so tired of learning lessons from ill-equipped teachers.

If I were an optimist, I would say the steps I've taken, while messy, ultimately lead me here, implying this has been a life well lived. But I'm not an optimist, so I would never say that. Mostly I'm just tired.

I'm tired of making bad choices and adapting to harsh new realities. Even now, waist-deep in my dream come true, I'm exhausted. Most people would think I'm crazy to hear me admit this, but I don't want to move into the new house. Croy and I have finally settled into a nice rhythm with one another and synced our routines, only to have it thrown in the air again. I don't want to go back to living in different timelines and feeling invisible.

Lost in thought, I turn into the driveway and startle when I see a car I don't recognize parked by the house. The sight makes my heart leap into my throat. The builder told Croy yesterday everything was finished and we were good to move in. So, who's car is that and why are they here?

My heartbeat quickens as my anxiety skyrockets. I can't very well sit here and do nothing, but what are my options? Who would be here and why isn't Croy responding to any of my messages? When I mentioned his brother, he seemed off and asked me if he was sitting on our couch. That was weird, but I didn't think much of it until now.

I take a photo of the car and the back license plate as I walk toward the front door, this way, if I'm murdered, the police will have a solid lead.

If only I had pepper spray or some other useful means of defense, but I don't.

On week three at the jail, the newbies had a pepper spray and taser training day. Kelly and I, being the newbies. That experience was anything but a good time, but the memory makes me smile because I didn't have to go through it alone. We got dosed at the same time and I swear I thought my eyes would burn forever. My throat felt like it was sealing shut and there was snot pouring out of my nose. It was not a cute look.

Before getting pepper sprayed, the training officer zapped us each with a taser. Without a doubt, if I had a choice between the two, I would pick the taser, every time. The electrical current shoots through your body and your muscles lock up, causing you to fall to the ground. Since it was only training, they let us kneel, so we didn't have as far to go before hitting the mats. For weeks, there was a lingering vibration, but nothing crazy. Come to think of it, maybe that's why I always shock Croy when I touch him. It's the leftover electrical pulses escaping through my fingertips in the presence of his mechanical framework.

The purpose of the training was for us to fully understand what it felt like. They wanted us to make an informed decision, if and when we sprayed or tased someone else. Sure, I got that and I was willing to play along, but I also think it was a sort of initiation, though the other officers would never admit that.

My thoughts ping-pong back and forth between past and present as I make my way along the path. What am I even doing? Am I being stupid? Am I about to get raped and killed over some copper piping? I have not mentally prepared for this.

When I left the condo, I was thinking about what order I should clean the house in, and now here I am, walking into a situation blind. Goddamnit! Why isn't Croy texting me back?

My hand shakes as I grip the handle on the front door, and when it swings open without resistance, I attempt to swallow my fear. No signs of forced entry. Okay, so probably not a break-in. I exhale slowly and tentatively step inside. "Hello. Is someone here?"

Croy can unlock the door with his phone, so he must have let them in, whoever it is. But why wouldn't he mention it to me, unless he thought they would be in and out before I got here? "Hello," I call out again, a little louder this time, but still there is no answer.

> : Why aren't you texting me back? I'm about to get murdered and you can't even be bothered to respond? Who the hell is here?

Alright, I guess it's now or never. Time to suck it and be brave. I'll do a quick sweep of the inside, and if I don't find anyone, I'll check the perimeter and the gym. After that, if I still can't locate the owner of the blue hatchback parked outside, I'll call the police. In the meantime, maybe Croy will text me back and we can sort this craziness out. Or I'll already be dead.

From the entryway, I take a quick peek into the kitchen and living room, but both appear quiet. With no furniture in the rooms, there aren't exactly a lot of hiding places available. The house is little more than a big, open space, flooded with morning light. If I wasn't so scared, I'd be in awe of what's been accomplished in the last few months.

I'm already standing to the right, so I walk into our bedroom first. Again nothing. The bathroom is empty and clean, with no signs of any damage. So far so good, but there's still plenty of time for things to go left.

I call out, my voice steeped in hesitant weakness. "Hello."

Pathetic. Where's the girl who used to go toe-to-toe with wife beating criminals? What happened to all of my sarcasm-laced confident determination? Maybe she really is lost, and here I stand in her place, as an impostor. "Hello?"

Whoever is here either can't hear me or intends to keep their location private.

> : I need you, you asshole. Where are you? I'm scared out of my mind. I'm about to check Verlaine's bedroom and bathroom, and then I'm heading outside. If something happens to me, I want you to know I truly did love you. You made life worth living. But I swear to god, if you ever date again, I'll haunt you to the brink of madness.

I pop my head into the second bedroom, searching for my undoing, and hear the shower as it turns on.

> : Someone is in Verlaine's bathroom, taking a shower. What should I do? Babe, I'm freaking out!

What the hell is the point of having a big, strong, scary husband if I have to deal with this shit on my own? I swear, if this is some kind of prank, and he's in there waiting to jump out at me, I'm filing for divorce.

Alright, this is it. No more stalling. It's now or never. I might not be the girl I was six months ago, but I do remember her. Officer Belk was fearless because she had nothing to lose. She was also mistakenly confident help would come from the others she vowed to protect.

"I only live for your love and your kiss. It's paradise to be near you like this..." The song hangs in the air, as her voice fills the previously empty space.

One by one, the knots of tension begin to loosen and release. The stranger in my house is a woman. That single piece of information changes the entire dynamic, swinging the odds of our survival back in Croy's favor. I grew up with older brothers, so I'm not entirely worthless in a fight.

With each step, my feet grow heavier, until I'm mere inches from the open bathroom door. One last deep breath, and then it's go-time.

Nope. That was a mistake.

My lungs fill with lavender-scented fumes and I'm coughing and choking uncontrollably as the silhouette of our mystery woman appears in the doorway. I wipe the tears from my eyes and attempt to regain my composure, as a hand comes to perch atop my shoulder.

"Oh, my goodness gracious. Sweetheart, are you alright? I'm terribly sorry. Do you need me to get you some water?" She attempts to comfort me, patting my shoulder while continuing to apologize. "I'm finished cleaning in the bathroom and... I am so sorry. I didn't know anyone was here."

So, this is how I die? Incapacitated by cleaning product fumes and then scared to death by a little, five-foot-two grandmother, wielding window cleaner and a rag. How embarrassing. No wonder Croy didn't want me to take a job at the state prison. I would've been eaten alive on day one. When did I become such a joke? If I ever walk outside again, I'll have to make sure to always face the sun, otherwise, I'm likely to be frightened by my own shadow.

"I'm okay," I say before releasing one final cough. "My husband neglected to mention anyone would be here. I'm so sorry. I apologize if I startled you." My lungs continue to smolder in my chest.

And in typical Heather Jepsen fashion, here I am, apologizing to my killer. Heaven forbid my death be an inconvenience to anyone's day.

Thirty-Six

TURNS OUT, my would-be assassin is none other than the housekeeper, hired by my sister-in-law. Upon learning this, I instantly jump into my feelings, as emotional pregnant ladies struggling with bipolar depression are prone to do. My irrational anger seems fueled by Astrid's audacity and my husband's lack of communication. How dare she send someone to clean my home? As if I'm incapable. And why didn't Croy tell me? He and I are going to need to have a serious talk.

The housekeeper, Linda, is a lovely woman, and we end up talking quite a bit. She insists on showing me the paid invoice to alleviate any lingering concerns I might have. It's unnecessary, but I indulge her.

"There's a bottle of champagne in the refrigerator and a card from your sister. I hope that's okay. I wasn't sure if it needed to be cold or not." Visible concern spreads across her face as she braces for my reaction.

Clearly, Linda is used to dealing with women who are far more uptight and particular than I am. Even still, no matter how accustomed one is to being scolded, it still hurts. I imagine this is what my face looks like when I'm around Croy's family.

"I don't know much about champagne, but I'm sure it's fine.

Feel free to take it with you when you leave. Knowing Astrid, I'm sure it's expensive and delicious." Part of me understands the people in my life are well-intentioned, but I hate the sneaky way they go about injecting their assistance.

My phone begins to vibrate in my pocket, but it seems rude to answer a call while I'm mid-conversation. Anyway, it's probably Croy finally getting back to me, and I need a moment to think before I talk to him. I was on the verge of a panic attack ten minutes ago, but now I have more of the picture colored in, the alarm I was feeling seems a little silly. I'm not happy with the situation, but I'm also not angry. I don't want to pick a fight over nothing, but I also don't want to sweep my feelings under the rug.

"I should be on my way. If for any reason you're dissatisfied with my work, or if you'd like for me to come back to clean again, I'll leave my card on the counter and you can call me directly. It was lovely to meet you. This is a beautiful home." Linda's kind words melt away the last of my unhappiness. "A beautiful home for a beautiful family."

"The house looks great. You did a fantastic job. I have no complaints." At least, I have no complaints that need to be directed her way. "It was lovely to meet you as well."

Pacing back and forth across the living room, I gaze out the back windows, attempting to collect and organize my thoughts. As I count my steps the phone in my back pocket alerts me to an incoming text. Again, I'm sure it's Croy. If I don't respond soon, he'll send the national guard to check on me.

Croy: Call me back!

: Everything's fine. We can talk later.

Croy: Answer the phone when I call you or call me back. I need to hear your voice.

: I'm fine. Let's not make it a thing.

Croy: Where are you?

: Can we talk later?

Croy: No. Answer your phone!

If I refuse to answer, he'll leave work and drive here for no reason, and I don't want that. "Hello."

"What's going on? Are you alright? I was in the middle of a tour with the president of the company when I read your messages and I'm pretty sure my soul left my body." There is no hint of his usual lighthearted joking. In truth, he sounds upset.

"I'm fine. I'm sorry. I shouldn't have bothered you." It's stupid, but I can feel myself shutting down.

"If someone's there and you're in trouble, tell me."

"No. There's no one here. No worries. Go find your soul and get back to your tour." This isn't the conversation either of us needs, but it's the one we're having. I want, more than anything, to reassure him I'm okay. I want to explain in detail what happened and laugh about it, but I can't force my mouth to cooperate when my depression is overriding my decision-making.

"To hell with the tour. All I care about is you. Do you need me?" What an interesting question. One I wasn't expecting him to ask.

And just like that, the spell is broken and I'm back in control.

"I always *need* you, but right now, I need you to stay at work and finish out the day. I promise you, I'm fine. The strange car in the driveway belonged to the housekeeper your sister hired. The one you neglected to tell me about. But we can discuss my feelings about that situation later, at home. I love you."

"Shit. Astrid told me she talked to you this morning. I

thought that meant... No. It doesn't matter. I should have told you. That was my fault."

"Don't worry about it."

"I love you so much. I need to get back out there but I'll call you when I'm on lunch, okay?"

"Okay."

"Baby, I am genuinely sorry. I promise one of these days I'll stop messing everything up."

"Please don't say that. I like it when you mess up. It makes me feel less insecure about my shortcomings."

"You're perfect."

"And you're perfect, so I guess we're a matched set."

"Can't argue with that logic. I love you."

"I love you too." I hang up the phone, happy we talked and relieved I didn't escalate the tension further by being an asshole.

Now that the last of the external chaos has subsided and all is as it should be, I have a choice to make. The cleaning is already done. So, I can either start unpacking one of the pods on my own, or I can call it a day and go home. Am I able to salvage what's left of the morning, and get some work done, or is the plan derailed and therefore dead?

I feel like a normal person would be able to shift gears and move on to a new task. For them, the transition would be effortless. They wouldn't need time to regroup. A normal person would be happy the cleaning was done. They would choose another item off their to-do list. If they even have a list. Maybe normal people can get through the day without planning and overanalyzing every detail and possible outcome.

Where's my mania when I need it? I could have this place unpacked and decorated by midnight if I could just get a small hit of the good stuff.

Despite my longing, I'm unable to will my frenzied passion and heightened exuberance into existence. So, the morning is a wash.

Thirty-Seven

BACK IN THE comfort of familiar surroundings, I manage to accomplish a few tasks before settling onto the couch to relax. I'm finishing the last episode of my new favorite series when Croy calls. Without my watch on, I'm not sure of the time, but I can assume it's his lunch break.

"Hello, my love." I answer the phone with a singsong voice, currently in a fantastic mood. For once, a show ended with the main character choosing the right guy. I swear, had she chased after the older brother with the poor attitude, simply because she'd been pining over him since they were kids, I would've thrown the remote. Not that I think people with shit attitudes are unworthy of love. Otherwise, I'd be single.

"I'm glad to hear you still think of me that way. I want to come home, right now, and cuddle on the couch with you." Croy sounds like he's ready for a shower and his relaxing clothes. It's cute. Unfortunately, his adorable tone evaporates faster than water boiling in the kettle. "I have to tell you something, and I want you to know that I feel terrible. My sister told me about the housekeeper and I unlocked the door this morning to let her in. I intentionally didn't mention it to you because I knew you would get pissed. You always want to do everything yourself, and I love that, but I wish you would accept help once in a while."

"That's a fair criticism, Croy. However, scaring me half to death sort of nullifies the kind gesture, don't you think?" Using his first name is a subtle signaling of my displeasure, without needing to raise my voice. I'm not happy about the situation, but I understand where he's coming from. This is not the first time my husband and I have had a conversation about my inability to accept gifts, encouragement, compliments, assistance, or whatever it might be. I'm more comfortable giving, than receiving.

"I never meant for you to get scared. I thought she'd be gone before you got there. Then I got busy at work and I couldn't check my phone. It doesn't matter. I messed up, and I'm sorry."

"Okay, I get it. I don't need any more apologies." I appreciate the acknowledgment of guilt, but enough is enough. Let's move on. "Are you going to be stuck at work late?"

"Hell no. I have the next nine days off and I'm looking forward to spending every second with you. I'll be home on-time, if not earlier." Croy's momentary excitement sparks and fades. "Seriously though, I need you to talk to me."

"I am talking to you."

"Yes. You are. And you're doing an awesome impression of someone who's in a good mood, but I'd rather you be honest with me about how you feel. I know you're mad at me. You're probably pissed at Astrid too. So, let's talk it out." Bait the hook and cast the line. Croy's chartered a boat for his fishing trip, and he's hunting for unabashed honesty. So, here it is.

"Was I pissed when I found out your sister hired someone to come clean *our* new house without asking me? Yeah hun, I certainly wasn't happy about it. Stop paying people to do shit I can do! I hate when you guys treat me like I'm incapable! I was mad. I can admit that, but you know what, I decided to let it go. Why? Because I don't have room for those feelings right now. I'm so tired of feeling like the worthless little wife who brings zero value to the relationship. And I'm sick of you not communicating with me. There was no reason for any of that to happen, had you opened your mouth or sent a text. You say you love me. You say you want to protect me. You tell me I'm the most important thing in your world. Bullshit! If that's true, stop lying to me. You're over here digging graves, trying to bury secrets, and I'm simply asking you to put down the shovel." Well, that escalated quickly. Now my heart is pounding and I can feel a twitch behind my right eye, which usually telegraphs the arrival of a migraine. I didn't want to have this fight, and yet here we are.

"You know I love you more than anything, and my sister thinks the world of you. The cleaning was meant to be a house-warming gift, for the pair of us, because she's excited. No one meant it as an attack on your ability."

"You asked me how I felt and I told you, now can we drop it?" No matter what I say, I can't win. If I pretend like everything is okay, I'm a time-bomb. If I'm honest about my feelings and speak up, I'm a Debbie Downer. People don't care about the truth. What they seek is absolution from their guilt. "No. You know what, forget it. I think I'll say goodbye for now."

"Please, don't. We can talk about whatever you want, I need to hear your voice."

"Okay, then tell me about your brother." Fair is fair. If Croy wants me to be more honest, then he needs to be willing to do the same.

"That's a long story, babe. Can I tell you over dinner?"

"I'll talk to you later." I rush through the words and hang up the phone. When Croy wants answers, he wants them *now*, but when I ask about something, it's always later. How the hell can two people who are mirror opposites have so much in common?

Croy: I know you're upset, but don't hang up
on me.

Croy: My half-brother's name is Anders. He's five years older than me but we didn't grow up together. As a teenager, he would move in for a few months when he was fighting with his mom, then he would leave. The disruption caused a lot of tension between my parents. The guy is an asshole. Even as a kid he would beat me up and break my toys. And he would count everything. Comparing and complaining. Always annoying shit. He would go on and on if I ate two cookies out of the package and he only had one. Like, take another cookie and be done with it, it's not that deep.

Croy: I told you about an incident that happened while I was in college. I came home, got into a fight, and my mom called the cops, but what I didn't tell you was that the fight was with Anders, not my parents. I came home for a visit and walked in on him having sex with my girlfriend, in my bedroom. I snapped and I wasn't a little kid anymore. So, I beat the shit out of him.

Croy: After that, he went out of his way to sleep with every girl I dated. So yeah, I don't talk about him and I don't consider him a brother and if I see him within 500 feet of you, I'm going back to jail.

: Did you get arrested when your mom called the cops?

Croy: Yes.

: Did you do time in jail for assault?

Croy: Yes.

: And you never told me! Are you serious
right now?

Croy: Will you please call me before my lunch
ends?

The phone barely gets half a ring off before he answers. "Please let me come home and explain everything. I'll go in, grab my computer, and come home, okay?" Croy sounds deflated like a foil helium balloon whose sides have begun to cave in, long after the cake is eaten and the party's over.

"You don't need my permission to come home, but I don't want you to get into any trouble, so maybe you should stick it out at work." My heart hurts every time Croy opens up about his past. I know parts of him inside and out, and yet still so much is a mystery. Who the hell did I marry?

"Do you still love me?"

"Nothing will ever change that." I'm not someone who walks away, even if I have every reason to run.

"With the holiday coming, a lot of people put in for vacation, so no one would care if I left. Plus, everyone knows we're moving." When it comes to making decisions about things that have nothing to do with me, Croy is always asking for my seal of approval.

"We're fine. Finish out the day and I'll see you in a few hours. I could use a little time to process what you've told me." I try to remain calm and avoid reaction, but this is a lot of information to dump on a person, especially after such a disastrous morning.

"I'm not that person anymore."

"Then why didn't you tell me any of this before we got married?" Every stone I kick over conceals another lie, and I see for the first time that I'm standing in the middle of a rock quarry.

"You were a goddamn corrections officer when we met. I was lucky you gave me the time of day as it was. Had I told you that was my third time in jail, you would've lost my number and stayed with Kelly."

"Third time?" My brain is about to explode.

"Underage drinking, at a frat party. I was out by morning."

I'm at a complete loss, as though the words actively evade me. I knew eventually, time would tattletale on us both and the skeletons would all come spilling out of the closet, but I wasn't expecting it to be today. As upset as I should be, I'm not. I'm sort of relieved.

Better him than me.

There's a lot Croy doesn't know because I haven't told him, and I need to keep that in mind. I could let slip a confession or two of my own, to balance the scales and ease his suffering, but what if I admit the wrong thing? Shining the spotlight on my past could be our undoing, and I'm not sure which revelations will be a bridge too far.

Turns out, my perfect husband is as flawed as the rest of us.

"Are you going to leave me?"

I didn't realize how much time had passed while I was lost in thought. His break ended five minutes ago. "No. But I should let you get back to work. I love you."

"Promise?"

Thirty-Eight

EVERY TEN MINUTES OR SO, I look toward the front door, half expecting Croy to come home early, but he doesn't. Time passes and he remains absent. I know I'm the one who told him to stay at work, but I would've bet money on him leaving early. A gamble I would've lost.

Turns out, I don't know my husband as well as I thought I did. Today's conversations have been chalked full of so many twists and turns that nothing makes sense. It's like reading a choose-your-own-adventure book cover to cover, without skipping around.

I have time to think about Croy's recent omissions and compare them to the list of my own. I understand why he didn't tell me, even though I'm not happy about it. Anders sounds as toxic as they come, and I wouldn't want a guy like that anywhere near us. As for the three trips to jail, I admit it sounds like a lot to a person who's never been there, until you look at the crimes.

In hindsight, maybe I should've done more to reassure him after his confession. Croy worries about losing me, even though it's never going to happen, but I guess when you have a history of brother fucking ex-girlfriends, it's easy to become distrustful.

That's probably one of the reasons we bonded so quickly. Croy and I both know what it's like to be cheated on, lied to, and abandoned by the people who claimed to love us. In the past, even though we saw the red flags whipping and cracking in the breeze of the oncoming storm, we stayed. We remained committed to crumbling relationships because the love we had to offer was unconditional.

As the hours pass and the afternoon sun begins to fade, I attempt to stifle my growing concern. It's nearly two hours past Croy's usual arrival time and he isn't one to be late. It's been a long day, and I'm worried about him, but I don't want to be the clingy wife who feels the need to track his every move.

Screw it!

: You good?

Croy: Yeah, sorry. I should've texted you.

: Are you coming home tonight?

Croy: You don't ever have to worry about that.
I'll always come home to you.

Now that I've received proof of life, I can continue with my evening. As my eyes drift across the room, I weigh my options. Television is an easy distraction, but it's loud and bright, and I'm in the mood for something peaceful. My shifting gaze drops and settles quietly upon a half-finished romance novel calling to me from the lower shelf of the coffee table.

Like most people who enjoy reading, I have a stack of books on my dresser calling to me. Their uncracked binding and pristine pages sit patiently waiting, like a destined lover on a park bench I've yet to introduce myself to. Books are not my escape. I don't step into their pages hoping to be lost, but instead longing to be found.

Initially, my ideas about *love* grew from those black-and-white pages. So, imagine my surprise when the cold hard reality of dating in the real world smacked me in the face. And no, I'm not talking about Kelly. I'm referring to the string of liars and cheaters who preceded him. Sure, I can acknowledge my wrong-doing, and by no means am I the blameless victim. I was an active participant in the revolving nightmares.

If I'm being honest, I set myself up for failure. I never made myself the priority. So no one else did either. Croy was the first person to come into my life and care about my thoughts, feel-ings, goals, dreams, fears, and insecurities. He supports and nurtures me, in the most unselfish way.

When I hear the front door begin to open, I shove the book-mark into the pages, drop my book on the coffee table, and jump up from where I'm seated on the couch. I can't always be a passive observer in my life, waiting for things to happen to me, instead of making them happen for myself.

I sprint to the door and wrap my arms around Croy before he has time to remove his shoes or drop his bags. This hug is my happy place.

"Let me put all this stuff down so I can give you a proper hug."

When I refuse to release my grip, Croy lowers the bags as close to the floor as possible before allowing them to drop from his hand. I can't see what he's doing because my eyes are shut tight, but I can feel the way his body moves within the limited space I have afforded him. Hopefully, he didn't bring home wine.

"I've needed this all day." His arms come up around me, swallowing the entirety of my narrow form. Croy makes me feel small, yet significant, which is what I've always wanted. We stand silently in this lover's embrace until the smell of takeout food reaches my nose, causing my stomach to grumble.

"You're even better than the version of you I fell in love with in my dreams."

"How so?" he asks.

"Because you're real." I cling to him like plastic wrap as we rock from side to side. "And because you bring home dinner so I don't have to cook."

I refuse to imagine my life without this man standing forever by my side. We are a bonded pair, tethered to each other as we float through space and time. Separate us, and we will wither away to nothing and die.

Seriously, I'm not being dramatic. Those were pretty much our wedding vows, if I'm remembering correctly. There is us, or there is nothing.

My eyes open as I angle my head upward, meeting his gaze along the way. "Hey, you got a haircut. It looks nice."

A smile plays at my lips as I rub my fingers over the short prickly hairs on the back of his head. What is it about a man with a fresh haircut that's so alluring? I mean, goddamn! He's a ten even on a bad day when I'm mad, but right now he's an eleven. Naturally, I may be biased, but since mine is the only opinion that matters, it's about to be his lucky night.

"I have something that will make you feel better, and all you have to do is lay there," I say with a wink, though I'm certain my words are enough to guide him in the right direction.

"Well, that hardly seems fair, but I would never dream of saying *no* to you." The charismatic tone of his response makes my knees weak.

"Smart man." I'm turned on by the mere idea of him and the things I want to do. Thankfully, muscle memory kicks in and I find myself walking into the bedroom, with Croy in tow. It's impossible to think straight when he's here, looking the way he is. His dress shirt is at risk of losing its buttons if he doesn't remove it in the next few seconds.

I bite my lip and attempt to locate my composure, while I unhook his belt.

"Do you want to take a shower with me?" His hands brush against my skin as he slowly removes my t-shirt. "I want to play around a little before we get too close to the finale."

Oh my god, why is he doing this to me? I want him so badly it's painful. Why does he insist on teasing me? This was supposed to be about taking care of him, not me.

"Wherever you are, that's where I want to be. So, I guess I'm joining you in the shower." Foreplay it is, since sex in the shower is off the table. Croy is too damn tall and I'm terrified of slipping and cracking my skull in half. However, I might be willing to drown on my knees.

Standing in the doorway of the bathroom, I watch as he undresses. My eyes rake over him slowly as he unbuttons his shirt and lets each article of clothing fall away to the floor. I've always tried to be a good person, to follow the rules, and put others first. Maybe Croy is my reward for twenty-nine years of valiant effort. I wonder if when he looks at me, he feels equally compensated.

He must feel something because we've barely started and he's already turned on. "Now be a good girl and get in the shower."

My breath catches in my throat and I nearly choke. "What?" Over the course of our time together, Croy has said some kinky shit, but never once has he said *good girl*. He seems to be trying something new, and I'm not mad at it.

"Do what you're told, or I'll have to punish you." His bedroom voice is one hundred percent pure, chocolate covered sex appeal. "Do you want me to punish you?"

"Well, shit babe, I do now." I have no idea what I'm agreeing to and I don't care. I need him. Period. End of sentence.

"Take your pants off and get in the shower. Now! Otherwise, I'm going to take you against this wall, and I'm going to hurt you." Croy's hand presses to the base of my throat, as he pushes against my chest. The few inches of space between me and the wall disappears instantly and I'm pinned in place. "It's your choice, babygirl."

I slide my thumbs into the waist of my pants and push them over my thighs. Desperately, I search for some sign that my husband is still himself and find nothing. Until he smiles, a full-face smile that reflects in his eyes. He winks and kisses the top of my head.

"You know I love you too much to ever hurt you." He takes my hand and guides me towards the shower, where he's quick to join. "I was playing around, trying to be like those guys you follow online. Guess I didn't do it right."

"No. You did it perfectly. I was about to call you *daddy* and melt into a puddle."

Croy squeezes body wash onto a loofah and starts to wash my back. His left hand grips my shoulder while his right moves in circular patterns across my skin. It feels amazing. I allow the sensation to spread throughout my body. My eyes close and I tilt my head back until it comes into contact with his chest. Both of his arms wrap around me as the length of his body presses into mine.

"Oh, you can still call me daddy, if you want, but first I feel like I owe you quite a few apologies." Croy brings his chin to rest atop my head with a somber tone.

"I don't want them." I bring my hand up behind me, to the place where he's poking me in the back. "So, if you want to make amends, stop talking and take me into the bedroom." I'm not trying to be harsh, but I want to get the sexy mood back before he kills it with all his unnecessary guilt.

Croy reaches forward and turns the shower handle, bringing the flow of water to an immediate stop, before stepping out onto the rug. He doesn't bother to grab a towel for either of us. He simply rubs the bottom of his feet back and forth on the gray bath mat, then picks me up and carries me into the bedroom, laying me gently on the mattress.

"I want you to play with yourself while I'm inside you." Croy positions himself between my knees, pushing my legs apart, then leans forward to kiss me, placing his hands on either side of my head, before whispering into my neck. "Now be a good girl, and show daddy how much you love him."

Thirty-Nine

MY LEGS TREMBLE as I make my way to the living room, an after-effect from incredible sex. This is a feeling I could get used to. Croy is already on the couch in comfortable clothes, waiting for me with our dinner arranged across the top of the coffee table. He must've picked up all the bags while I was getting dressed. I imagine our food is room temperature at best, but I don't mind.

On the dining table, there's a gorgeous bouquet of red roses in a clear glass vase and an envelope with the words *My Love* written across the front.

I'm not a great receiver of gifts, but I am a huge sucker for sentiment. So, while I do like the roses, it's the card that has my interest piqued. Of all the gifts I've ever received, my favorite is Croy's endless devotion. For once, someone loves me with the same unshakable determination as I offer them. He is too much, in a way that always works out to be the perfect amount.

"A haircut, dinner, flowers, and a card. No wonder you were late getting home. What did I do to deserve all of this?" I bend slightly at the waist, allowing my nose to hover above the most attractive rose, and breathe in its scent. Then, I pluck the card from the table and join Croy on the couch. "How did I get so lucky?"

He answers by shaking his head and pulling me to his chest, where I make myself comfortable by sinking deeper into his embrace. Something from today is still bothering him, but I don't want to venture a guess or make assumptions. Perhaps if I remain quiet for long enough, he'll open up.

As far as I'm concerned, everything that happened today was forgiven hours ago. I know the housekeeper coming to clean was meant with good intentions, and had I not been so scared, I might have appreciated the kind gesture. It's one of those things I can laugh about, in hindsight, even though I was on the verge of tears in the moment. And finding out about Croy's half-brother and the multiple trips to jail was surprising, but it's not my place to be upset with him about any of that.

No one goes into a relationship spilling their guts about every detail. That simply doesn't happen. We all have secrets, and stories we reserve for down the line or maybe never. I have items in my past I've never shared with anyone, things I'm too afraid to tell Croy. Not because I'm afraid he won't love me anymore, but because I know him, and he'll feel guilty he wasn't around to protect me.

After what feels like five excruciatingly long minutes of silence, Croy finds the words to explain what's on his mind. "If I would've known, when I was younger, that I had someone like you waiting for me, I would have done things differently. I would have found you sooner and asked you to be my date for prom. I would have let you wear my jersey to school every Friday before the football games, and I would have waved to you from the sideline as you watched from the stands. I would have gone to whatever college you wanted and got us an apartment off campus. I would have spent my nights on the couch with you instead of at the bar trying to drown my loneliness. I would have spent the last twelve years investing in us, instead of myself. And I would have been smart enough not to let my anger get the best of me. I would've had a reason to stay on the straight and narrow path had I been standing next to you. I'm sorry I didn't tell you about my asshole brother and the real reason my parents had me arrested. I should have. I should have told you everything from the beginning, but I was embarrassed and I was too afraid of losing you."

"We can talk about it if you want to, but we don't *have* to. If you tell me there are people you don't waste your time with, I don't need to know them. To hell with your brother." I do wonder what Anders looks like, but I'm not about to ask. It's just that I can't wrap my mind around the fact a woman could have Croy and cheat on him. Then again, I'm married to the man and still had sex with Kelly, so maybe I'm not any better. Although, I would argue a threesome among consenting adults is different than an affair.

"I'm more concerned with how you feel about me going to jail three times. Is that going to be the deal breaker for my sexy law-abiding, former corrections officer wife?"

I try not to react, but it spills out. And what's worse is, it's the kind of full body laugh that ripples through me from head to toe. My stomach muscles contract and release, as I attempt to mute the sound by putting my hands over my face. "No offense, but the image of you as a criminal has pretty much been seared into my brain since day one. We met in a jail! How could your record of petty crimes be a deal breaker?"

"I don't want to make myself sound worse, but I did put him in the hospital, so... I wouldn't call that one a petty crime."

"I expected nothing less, but my point still stands. You need to give me more credit here, or maybe less depending on how you want to look at it. I'm more understanding than you know because I'm more broken than you realize." When will Croy truly accept the fact I'm not going anywhere? I have no place to go, and I can't exist without him.

I'm about to continue when I hear my phone calling from the

bedroom. The text alerts come one after the next, in rapid succession.

"Maybe you should get that? It could be important." The arm Croy was using to support my weight adjusts me into a full upright position.

"It's probably your sister. She asked us to get a case of wine for Thursday and I told her we'd pick it up after you got home from work. I completely forgot, so it's probably good she decided to check in." There aren't very many people who talk to me, especially as of late. My mom usually calls in the morning, and Croy will text me throughout the day while he's working. Other than that, my phone doesn't see much action. I don't have any friends left, and the builders have all come and gone, so I've stopped carrying my phone around with me in the evenings.

"Ugh. Can we go to the winery tomorrow? I want to hold you right now." He pulls me back into his chest and I snuggle in. That is, until the phone goes off again. "You better grab it, hun. There's no way that's my sister. Astrid is not a repeat sender. She wouldn't fire off half a dozen messages one right after the next. If it was *that* serious, she would've called me."

"Why don't you grab my phone and deal with whatever it is." I slide off Croy's lap and begin to pull open the envelope I've been patiently holding in my hand. Whoever is texting me, I don't care, because I already know who it isn't. At this point, I've cut ties and burned bridges with pretty much everyone, not because I had to, but because those relationships no longer served me. Anyone who felt the need to share a negative opinion about my husband was snuffed out faster than a candle on a birthday cake.

As my grandmother used to say, "good riddance to bad rubbish."

I carefully open the flap of the envelope, remove the contents, and slide the tip of my finger across the embossed face of the card. It's beautiful. But before I can get to the handwritten part of Croy's card, he walks into the living room carrying my phone.

Holding it out to me, he says, "I don't think you want me handling this one."

I know who it is without having to look. There's only one person in my story who elicits this response from Croy. It's a mix of disappointment, anger, annoyance, and helplessness. Kelly is the one messaging me, and I'm not sure I even want to look.

"If you don't want to deal with him right now, then neither do I. Shut the ringer off and toss it back in the bedroom. I'm in the mood for a Hallmark Christmas movie. Are you game?" I love light-hearted romance and Croy is obsessed with Christmas movies, so we're entering into the perfect time of year. As for Kelly, I can deal with him and all his feelings another time.

Croy has the next nine days off work, and a lot of our time is going to be spent moving and unpacking. I want to enjoy tonight, before we're forced to succumb to the chaos of tomorrow.

He emerges from the bedroom with a smile on his face. "You don't have to ask me twice."

Forty

I CAN'T REMEMBER the last time we woke up in bed together, without an alarm. If heaven is a perfect moment, where the laws of time and space no longer exist, then let this be my eternity. To merely state I love Croy doesn't begin to do those feelings justice, and calling them feelings also falls short of the mark. My love for him is an irrefutable fact and anyone who wishes to question this will be stricken from the record.

Croy is exceptional, in all the ways you would expect a soulmate to be. He is understanding of my shortcomings and accepting of my flaws, of which there are many. He would argue those are some of the things he loves most. The parts I refer to as damaged, he views as the individual qualities that make me the woman he can't live without. And I would argue he's crazy, except I feel the same way about him.

Every time I find out some new piece of information, something he worries will be a bridge too far, I fall deeper into my love for him. Sometimes I look at him, and I see our whole future there, laid out in front of me. Croy provides me with so much, but beyond all of that, he gives something the other men never even knew to suggest. Croy offers me certainty.

No matter how far into the future I look, he's always by my side, protecting me, supporting me, and loving me, not only for who I am today but for any version of myself I'm meant to become.

Forty~One

BRUSHING the tips of his fingers along the length of my exposed arm, Croy smiles and leans in to kiss me. "Before we dive headfirst into the chaos of today, I need to ask you a couple things."

Our hands meet in the center of the bed, halfway between us, and his fingers lace into mine as he pulls it to his lips. Whether or not he does this as a means of calming me, I'm not sure, but the effect is achieved nonetheless.

"Yes, I still love you. And *no*, you *cannot* hook up all of your video game systems in the living room. That's why you have a television in the gym." I smile, having no idea what he really wanted to ask me. My random answers were meant to lighten the mood, in case a heavy topic rests on the horizon.

"My hope is you'll always love me. As for the video games, that's fine. Verlaine will let me hook them up in her room, and we'll play without you." He gives my hand a playful squeeze while keeping his eyes locked on mine.

"You can play all the Xbox you want in there, so long as you're changing diapers and mixing bottles of milk." Even though this conversation is a joke, I can picture it all so clearly, playing out in my head. I'm glad our daughter has one good parent lined up, eagerly awaiting her arrival. As for myself, I'm still terrified. I don't do well with uncertainty, and everything about being a new mom is one giant question mark.

"Deal! Now, on to my real questions." Croy's expression changes. His face conveys the seriousness his tone is about to reiterate. "Are you going to respond to Kelly's messages from last night?"

"Nope. I haven't even looked at them, and I don't intend to. I'll deal with it on Monday, after the holiday." I get to spend the next nine days with Croy, morning, noon, and night, and no one is going to mess that up for me, including myself. It's bad enough I have to deal with his family on Thanksgiving. I have no intention of talking to Kelly about things I have no answers to.

"Babe, you can't tell a guy he might have a kid on the way and then leave him on read for a week and a half. I don't like Kelly, and I don't like the possibility of him being in our lives forever, but ignoring him isn't an option anymore."

"Okay. You're right. I get it." I shut my eyes tight, pull my hand away, and move to sit up. "Before I'm willing to throw myself into a depression-death-spiral inducing conversation with my fake ex-boyfriend, what was your other question?"

"Do you want to go to breakfast before we have to meet everyone at the house?" Croy sits up and repositions himself behind me on the bed, his arms and legs wrap around me like squid tentacles. "Babe, if you want me to deal with Kelly, I will, but I think it would be better coming from you."

"I know. I'll talk to him." I lean into Croy's embrace and allow him to support my weight. "And *no*, I don't want breakfast. You've murdered my appetite."

"Avoiding the conversation would be worse. My advice is to read the messages, respond, and put the situation behind you. No reason to let it ruin the whole day." Croy is talking about letting this go as if that's a possibility. It's like he's giving advice to a normal person, instead of the woman he's married to.

The last month has been miserable, and I've cried more times than I can count over my dissolved friendship with Kelly, since he walked out and never looked back. I do my best to keep the tears locked away, holding back until I'm alone, but sometimes my best efforts aren't good enough. Croy has held me together on a handful of occasions, and I imagine it can't be easy for him, listening to his wife cry about how much she misses another man. I'm not sure why he puts up with it, but he does.

"I'll make coffee and text the guys. If you need me, I'll be in the kitchen, okay?" Croy gets up, leaving me sitting on the bed. Alone. "You're so much stronger than you give yourself credit for." He leans down to kiss my forehead before leaving the room and shutting the door behind him.

There's no part of me that wants to deal with these text messages right now. I've not planned for any of this. I thought I was going to wake up, have one last cup of coffee while looking at the lake, and then plant both feet firmly in my new life. Moving Day 2.0 was meant to be exciting. I wanted to make memories and put down roots. I wanted to watch my super sexy husband and his attractive friends move heavy objects. Was that so much to ask for?

My phone sits silently on the bedside table where Croy left it before the movie. Why is he making me do this? Last night, he was more than happy to silence my ringer and ignore the conversation, but today, it's at the top of the to-do list, and I don't get it. Since when does he care about Kelly's feelings? Croy is the one who initially convinced me to keep everything a secret, saying it wasn't worth the trouble until we had more information. Now that everyone is in the know and ready to talk, I'm just supposed to meet them at the table?

What is it that people always say, "You've made your bed, now lie in it." Seems like the time for lying has passed. Now I have to accept the unpleasant consequences of my promiscuous actions. Perhaps if I had spent less time lying in beds that weren't mine, I wouldn't be in this mess.

Kells: I don't know where to start or what to say. I know you, so I'm not even going to ask if you were being serious.

Kells: Realistically, what are the chances this baby could be ours? Is this like 50/50, or 80/20? I assume you and Croy had sex a lot more than we did.

Kells: Sorry, I'm not doing that. I just need you to tell me what you expect from me, if I'm the one who got you pregnant.

Kells: I'll be honest with you, I am seeing someone, and I'm happy. But I love you, and I'm not going to leave you to deal with this on your own. Are you and Croy staying together, no matter what the outcome is? Or...

Kells: Goddamnit, babe, this is all my fault. I know that. But why the hell didn't you tell me as soon as you found out? Why did you get married to him? You had options. I would've taken care of you and given you a good life, you know that.

Kells: I don't want to be some every-other-weekend dad who everyone ends up resenting. And I have a feeling you aren't too worried about the child support payments. So, am I out of line if I offer to sign my rights away? Do I even need to? If there's no paternity test, would anyone question it? You and Croy could go live happily ever after and over time we'd all forget there was any other possible outcome.

Kells: Am I being stupid? Or worse, an insensitive asshole? That's not my intention.

> Kells: You matter to me, a ridiculous amount,
> but I'm not sure what you need from me right
> now. If you tell me to go away, I will. It'll kill me
> to lose you, but it would be worse to stay and
> watch you grow to hate me.

> Kells: If there's a chance Croy would divorce
> you over this, I need you to tell me sooner
> rather than later, okay? Please.

I read through the messages one by one, absorbing their context while doing my best to hear each line delivered in his voice. If he were here, sitting next to me, we could sort this out as friends. But knowing us, we'd brush over the details and end up making out or something. Kelly isn't the villain of this story. More and more, I think it's me.

"Babe!" I shout through the thin interior wall. The door is quickly replaced by a figure who fills most of the available space. "Is there any chance you're going to divorce me if we do a paternity test? Kelly needs to know, ASAP."

"Tell Kelly to find his own wife. Mine isn't going anywhere." Croy's legs are so long, it only takes him a second to close the distance between us, knotting his fingers into the hair at the back of my head. He leans in, his lips falling short an inch from mine. "I'm not losing you."

"You don't have to worry." My voice is soft, but audible.

Why is Croy so angry, when he's the one who insisted on me facing my issue with Kelly head-on? I haven't even responded to the messages. All I did was read them.

"You're mine. Do you understand? The days of me sharing you with Matt Kelly are over." Croy's fist clenches, pulling my hair tighter.

"Are you being serious, or is this some dom fetish thing you saw online? Because I'm confused and turned on, but also a little scared." The moment the word *scared* passes my lips, Croy releases my hair and steps away from me.

"I'm sorry. I didn't mean to be so intense." He steps forward and drops to his knees. his arms wrapping around my waist as his head falls into my lap. "I panic when the word divorce gets thrown around, and it feels like my heart is getting ripped out of my chest. I'm sorry I scared you."

"No. Come on, don't do that. Please. I want the big scary guy back. He sounded like he knows how to take care of a girl, and lord knows I need to be taken care of." I run my fingers through Croy's hair, coxing his face to angle toward mine.

He forces a smile and licks his lips, falling back into character.

"First, I'm going show you how good you have it. And when I'm finished, you're going to tell me about the conversation you had with that piece of shit loser you were fucking when you should've been home with me." His words come out in a growl as he pushes me back, laying me across the center of the bed. "Tell me you belong to me, and I'll give you the world."

Now is probably a terrible time to mention I've yet to have a conversation with Kelly, right? I'd have to be an idiot to stop this one-way train to euphoria. And while I'll admit I am prone to making questionable choices, I'm not a moron. Instead of pumping the brakes, I buy a ticket and jump on. Metaphorically speaking.

"You were going to give me the world anyway, because you already know I'm yours."

Forty~Two

NOW THAT EVERYONE'S in a better mood, I agree to have breakfast at our favorite local spot before heading to the house. Croy and I discuss the messages and take turns passing my phone back and forth across the table. We talk through the various paths ahead, weighing the pros and cons.

While it seems like Kelly is willing to *do the right thing*, I also get the feeling he would be just as happy to wash his hands of the entire situation. With the financial burden and responsibility in Croy's capable hands, Kelly would be free to run off and dip into his flavor of the month.

Gross.

That revolving door of women is the last thing I need in my daughter's life.

On the drive to the house, I decide to text Kelly back. I start to type out my message, stop, delete, and start over. It's hard to know what to say, especially with Croy sitting next to me. I craft what I deem to be an adequate message and hit the send button, refusing to overthink every detail of the outcome.

"So, come on, don't leave me in suspense. What'd you say?" As we pause at a stop sign, Croy squeezes my leg and smiles.

"Read what you *actually* wrote, and I promise I won't get jealous."

I roll my eyes and return the smile. I love my husband and I applaud his effort, but when it comes to Kelly, I know to expect a splash of jealousy. What he said earlier was not lost on me, I simply failed to respond because I didn't want to spoil the mood of the moment. But when Croy uttered the words; *you were out fucking him when you should have been home with me*, I knew that was the truth slipping out.

"I didn't know what to say to him, so I went with… Croy and I are NOT getting divorced, so please remove all futures where you and I end up together from the equation. I miss you, but this decision shouldn't be about our feelings for each other. Take some time and think about what you want. I'm not going to tell you to go away, but I'm not going to beg you to stay either. I regret not telling you sooner, and I'm sorry. As for the odds, they're split evenly." I'm wishing now I would have sent something else. Anything else. Reading my message aloud, I can hear how it sounds, and it's not pretty.

Croy pulls into the driveway but stops at the end and parks near the street. "Why do you always do that? You give him just enough to keep him on the hook, and I want to know why. Why do you feel like you need a backup plan? Do you think I like him waiting in the wings, ready to step in the second I fuck up? Tell me why you need him. Why can't I be enough for you?"

I hang my head and close my eyes, attempting to quell my tears. "I don't know."

"Heather, look at me." Croy takes my face in his hands and uses his thumbs to wipe the tears from my cheeks. "I'm not mad at you. I've known who you are from the very beginning. You're someone who loves with your whole heart, sees the best in everyone, and doesn't know when to give up. I adore those qualities as much today as I did back when they worked in my favor."

"It's weird hearing you call me Heather when I'm awake."

Normally, he reserves this form of address for when I'm lost in the nothing place. Perhaps he saw me on the verge of drifting away.

"My wife. My love. My everything. My reason for living and breathing. I'm not going anywhere, so be honest with me once and for all. Why do you feel like you *need* him in your life?"

"Because I like the way it feels when he sees me. Kelly reminds me of every asshole guy who's treated me like I didn't matter. So, when he acknowledges my existence, it fills the need I've had my whole life to be seen by them. Like I finally exist in their orbit. But I don't need them and I don't need Kelly. You are enough, but what you offer fills a different hole." Having this conversation only serves to solidify my need for serious professional help. I need someone to Marie Kondo my emotional baggage because this shit is not sparking joy.

"You better not be talking about intercourse."

"Oh god. I wasn't, I promise. Gross." I shake the words out of the forefront of my mind, allowing them to rattle around to the back. "I'm not using you for sex. I swear."

A car horn honks behind us, causing me to jump. Brian and Nate have come to help Croy with the heavy lifting while the wives are on unpacking duty. Megan and Taylor both keep a nice, clean, organized home, so I'm happy to have their assistance. And per usual, all final decisions run through me, so I'll be wearing my onsite foreman hat today and possibly again tomorrow.

Croy pulls up and parks by the house. The second the ignition dies, he jumps out of the driver's side door like his pants have caught fire. I'm taken aback for a moment, until I realize what's happening. The last couple times we've been here, I've opened my own car door, which has caused him noticeable distress. It seems like an odd thing to be troubled over, but if it's important to him, then it's important to me. I remain seated until the door to my right opens on its hinges.

I start to swing myself around and out, but Croy leans in,

stopping me before my butt can leave the seat. "Real quick, before we join everyone and get things started, I want you to know I love you and I'm not upset about the text. I'm not mad about him or your history or your friendship or the fact that there are times when you choose him over me. I'm sorry I've been such an asshole about it. I've always regarded him as your backup plan, but Kelly isn't my competition, he's your solace."

The instant Croy's lips touch mine, I forget where we are and who I used to be. My arms come around him, pulling him in closer. This kiss could last forever, and it would never be long enough to quench my desire for him. I pull tighter, knocking him off balance, but he catches himself and leans in deeper. Our kiss continues without pause, gradually intensifying.

It isn't until I hear Brian's voice that I remember we have company. "Alright already, break it up. We didn't come all the way out here to watch you two go at it in the driveway."

"Oh leave 'em alone. When's the last time you kissed me like that?" Megan chimes in, and her question makes me laugh so abruptly I almost bite the tip of Croy's tongue.

"They're even worse at the gym. Both of 'em. They spend the whole time watching each other work out, smiling like a couple of love-struck teenagers. It's highly distracting." Nate adds his two cents to the onsite commentary.

"That's what newlyweds do. Or have you forgotten? You used to watch me fold laundry like it was some sort of mating ritual," Taylor says with a laugh.

Croy places one last small kiss gently on my lips, then whispers, "Let's go make this place feel like home. You with me?"

"Until the end," I reply, keeping my voice low. We don't need to give the peanut gallery more ammunition, and they already think we're a couple of love-sick saps.

Extending his hand, Croy offers support as I locate my footing. His SUV always seems so high off the ground for some reason. Plus, I find myself losing my balance more frequently the further I get into pregnancy. I'm sure the combination of low iron and unequal weight distribution has something to do with it. I still don't have much of a baby belly, but I've seen her growing on the ultrasound, so I know she's in there.

At the front door, Croy stops to look at me. "I'm doing it, and I don't care what you have to say about it."

"Oh god. Please don't." My cheeks flush with embarrassment.

"It's happening." He swings open the door, scoops me up in his arms, and steps through without so much as grazing my feet or elbows on the frame.

I bury my face in his chest, attempting to block out the audience. Without warning or intention, I'm transported back to the night of the fight, when Grant carried me out of the blocks. I can feel their eyes on me, and their whispered thoughts amplified in my subconscious mind. Caught between then and now, my heart pounds as I struggle to breathe and I feel myself falling.

I slip away from both my memories and the present.

Forty-Three

I CAN STILL REMEMBER the first time I was lost here, in the place absent of all things.

It was a morning like any other, except on that day, my mom was curling my hair for school. I was kneeling in front of the sink, in a bathroom whose walls had been adorned with a brown and black plaid wallpaper. It sounds odd but it looked awesome. The decor was mature for a girl not yet in her teens, which made it all the more special.

My mother, being relatively short in stature, couldn't see the top of my head if I was standing, and there was no good place to sit, so I knelt on the rug as she twisted my hair around the iron. My eyes focused on the wood grain of the cabinet, searching for hidden pictures, when I started to feel warm. Initially, I assumed the proximity of the hot iron to my scalp was causing my discomfort, but the room began to spin and my vision blurred. The only thing I said was, "I don't feel so good," and then I disappeared.

I fell back, hitting my head on the base of the shower stall behind me.

That morning, it was my mom calling my name, her voice leading me back. I'm not sure how long I was out, seconds, maybe half a minute. Time works differently in the nothing place.

At the sound of my name, I knew I had to go back.

When I opened my eyes, the panic on my mother's face matched the alarm in her voice. I did my best to reassure her I was okay, even though I was drowning in confusion and hazy recollection. It always felt like my duty to be strong, so others could be weak.

I remember going to the doctor at some point, but I can't say with confidence if it was the same day or a few days later. I suppose it doesn't matter. What I do know with one hundred percent certainty is that every day since falling and hitting my head, I've had a headache, and when I'm sitting still, my leg jumps around until I consciously will it to stop. The second I stop thinking about it, the shaking starts again. This has been a bone of contention for many of the people I've dated in the past, so I began sitting with my legs tangled together underneath me, criss-cross applesauce.

The first time Croy commented on my jumpy frog leg, was in the hospital during our dinner date. He asked if I was nervous, which I was, but not in the way he assumed. I assured him I was perfectly comfortable in his presence, and made every effort to keep still for the rest of the evening. Since then, he hasn't commented, but occasionally, if it happens while we're sitting next to each other, he'll gently rest his hand atop my leg and give my thigh a small squeeze. Oddly enough, it helps.

Over the years, I found other ways to get back to the nothing place. I would drink cheap vodka until the ground fell away beneath my feet. Even in high school, I had a reputation for drinking guys under the table. I would do shots and smoke weed until everything disappeared. When that wasn't enough, I experimented with drugs until I found something I liked, and then pushed my limits to the brink of self-destruction. I didn't care about myself or the consequences of my actions.

Life and death were meaningless. Every day felt like torture and I dreamt only of escape. When I tried telling people about the war raging inside me, they chalked it up to teenage angst and sent me on my way without aid.

Since no one cared, including myself, I was free to do anything and everything I wanted. In college, I made a game out of sleeping with random guys in the dorm, because for the first time, I could. After having surgery and losing weight, I could get anyone I wanted. Sex meant nothing to me, and love was never offered. My physical safety was an afterthought at best, and I'm not sure how I survived this long. Good decisions are rarely made when one is floating outside oneself.

It wasn't all bad. On two occasions, my omnidirectional course crossed the path of a kind-hearted soul. We fell in love, enjoyed each other's company, and spent every second entertaining one another. But despite every effort coming from both sides, it was never enough. I always needed more. In those days, I did things I deeply regret. Horrible things that can't be undone. I hurt people I truly loved and an apology was never going to erase that.

I made an art out of disappearing because what did it matter if I was invisible anyway? After college, karma spent several years with its foot on my neck, so I hid myself away every chance I got. I dove into one bad relationship after another, swallowing the lies.

True love is far more effortless than we're led to believe. A fact I'll be sure to share with my daughter when she's older.

As it turns out, my need to see the best in others is entirely selfish. If people, in general, are beyond redemption. That includes me, specifically. Which would mean I could never deserve my husband or the life we're building together. I might frequently consider the possibility that I'm irredeemable, but I refuse to truly believe it.

Croy and I belong together. For better or worse.

Forty~Four

"HEATHER, I need you to wake up." Croy's voice cuts through the commotion, which has flooded the quiet darkness. I can't make out the other voices. Only his words come through clearly.

My hands come up over my face, as I attempt to get my bearings before letting in the light. Once I'm confident that I am actually laying on the floor of the new house, with Croy kneeling by my side, and an audience of our friends looking on, I let my hands slide back into my hair. Now, with my face shielded by my arms, I open my eyes.

"Sorry about that. I'm fine." I know this feeble attempt to reassure him will be fruitless, but I have to try. "You certainly know how to make a girl swoon."

"I'm gonna take you to the hospital, okay?" He kisses my forehead before turning his face toward my ear. "Let me take care of you."

"I'm fine. I swear. I just need to get up." The spinning slows to a near stop as I move to sit up. "Can you help me stand?"

This is not how I expected this morning to go. My game plan was prepared with meticulous detail, but at no point did I factor in time for blackout breaks. Now that I've ended up on the floor,

Croy isn't going to let me carry so much as a pillow. This day is a complete wash.

Brian comes through the front door carrying a patio chair he found in one of the pods we're all meant to be unloading right now. He's out of breath, which makes me laugh. These guys, with all their muscles and time spent in the gym, fully undervalue the benefits of cardio training. Now I have five people encouraging me to rest when all I want is to get to work.

It takes some convincing, but eventually, I agree to sit, if everyone will stay to help with the moving, as planned. I'm not sure why I blacked out this time. Perhaps it was the sudden shift in elevation or the overwhelming combination of emotions coming at me from all sides. Whatever the reason, I really am fine.

The second Croy stops looking, I jump up to assist the ladies in the kitchen. "Please let me help with something before I go crazy," I say, nearly begging. "I hate watching my life unfold from a distance."

"I can't take my eyes off of her for one second." I hear Croy say from the other side of the wall as the guys come in carrying pieces of the living room furniture. I'm able to hop onto the island countertop before we are in full view of one another. He can't complain too much if I'm still sitting down. When his eyes meet mine, his disapproving scowl is replaced by a smile. "Please be a good girl, or I'm going to have to punish you."

Megan's mouth falls open and Taylor nearly drops the drinking glasses she's unwrapping. Both women stare as Croy sets down the coffee table he's carrying and walks over to where I'm sitting on the counter. He pushes my knees apart and positions himself between my legs, with his hands on my waist.

"Look at me, sitting here doing nothing. I am being good." I lean in to kiss him, as the background melts away. Normally, after six months with someone, I'm bored, but Croy's kiss excites me as much today, as it did on our first night together.

"I know you are, but now I sort of want you to be bad so I

can send everyone home." Croy's hands grip onto my hips, pulling me tightly against him, before lifting me away from the marble countertop. He carries me to the living room and gently places me on the couch the guys have just brought in.

"Bro, seriously. What the hell? My wife is watching this shit and now she's going to expect me to carry her around the damn condo like that when I get home. Can you stop with all this romantic bullshit? I thought we were friends. You know you're making us look bad, right?" Nate sounds like he's only half joking.

Croy kisses the top of my head and walks away, shooting Nate a look as he goes. Maybe we should send the other couples home. If I'm not allowed to help in any substantial way, I'm not sure I want to be here. This was supposed to be our big move into the new house, and I ruined it by temporarily checking out, sending Croy straight into overprotective mode.

Nate comes to sit next to me on the couch, catching me off guard. He's always friendly, but this side-by-side proximity is a new one. In fact, this might be the first time he's come within ten feet of me since the incident at the gym, where his misinterpretation of the moment nearly cost him his friendship with my husband.

"Heather, you should let Croy take you to the hospital. We're all pretty worried about you. Go and get checked out by a doctor. Brian and I can carry in the heavy stuff and the girls will organize the boxes. Everything is labeled, and we aren't going to steal anything. Just go. Nothing happening here is more important than your health."

"I'm fine, Nate. I appreciate your concern, but it's not necessary. I'm glad you guys stayed to help, but I'm not sticking around because I'm afraid of you stealing the furniture." I laugh. What an odd and unexpected conversation to be having. "I got dizzy when Croy picked me up. It's no big deal."

"I'm starting to understand why your husband keeps such a close eye on you. For a long time, I thought it was jealousy, especially after I met your *friend* Matt. There's no way I would let Taylor hang out with a guy who looks like that. Let alone a guy who's totally in love with her. But you have a real knack for downplaying reality."

"I'm not sure what you mean exactly. But if it makes you feel better, Kelly and I don't talk anymore." I don't understand where Nate's going with this line of conversation. Maybe he knows something I don't. "Croy has no reason to be jealous, and Kelly isn't in love with me."

"I honestly can't tell if you're joking or not." Nate's expression looks puzzled, as though my words are an enigma he can't riddle out.

Catching the exchange, Croy sets down the chair he's carried in and takes a seat. His eyes lock on Nate. "Joking about what, exactly? Maybe I can help you sort it out." The whole house goes quiet as the two guys stare at each other.

I'm not sure where all this tension is coming from. These two men claim to be friends, but at the slightest infraction they're prepared to come to blows. Brian positions himself behind the couch, over Nate's shoulder, undeniably choosing a side. I want to help calm the situation, but I'm still knee deep, wading through the confusion of our previous conversation. For some reason, I can't seem to catch up. I'm watching everything unfold, but my reaction time is set on a ten-second delay.

My head feels too heavy for my neck to support on its own, so my hands come to lend their assistance. With my elbows on my knees and my fingertips on my temples, I take in a deep breath and exhale slowly. "Hey babe, do you think you could do me a favor?" My head sinks deeper, catching in the palms of my hands. "Can you take me to the hospital? I don't feel so good."

Forty-Five

I'M in Croy's arms before I can collapse in on myself any further. Safe again, for the time being. No further words are exchanged. He carries me to the car and loads me gently into the passenger side, reclining the seat back as far as it can go.

The gravel tings against the metal undercarriage as we accelerate quickly in reverse. Speed limits seem to no longer apply as he makes his way to the freeway on-ramp. After ten minutes, we pull into the emergency room parking lot. If Croy ever gets tired of working behind a desk, he should consider driving an ambulance.

On occasion, I've fantasized about him in uniform, as a cop, but I don't think he'd ever go for it. Not that he even could, with a DUI, underage drinking, and assault on his record. But maybe in the bedroom, I could convince him to play the part for my eyes only. That would be interesting. It would have to be a real uniform, not one of those cheap Halloween costumes. And handcuffs. He would definitely need handcuffs. I think I might have a few new ideas for Christmas.

Thankfully, the hospital is quiet and they're able to get me into a room without having to wait. I'd feel guilty if I was taking attention away from more severe cases, but I haven't heard anyone screaming out in agony.

Croy lists off my symptoms and informs the medical assistant I'm six months pregnant. She looks at me, skeptical of his claims, then rattles off a new catalog of questions. She records the information as it's given, conducts her pre-exam, and adds low blood pressure to the list. "The doctor will be in shortly to see you."

"What the hell was that about, back at the house? I thought you guys were okay with each other again?" I ask, still confused about how we got here. I'm glad we're sitting next to one another, nice and low to the ground.

Croy wraps me in his arms and pulls me onto his lap. "You tell me. All I heard was Nate say, 'I can't tell if you're joking or not.' and you looked uncomfortable. Then he puffed up his chest in typical fashion, and decided to have a staring contest. I thought we were going to have to measure our dicks or something. What was he saying to you?"

"I don't know. He said I should go to the hospital. Then he brought up Kelly. And something about how I downplay reality. I don't know what point he was trying to make, but it wasn't anything to get worked up about. You two turn on a dime so quickly. It's probably best we're moving before you guys kill each other."

"What was the last thing you said before I got there? I doubt you were telling a joke." Croy's words rustle my hair as they pass through, and I wonder if us sitting this way, here in the hospital, is inappropriate. Or is a husband comforting his pregnant wife a natural thing?

"I said something like, 'Croy has no reason to be jealous and Kelly isn't in love with me'."

"Ah! Well, he's an asshole for bringing that up!" The tips of Croy's fingers stretch up and down my leg in a repetitive motion that's beginning to unnerve me. "Okay, so something happened the morning Kelly went to the gym with me, and I never told you. But I think we should talk about it later, at home, after we get you checked out and we know you're okay."

"Yeah, I don't think so. You should probably tell me now!" I push his hand away from my thigh but don't move from his lap.

"I need you to understand that when all of this happened, there was a lot going on. It was the morning after I watched you two hook up. He and I had that talk about you on the couch. There was the fight with my parents. You took your ring off. My head was not in a good place. So, when he said he was in love with you…" Croy laces his fingers into mine and places them in a pile atop my leg.

"I wish you would get to the point." I hate being the last person in on a joke. It makes me feel like I'm the punchline.

"I know, babe, but it's not that simple. Can we please talk about this at home?"

"You're making it worse by stalling."

"Fine. While we were at the gym, a lot was being said in front of the guys. We were lifting weights and I was getting cocky. Things escalated and my arrogance turned into stupidity, trying to save face in front of my friends. I told Kelly you were free to make your own choices and if he could get you to leave with him, he could have you."

My heart plummets, crashing into my stomach, and causing a wave of nausea to flood into the back of my throat. Before I have a chance to respond, the doctor walks in, placing our conversation on a permanent hold.

The rest of the appointment is a blur. I go through the motions, but my thoughts are elsewhere. How could my husband, the man who claims to hold me as the center of his universe, casually offer to give me away? I'm not looking to overreact, and maybe there's more to the story, but I'm a little annoyed that this is only now coming to light. I love Croy, but I'm getting tired of these lies of omission.

Hell would freeze over before I would encourage some woman to shoot her shot with my husband. Watching Sarah lick his stomach during a game of Truth of Dare had me contemplating homicide. Had I not been so distracted by the next dare, who knows how that night might have ended? Then again, I can't imagine Croy was too happy about my kiss with Kelly, so yet again I'm the bad guy. How the hell am I the villain of my own story?

"Have you scheduled the iron infusions your OBGYN ordered? That could be why you're experiencing a lot of these symptoms." The doctor is using his stethoscope to listen to my heart, so I don't respond to his question. "It's important you eat enough, take your vitamins, and give yourself time to relax. It sounds like you're trying to do too much and running on an empty tank."

Repositioning the exam table, the doctor gently presses against my shoulder in hopes of getting me to lie back. "Everything with mom looks okay. We're going to check on the baby and then you'll be on your way. Try to relax and breathe."

Croy moves into the chair closest to me and takes my hand. His touch is all I need. I can feel the clenched muscles throughout my body release one by one. As promised, the ultrasound tech comes in with an equipment cart in tow.

A black and white image of Verlaine swishes around on the screen as the tech looks for fingers and toes, heart and face, spine and placenta. Everything appears to be fine, so we're free to leave.

"Get those infusions scheduled and you'll feel a lot better. Take care of yourself, and that little girl." The doctor smiles as he opens the door. "You can check out up front when you're ready."

The ride home is quiet. The only thing Croy asks is if I want to talk about it. But whatever *it* is, I'm not in the mood for a discussion. This has been a very long, disappointing day and all I want is for it to be over. "Can you please drop me off at the condo before you go back to the house? I'd like to close my eyes for a bit."

Sometimes I wonder if men are really worth the trouble.

Forty-Six

THE NEXT FEW days go more to plan. Unpacking with Croy is a lot less stressful, and I'm able to move at my own pace without feeling like our friends are passing judgment on my every move. Croy and I work well as a team and we tend to use a lot of made-up words or shorthand to describe what we need the other to do. I wonder if I need to speak at all. When it comes to the house, Croy doesn't fight me for power, he allows me to take the lead and is quick to do as he's told.

By Tuesday, we're able to get the pods unloaded and hauled away, the boxes unpacked and broken down, and even started moving things from the condo. It was then, a day and a half before Thanksgiving, that I realized I was in serious trouble. As soon as I saw the bottle of champagne in the fridge, I screamed for Croy.

"Babe! We messed up." I can't believe I forgot. Astrid is going to kill me. "Come on. We have to go. Now!"

Croy grabs his keys off the counter and slips on his shoes. "What happened?" He closes the front door behind us, and I'm nearly to the car when he catches up to me. "What are you doing?"

"Can I drive?" In all the time we've been together, I've yet to drive Croy's big fancy SUV. Not that he wouldn't let me, I've simply never thought to ask until now. Unsurprisingly, he opens the driver's side door and helps me in.

"Are you planning on telling me where we're going in such a hurry?" It's funny seeing him in the passenger seat of his own vehicle.

I've never driven anything this expensive, and I won't lie, it feels pretty good. There is a teeny tiny little itty-bitty part of me that wants to let Croy buy me a car like this, but then I would feel like an even bigger financial burden, so I'm keeping my car until it falls apart around me.

"We forgot to buy the wine for your sister's dinner, and I'm not sure if they'll be open tomorrow. Heck, I'm not sure if they're open at all this week, but I have my fingers crossed." I pull out my phone in hopes of checking the winery hours, but Croy snatches it from my hand.

"Hands on the wheel and eyes on the road, my love. I don't need you driving us straight into the ditch. Anyways, looking up hours and directions is my job as the passenger. I also get to be the DJ." He scrolls through his phone for a moment before choosing a playlist. "And here it is, I have the perfect thing."

As soon as the first song comes on, I recognize the playlist. It's the one that made him cry for 20 minutes on his drive to work. Honestly, I'm not sure why he got so emotional. These songs aren't even that sad. Half of them are on my current gym playlist, and I'm not exactly crying into my shoes on the tread-mill. Then again, sometimes I forget that Croy has a whole life-time of emotion bubbling up inside of him, like a volcano that's lulled the world into a false sense of security by lying dormant for a few hundred years. One of these days, the surface tension holding Croy together is going to slip, and he's going to burn our fairy-tail romance to the ground.

As the song approaches its chorus, I begin to sing. *"All because of you... I haven't slept in so long... When I do I dream of drowning in the ocean... Longing for the shore where I can lay my head down... I'll follow your voice... All you have to do is shout it out."*

I continue singing quietly, under my breath, as I turn off the main road.

"Why'd you stop? I love when you sing along to the radio. That's why I put on this song." He leans over and kisses my shoulder. "You would've made a sexy lead singer. If your ex had been smart, back in the day, he would've utilized your vocal talents in his little rock band."

"I was in college at the time and he was in a heavy metal band. Not sure I would've been much help with his music career. But it's funny you say that. I used to write him songs while I was in class, and when we got a chance to hang out, I would sing while he played guitar. Those are some of my favorite memories from back then. Maybe I should look him up online and reach out. See if that music career of his ever worked out."

"I'm sorry I brought it up. Oh look, we're here." Croy pretends to be excited about our destination, although I know he couldn't care less. "I ordered everything and paid for it online while you were driving, so I'll be right back." He leans toward me but stops before he reaches my lips. "I'm really impressed with what you've accomplished at the new house, and I want you to know that I appreciate you."

"Well, I appreciate how hard you work in order for us to have the life we do." I'm not great at accepting compliments, so I toss it back to him. "Hard to believe we're about to start another new chapter when we were barely settled into the last one."

"You're okay with leaving the condo, aren't you? I guess we haven't talked about that part." Croy's lips are playfully close, but still, he doesn't kiss me. It makes the conversation feel a lot more intimate than it is.

"Wherever we are together, that's home. I suppose it doesn't matter if that's the condo or the new house. Give me a little time to adjust, and I'll be happy about the move." Tired of waiting, I lean forward and press my lips to his.

What initially starts as a tender moment, quickly heats up. This sort of kiss usually leads to something else, but a parking lot in broad daylight is not exactly where I want to get caught with my pants down. Maybe in my younger days, when I was more adventurous, he would've convinced me, but I'm getting a little too old for this sort of risk.

I push against Croy's chest, signaling my need to stop. "Why don't you run in and get the wine so we can continue this at home? I'm not trying to get busted having sex in a parking lot."

"Alright. I'll be quick." He kisses me one last time before getting out, leaving me with the lingering feeling of his touch to keep me company in his absence. Out of the two of us, Croy is the more affectionate one, whereas I desire the need for certainty. After a few steps, he looks back with a smile.

I spent so many years being invisible, which plays on a person's self-worth. Over time, I learned to navigate life cloaked in unimportance, silently operating beneath the vale. But as much as I might have pretended to be okay with anonymity, I truly longed to be discovered. I dreamt of being explored and conquered and claimed. And now, to be seen so completely can be jarring. There is no place I can hide where Croy won't venture to find me. It's an intense adjustment. One I'm still getting used to.

After what seems like a while, I start to worry the winery might have run out of the bottles I've promised to deliver. If only I had remembered to come here sooner. I'm not typically someone who puts things off for tomorrow, but my memory as of late has been spotty at best. I'm about to text Croy for an update when I spot him standing on the patio, talking with a woman.

We've parked quite a way from the building, but my distance vision is impeccable, so I might as well be looking through binoculars. Croy seems to be sharing a glass of wine and engaging in conversation with a brunette woman I don't recognize. I'm doing my very best not to jump to any conclusions, but what the fuck!

There are things Croy allows me to do that I would *never* tolerate from him. Basically, everything involving Kelly. Between the two of us, I'm the jealous one, and he knows this. So, what the hell game is he playing?

: Making friends or interviewing my replacement?

Croy: NEVER. You are the only woman for me, my love. I was about to text you, but I forget you have that damn sniper vision. It's Sandy and her husband Frank, from work. Come over and hang out for a minute.

: I'm in my work clothes and I look like crap. I can't walk in there dressed like this.

Croy: I'm dressed the same way you are, babe. It's fine. Come to the side and I'll lift you over the railing. You don't have to go inside.

: But you're YOU!

Croy: What does that mean?

: It means that you look fricken hot no matter what you have on, and I look homeless.

Croy: You're always beautiful. I only shine as a reflection of your light.

: You're too much... I'll be right over.

I attempt to smooth my hair and find my nerve. Taking a deep breath in, inhaling for five beats, and then letting it out. "You can do this." These attempts to psych myself up rarely work, but I make the effort nonetheless. I wonder if I'll ever get over my social anxiety. When I was a teenager, the doctor told my parents it was a phase I would grow out of. Evidently, I'm still growing.

This late in the year, the days turn to night almost out of nowhere. When Croy went in for the wine, it was light out, and now the sun has dimmed, allowing space for artificial light. The patio is outlined with hanging strings of Edison lights and crackling open flame fire pits. Of all the wineries this town boasts, this one is by far my favorite.

Before Croy came into my life, even before my parents moved here, without any ties to this town, I used to come here with my girlfriends from work. Or rather, they were all friends with each other and extended the invitation to me on a handful of occasions. We would stop in at a winery, share a bottle, and then move to the next. Every time we got here, I wanted to stay, but it wasn't my show, so I never spoke up.

Croy's eyes have been on me since I stepped onto the parking lot, and now that he's able to see me clearly, there is a playful smile on his face. Gloating about the fact that he got me out of the car, no doubt. I swear, he's impossible to say no to, and he revels in it.

The railing around the patio is past my waist, so I have zero hope of stepping over on my own. I suppose I could go inside, but then I'd have to endure the disapproving glares from fancy-pants patrons. Croy is waiting there, poised to greet me, as I approach. He leans over and kisses me before lifting me off my feet. The effortless way in which he scoops me up is a gigantic turn-on, and I'm suddenly wishing we were back in the car. The way I'm feeling right now, I could be convinced to break a few laws.

He sets me on my feet but continues to support my weight. Perhaps he's concerned about another fainting spell brought on by a sudden shift in elevation. This time I feel perfectly fine, minus the flush of embarrassment, as I notice everyone staring at us.

Thankfully, once I take a seat, most of them stop looking and go back to their previous business. Any lingering stares are coming from female eyes, so I can only assume it's Croy who has caught their attention, as opposed to me. I understand, but that doesn't mean I appreciate it.

"So, you're the wife we've all heard so much about? It's great to finally meet you. Croy pretty much has us all convinced the sun rises and sets under your command." The smile on Sandy's face would indicate this is coming from a place of praise, though I'm not entirely sure. She might be calling me controlling through grinning teeth and a fabricated smile.

"I'm not even sure what that means, but I assure you, I hold no sway over the stars." I smile back, and everyone laughs.

"He thinks the absolute world of you, sweetie. You're his favorite topic of conversation."

As if on cue, a man arrives at the table carrying a clean wine glass and a bottle of water. He sets both items in front of me and takes the empty seat to my left. I can only assume this is Frank, Sandy's husband. "I got you a glass so you don't feel left out."

"Thank you. I appreciate that." I smile and relax. It's crazy that random coworkers can be so kind and accepting of me, but Croy's parents can't seem to look past their egos. You would think everyone who knows him would want to see him happy. I know I do.

We spend the next few hours making small talk and draining bottles. I'm relieved to be the designated driver because Croy is drunk. This is something we'll need to discuss in private after he's had a chance to sleep. It's not that I'm anti-drinking, but I don't like the idea of our daughter growing up in a house with casual drinkers, let alone parents who drink to excess. It sends the wrong message. Or maybe I only feel that way because I'm pregnant and can't indulge right along with him.

Once my husband is sufficiently pickled, he leans over and

whispers in my ear. "Babygirl, I'm ready for you to take me home. I have things I still need to do to you." Then he kisses my neck, sending tingles coursing through my body.

"And on that note, I think we should probably call it a night." We say our goodbyes and make our way to the parking lot. Thankfully, being of sound mind and body, I remember to grab the case of wine we need for Thursday. I have a feeling Croy is going to spend tomorrow on the couch nursing a wine hangover and a headache.

On the drive home, I'm distracted by a flirtatious hand rubbing the inside of my thigh and lips kissing my neck. It's taking everything in me to keep my eyes open and focused on the road ahead. Only two more miles and we'll be back at the condo, safe in bed.

"I like driving your car. Please don't make me crash." It's becoming increasingly difficult to focus, so I try to move the conversation away from sex.

"Will you finally let me buy you one?" His fingers tease along the inseam of my jeans, devoted to their quest.

"If I say *yes*, will you stop distracting me? I promise you can pick up where you left off when we get home. Unless you want to go to sleep." I bite my lip and contemplate pushing his hand away, but as much as I need him to chill out, I don't want him to stop.

"No such luck, babygirl. When I drink it takes me longer to get off, so plan on staying up. We can role-play if you want. I'll even let you call me by another guy's name."

"Which guy?" I ask, playfully. There is only one name that comes to mind, if it has to be someone other than Croy.

"Ugh... If it has to be that one, so be it. Whatever gets you there. I don't care, so long as you're with me." He leans in close, whispering against my neck. "I like watching you with him, even though I get jealous after. If he wasn't three hours away, I'd tell you to call him."

"Depending on where he's working tonight, he might enjoy

listening." I'm joking, but that doesn't stop the flood of memories from coming. Nights spent in the jail mix with moments shared in bed with Kelly. I think about both times Croy set aside his hatred and shared me with the one man he feared losing me to.

I pull into the designated parking spot in front of the condo and kill the engine. Once we're parked, he pulls my hand toward his leg so I can feel what awaits. He's ready to go, and I can't wait any longer. "Bed or backseat? Choose quickly."

He unhooks his belt, shimmies out of his pants, and reclines the seat. "I want you, right here and now, and we aren't stopping until you get off with me."

"Okay." I climb over the center console and settle myself on his lap. Leaning forward, I whisper. "Well, if that's the goal, you know what you have to do."

"Oh, I plan on it."

Forty-Seven

AS EXPECTED, most of Wednesday is spent on the couch cuddling while Croy nurses a hangover. During moments like this, I'm glad I can't drink. Truthfully, I'm not sure I'll even bother with it after Verlaine is born. Cherry vodka and red bull used to be my go-to vice, but I seem to have lost my taste for them, even before finding out I was pregnant. The last time I had a drink was on the back patio at the old house, while Croy and I discussed what dating might look like after I moved away.

That conversation seems funny now, since we only lasted about a day apart from one another. There was no way I could risk losing time with him. For what reason? Deep down, I knew he would never hurt me.

As for new vices, pretty much the day after Halloween, Croy and I switched from horror movies to Hallmark Christmas meet cute romances, and I'm obsessed. They give me all the feels, and I can't get enough. If heaven is bliss, then mine is being on the couch, under a blanket, snuggled against Croy's chest, watching Christmas rom-coms, in a room lit only by flickering candles and light from the television.

We're getting to the part where our couple breaks up over some silly drama instead of having a conversation when Croy pauses the movie and gives me a squeeze. "I've been wanting to ask you, how are you feeling about tomorrow?"

"I'll be on my best behavior, as always, if that's what you're worried about." If I'm being honest, I'm trying not to think about it. Between unpacking boxes at the new house and making the most of his vacation time, I've been too busy to dwell on what may come. Seeing Croy's parents is not my idea of holiday fun, but I'm married to their son, so I can't avoid them.

"No. That's not at all what I'm worried about. I don't want you to give up on me because my family is a pack of assholes." Croy's concern awakens my stifled anxiety. He needs to drop it and let things play out as they may before he convinces me to stay home.

"I don't think that's going to happen." I wish I could be more confident in my response, but family issues can be complex and insurmountable. I have quite a bit of previous experience in this area and it's almost all bad.

"The second you feel uncomfortable, we abort the mission and come home. If you say *cranberry sauce*, I'll know you've reached your limit."

"I'm not worried, and you shouldn't be either. Your mom caught me off guard the first time, but now I know better. There's nothing I'm going to walk into over there that I can't handle. So, let's finish the movie, and enjoy the rest of our stress-free evening together." These words are meant for his benefit. I already know I'll spend the rest of the night playing out worse-case scenarios in my head, but there's no reason Croy should suffer along with me. After all, I'm the one they'll be coming for, not him.

As expected, our perfectly matched movie couple falls apart the second someone looks sideways at them. Friends, to lovers, to broken-hearted saps, all in the span of an hour. Thankfully, a chance meeting in the cereal aisle of the local market on Christmas Eve was enough to rekindle what was previously thought to be lost. And just like that, it's a Christmas miracle, culminating with a kiss under the mistletoe. If only real life could look a little more like the movies.

"I'm going to iron my stuff for tomorrow. Is your dress in the closet?" He kisses the top of my head before getting up. My answer is irrelevant. Croy's funny when it comes to clothes, especially around his parents. He's going to iron the dress whether I ask him to or not, that's a given.

"Yeah, it's in there, but I only wore it one time, for like two hours. I'm sure it's fine." In twenty-nine years, I think I've used an iron once, and that was only because my mom was teaching me how to use one.

"Tell me you're joking. You did wash it after our date, right? It probably smells like after-dinner sex." He ducks into the bedroom as I jump up from the couch to follow.

"Leave my dress alone! It's fine." I give chase, finding him in the closet with my favorite fancy outfit pressed to his nose. "Don't you dare. If my dress gets messed up, I'll have nothing to wear."

"You're lucky. It smells like your perfume." He hangs it back on the hook and joins me in the doorway. "What am I going to do with you? I feel like you get a kick out of watching me panic."

"I don't. But it is a little bit adorable. You're the one who married a girl with no fashion sense, so, that's on you." I lock my fingers under his belt and pull. "There must be other things I'm good at, right?"

"Mm-hmm. You have several skills I thoroughly enjoy." The look he gives me causes my cheeks to flush and makes my heart thump uncontrollably as he moves toward my neck. "Why are you being a tease?"

"I'm not. I have every intention of delivering." As soon as the words part way with my lips, he picks me up and carries me over to the bed. When it comes to being a girlfriend or wife, my shortcomings are many. However, there is one particular skill I have honed over the years.

Being chubby in my teens, I avoided getting undressed at all costs, but I wasn't a prude. I blew through my High School like an F5 tornado. Some people might look back with regret, but not me. While other girls got dates to Homecoming, I had evenings in the parking lot with some of the best-looking guys in school. And now, my husband gets to lay back and enjoy the tips and tricks I've picked up over the years, so it's a win for everyone.

Croy is so good about making sure I'm taken care of, in and out of the bedroom. Last night, for example, when we were parked out front, he said some downright filthy things to me. And because of that, I was able to finish when he did.

Early on in our relationship, he discovered dirty talk was the key to unlocking my flood gates and he's always willing to say and do whatever it takes to get me there. So, on occasions like this, I'm more than happy to return the favor.

Forty~Eight

LAST NIGHT ENDED up being more than I bargained for, which resulted in a late start to the day. My husband, being who he is, has been up for hours, while I've been sleeping the morning away like a goddamn princess.

The smell of coffee tells me he's in the kitchen or close by, so I run out of the bedroom, still pulling on my shirt. "Why didn't you wake me up? We have to leave in two hours."

"I know better than to wake a sleeping dragon." He laughs and wraps me in his arms. "Anyways, I was just about to go in there. So, relax. We have plenty of time."

"This is about as relaxed as I'm going to get today. It's all downhill from here, I'm afraid. Sorry, not sorry." I wiggle out of his arms and turn on my heels. There is no time for cuddles and cuteness. I need to shower, do my hair and make-up, get dressed, and somehow transform myself into a woman worthy of the man I married. It's not going to be easy.

After connecting my phone to the Bluetooth speaker in the bathroom, I scroll right past my shower playlist and opt for something harder. If I'm going to make it through today in one piece, I need to get pumped up first. Gym playlist vol. 2 should do the trick. I used to listen to a lot of these songs before going to work at the jail when I needed a little confidence injection.

Hopefully, Thanksgiving dinner won't require backup.

"Is everything alright in there?" Croy shouts from somewhere in the bedroom.

Between the music and the running water, I barely hear him, so I don't bother to respond. I'm not going to lose my voice shouting back and forth with him about how I'm fine with not being fine. We can talk after I get out.

I'm about to start washing my hair when the curtain behind me slides to the side and a naked Croy steps into the shower.

"What are you doing? You smelled so good when I found you in the kitchen, I thought for sure you'd already showered." Not that I mind having him in here, but I'm kind of on a time crunch.

"Yeah, I did. I thought maybe you could use some company, that's all." He reaches past me, grabbing a loofah and the body wash. "Can I wash your back? And then maybe the front? You know, to help save time."

"I would never dream of saying no to you." I lather my hair while he soaps my body. I suppose this could save time if we're both able to keep our thoughts from sliding into the gutter.

"Now that's a good girl," he says, turning me around to face him.

"See. You say shit like that and get me all worked up." My head tilts back as he presses himself against me. I'm not sure what it is, but the feeling of shampoo suds and water cascading down my back gives me chills.

"Regrettably, we don't have time for all of that, but I will be having you for dessert later." His mouth says one thing as his body implies another, suggesting some part of him isn't interested in waiting.

"Now who's being a tease?" I laugh.

Croy's arms pull me in once again, and I'm content to spend the rest of the day here in the shower with him. In truth, I would prefer it. If I had any real choice in the matter, I would stay home and celebrate Thanksgiving with a turkey sandwich, BBQ baked potato chips, and a diet coke, but we gave our word to Astrid when we accepted her invitation, and I'm not about to disappoint the one family member who actually likes me.

As we stand, locked in a lover's embrace, I can feel Croy's concern seeping into my open pores. He didn't join me in the shower to be flirty, he came in here because he was genuinely worried. Normally, this would kick my anxiety into high gear, but for some reason, my need to reassure him is stronger than my fear of the unknown.

"So long as we're together, everything's going to be fine. I promise. Now, can you please get out of here so I can finish washing my hair and shave my legs?" I love him, but he's distracting as all hell, especially when he's naked.

Croy kisses the top of my head and steps out onto the mat. "We could stay home," he says, from the other side of the curtain while drying off.

"Tempting, but no. Let's make an appearance so we can be done with family holidays for the year." I wish he wouldn't have made the offer, even if it was a joke. Now I'm going to obsessively regret not taking the easy way out when things go left during dinner.

"Deal."

When I finish in the shower and step out, I half expect Croy to still be in the bathroom waiting for me, but he's not. Everything about this morning feels off. I assume it's my nerves getting the better of me, or a sign. Either way, promises have been made and the day is upon us. No backing out now.

The bathroom air is still thick with steam from my shower, so I take my make-up bag and hair dryer to the bedroom. Once I'm set up in front of the dresser mirror, it's time to get to work. Growing up, somehow, I missed the girly phase. So, to this day, I still don't wear makeup very often, and when I do, it's pretty basic.

Thankfully, due to my lack of skill and a waning desire to impress anyone, I'm finished with hair and makeup, with time to spare. Now all I have to do is find my dress. I look in the closet, but it isn't on the hook where I left it.

"Babe!" I don't mean to shout, but I'm starting to panic. "Do you know where my dress is?"

Croy walks in the room wearing a sheepish grin, carrying a freshly laundered and pressed dress that looks exactly like the one I told him to leave alone. "Don't be mad. You know I'm weird about clothes."

"I'm not mad," I say, snatching the dress from his outstretched hand. "I'm annoyed you feel the need to do shit behind my back. Thank you." I unzip the back of the dress and step into it. "Would you mind getting the zipper?"

He takes his time. The teeth of the zipper bite together in an irritatingly slow motion. Something about the way time is moving, jumping back and forth between hyper-speed and near stop, reminds me of nights spent dancing in underground rave clubs. The first time I did ecstasy, I went home, after a night of dancing, and took a shower. To this day, I would swear that I could feel every drop of shower water individually as it made contact with my skin. And while it was an experience, to be sure, I will encourage my daughter to avoid illegal drugs, in all their many forms.

"You look beautiful." Croy brushes my hair to the side and kisses my neck. "Thank you for going with me."

As if I had a choice.

Forty~Nine

MY UNEASE GROWS as our drive progresses. Although I'm not entirely sure where Astrid lives, I know we've entered the city limits. Maybe I can find a way to help in the kitchen and avoid being in a room with their mother. I'm willing to do anything. Scrub pots and pans, take out the trash, just point me in a direction and I'll happily engross myself in any task.

When Croy parks in front of a white two-story home with black shutters and immaculate landscaping, my heart sinks. Not for any reason pertaining to the house, or seeing Astrid, or my dislike of eating in front of people. My current anxiety is being stoked by a memory.

I knew his parents were going to be here. I've known since accepting the invitation. But seeing their car parked in the driveway is triggering in a way I wasn't fully expecting. "Hey babe, maybe you should go in without me, and I'll hang out here and wait for you."

"Okay, we're going home." Croy moves to restart the ignition, but I catch his hand mid-way and pull it towards my chest. "I'm not putting you through this, and I never should have listened to you when you said it was a good idea. I don't need them in my life. I need you."

"I'm fine. There's no need to be dramatic. I was merely making a suggestion. Plus, we have wine to deliver." I kiss the back of his hand and straighten my shoulders.

"Don't do that. It's my job to protect you, not the other way around." He holds me in his eyes.

"I hate when you say shit like that. As if our entire marriage is one-sided." I know that isn't what he meant, but sometimes that's how it feels. As if he's required to do it all on his own and I'm just along for the ride.

"That's not what I'm saying and you know I don't think that."

"Let's go in before I exhaust my composure." I push the door open and step out, no longer willing to flip through this book in an effort to get on the same page. Croy and I are never going to view this issue with his parents from the same vantage point, which means in regards to this particular issue, we will never truly be side by side. Family is the one wedge that could ultimately drive us apart.

He catches me halfway up the brick pathway leading to the front door. Taking my hand, Croy looks at me and says, "We do this together, or not at all."

I nod my head in agreement. Per usual, he's right. We are in this together, otherwise, what's the point? My misplaced anger is being directed at the one person who doesn't deserve it, and that's only because he's the easiest target.

When we arrive at the front door, I half expect a fashionably dressed butler to greet us, but when it swings open, Astrid is on the other side, smiling from ear to ear. "Ahhh! You guys came." She pulls us both into a giant group hug and squeals with excitement. "And you brought the wine." Noting the white cardboard carrier in Croy's left hand. "Here, I'll take it to the kitchen."

"Let me get that," I say a little too enthusiastically. "Just point me in the right direction." I slide my fingers around the handle as Croy transfers the weight of the box over to my possession. Hiding out in the kitchen, pretending to sort out the wine, is a far better option than stepping into the living room.

"Yeah, okay. It's down the hall and to the left. You can't miss it." She smiles at me wearily, sensing my need to escape.

The house is unbelievably attractive, much like Astrid herself. I guess I shouldn't be surprised. No doubt she had it detailed in preparation for the holiday, but I get the feeling it probably looks like this all the time. A single woman living in this house alone, with no pets, can't be that hard to clean up after. And if she's anything like Croy, this house has never seen a dish in the sink or a t-shirt on the floor. I admire her perfection, while also finding it annoying.

I slow-walk my way to the kitchen, being sure to poke my head in rooms that sound empty along the way. To the right, is the living room, where I can hear everyone talking. On my left is a room that looks like an office. I wonder if Astrid works from home, or if this is merely meant for show. A framed photo sitting on the middle shelf of her built-in bookshelf catches my eye. It's her and Croy at the Grand Canyon. I recognize the image immediately since I've seen this same photo on his phone.

I wonder what that must be like, to have a close relationship with a sibling. My brother and I could probably go years without talking or seeing one another and think nothing of it. Truth be told, if my mom didn't insist on having everyone gather a few times a year at her house, I think we might lose touch altogether. This is in no way due to dislike for one another, we simply aren't that close. Family isn't something I put a lot of stock in, but I can see Croy does. Yet another reminder of why I could never ask him to choose between me and them.

I'd love to sneak upstairs, but I've yet to come across a staircase. Plus, I worry that might be viewed as intrusive. Best to wait until a guided tour is offered, I suppose.

The weight of half a dozen wine bottles is beginning to become a strain, so it's probably best to continue on my way. From what I've seen so far, all the walls have the same white wooden wainscoting lining the bottom three and a half feet, and crown molding along the top. I am deeply obsessed with this look. I had considered doing something similar at the new house but didn't want to ask for anything to add further expenses. If I can say one thing for sure about Astrid, it's that she's got good taste.

Even without directions, I could've found my way to the kitchen. The smell of turkey cooking in the oven is so delightfully inviting, there might as well be a breadcrumb trail of stuffing and pumpkin pie lining the path. As much as I hate to admit it, being here might be better than a lunch meat sandwich and chips on the couch at home.

I hear what sounds like the oven door closing and a low conversation between two men. It's impossible to make out what they're saying, but I assume it's the chef and an assistant. Croy's mother is still loudly chattering in the living room, so I step into the kitchen assuming the coast is clear. Unfortunately, my heart is not ready for what I unexpectedly find there.

Leaning against the counter dressed in black pants, a black tie, and a white button-down with the sleeves cuffed to his elbow, is the last person I expected to cross paths with today. The shock is enough that the last of my failing grip abandons me and I drop the case of wine, sending it clattering to the floor.

"Oh shit!" He rushes over and wraps me up in his arms as the tears spill from my eyes. "Please don't be upset with me." The sound of Kelly's voice inches from my ear feels like a knife in the back.

Coming here today, I expected Croy's mom to throw daggers. That was a given. I ran through all the worst-case scenarios and practiced maintaining my composure. I thought of all the things I would say silently in my head while smiling through gritted teeth. I reinforced every wall and strengthened my defenses in case Croy failed to react. But never, not for one second, did I mentally prepare for an assassin-style assault from my best friend.

"What are you doing here?" For one fleeting second, I

thought he might be here for me, but then I did the math and pieced together the clues. Kelly told me he was seeing someone, but I never had the opportunity to ask who, because honestly, I didn't want to know. And Astrid mentioned there would be six of us for dinner, but again, I failed to dig past the surface. These two have been dating since they met at the condo, and neither of them felt the need to mention it to me. Honestly, with friends and family like this, who the hell needs enemies?

"I've needed this for a long time," he says, rocking me back and forth in his arms. "You have no idea how many times I've wanted to tell you everything, but I didn't know how. And then when we talked about the baby, and the possibility that she could be mine, I got scared." His words are comforting in an odd way. Or maybe it's simply that I've missed being in his arms. Whatever the reason, I melt into his embrace.

Getting lost in this moment could be effortless if I allowed myself to let go. But I can't. There is wine soaking into my sock and Croy's voice on the other side of the wall. It is these two things that keep me tethered to reality. "You could have anyone. Why would you start dating Croy's sister? That's so messed up."

"That's not entirely true, now is it? There is one girl I can't have, and I miss her." He tilts my face toward his, our lips dangerously close together. "We need to talk."

Croy steps through the doorway of the kitchen, loudly clearing his throat. "Did you know he was going to be here?" His question is directed my way.

I wipe the tears from my face as Kelly lowers his arms and takes a step back. "She didn't know." His words echo the response rattling around inside my head. And as good-intentioned as he may be at the moment, talking for me is an unwise choice.

"I'm not speaking to you, Kelly." Croy's tone is firm and direct as he makes a considerable effort to remain calm. "Did you know he was going to be here?"

"No." Is all I manage to say.

My eyes shift to the floor, and I appear to be standing in a bottle of blueberry wine, which is a real shame. I knew one of the bottles broke, but I was hoping it was the pear.

Fifty/Fifty

WHEN I CLOSE my eyes and picture my future, it's always Croy by my side. He is my better half, my best friend, my everything. There is no question as to who I would choose, time and time again, no matter the outcome. Since the moment my life collided with his, I've known where I belong.

Kelly seems to think I can be swayed depending on the results of a paternity test, but that isn't the case. Even if Croy left me, which he won't. But even if he did, I couldn't jump ship and crawl back into my old life. A butterfly is never going to be a caterpillar again. If life with wings doesn't work out, they die. Period. There is no going backward.

I've given a lot of thought to all of this over the last few months. Croy and I have spoken at length, walking every hypothetical path, and toiling over the details. It's been exhausting and informative.

If the test comes back in Croy's favor, nothing changes. Verlaine grows up in a home filled with laughter, dad jokes, made-up songs, and love. I've seen this version of my life so many times it's begun to feel like a premonition.

However, in the event of a test in Kelly's favor, the possible paths get muddy. I have no idea what he would want, so it's impossible for me to prepare in any meaningful way. Kelly suggested signing his rights away, but would he still feel that way in the moment, once everything becomes real? Will he use this as an opportunity to make my life a living hell, or see it as a way of keeping a piece of me forever? Will Kelly fight me out of a need to win or a love he can't let go of? Or will he finally walk away?

And now there is Astrid to consider. Is his relationship with her serious, or is it a fling meant to piss Croy off and make me jealous?

There is a paternity test that could be done now, but I've been too embarrassed to ask my doctor about it. Even though I didn't cheat on Croy, it would look that way, and I don't want everyone silently judging me while I'm trying to focus on giving birth.

On a scale from one to ten my stress level is officially at eleven, and we haven't even sat down for dinner.

Fifty~One

CROY MOPS up the puddle of wine with a clean towel while I inspect the remaining bottles. For all intents and purposes, I'm wearing blinders. My current plan is to carry on with my holiday as if Kelly is not in the room, and I will *not obsess* over how good he looks.

"The other five look fine," I say, desperately searching for a rainbow during the storm. "Do you think your sister would mind if I borrow a dry pair of socks?" At this point, I would happily drive home for new socks if need be. Anything to get me the hell out of this kitchen, while still avoiding the living room.

"Why don't I take you on a tour of the house and you can rummage through her dresser drawers. I would do it myself, but the last thing I need right now is to stumble across my sister's hidden collection of sex toys." He visibly shivers at the thought and takes my hand.

Behind us, the sound of stifled laughter stops Croy dead in his tracks. He doesn't want to think of his sister and Kelly together any more than I do, and this isn't the time or place to start exchanging words.

"Let's go upstairs and have a conversation, just you and I. Please." I gently push him toward the door, propelling him forward. Whatever part of him wants to remain in the kitchen and have it out with Kelly is overshadowed by his need to protect me. For that, I am happy. Otherwise, I wouldn't be strong enough to move him half an inch.

In order to keep up our current ruse, Croy begins giving me a very professional tour. One that leads us quickly past the living room and up the stairs to the second floor. Once we're in the master bedroom, he shuts the door behind him and sits me on the bed.

"What is going on? You swear you had no idea he was going to be here? Like, neither of them so much as hinted at the fact they've been dating?" He searches my face for answers and my eyes well with tears. "No, of course you didn't know. I'm so sorry, baby. My sister is such an idiot when it comes to guys! No offense. I know Kelly has a way of being charming when he wants to be, but why pursue Astrid, of all people? It seems intentional."

"I don't know. They did seem to hit it off when they met at the house, so maybe it has nothing to do with us." I can't believe I'm defending their secret relationship after being lied to and ignored for the last month and a half. Croy's face mirrors my shock as the words leave my mouth. "I'm surprised she didn't mention it to you. I thought you were her favorite brother?"

"Don't even mention his name, or he's likely to pop out of the mirror like Bloody Mary at some teenage girl's sleepover."

"He's not Beetlejuice." I can't help but laugh. "But anyways, let's focus on one issue at a time. What are we going to do about dinner? Should we leave or pretend like everything's fine?"

Before Croy can answer, the bedroom door swings open and Astrid steps into the room. "Oh, thank god. I was afraid you guys came up here to have sex in my room."

"So, you open the door without knocking? Gross!" The effortless banter between brother and sister is precisely what this moment needs. Looks like we're going to bite our tongues until we each drown in our own blood. Dinner should be fun.

"Matt said you needed a fresh pair of socks." She walks over to the dresser and pulls a fluffy pair of slipper socks from the top center drawer. "And he mentioned something about sex toys, which made mom choke on her wine. It was fantastic." Before exiting, Astrid turns to me and says, "You can't hide all day, it's time to eat. Honestly, I thought you'd be happy I called in back-up." And with that, she's gone.

"Does she mean Kelly is here for me? Are they dating, or did she invite him to dinner for my benefit?" Now I'm more confused than ever. It's like I'm in Wonderland and everyone's speaking in riddles. I wish someone would tell me what's going on in plain English.

Fifty~Two

WHILE I'M busy choking on my secrets, Croy's mother was more than happy to dole out her version of the truth. The way she's gushing over *Matt*, I can't tell if she's in love with him, or thrilled about the possibility of someday having the son she's always wanted. It's nauseating to experience from where I'm sitting, and I get the feeling it's even worse for her actual son. Croy is so tense he feels carved from granite.

I tap him on the shoulder and motion with my hand for him to come closer. "I need to tell you something," I say, as his ear approaches my lips. "You're my favorite person in the whole world."

He turns his face toward me and smiles before placing a soft kiss against my lips. "I love you, more than everything."

For a moment, time freezes, and I forget about the tension surrounding the dinner table until I hear a familiar voice speaking in a tone I recognize.

"Excuse me! Repeat what you just said." Kelly blurts out, cutting off Croy's mother mid-sentence.

"You two are so perfect for each other, it's disgusting," Astrid interjects, playfully lightening the conversation. "I think it's time for you to tell us, once and for all, how you *really* met."

I dread this conversation, even though it's one of my favorite stories. Croy squeezes my leg, and I wonder if his hand has been there the entire time. I've become so accustomed to the weight of his hand on my thigh that I only tend to notice when it's absent. Reaching for my glass of water, I take a sip and look at Croy in silent communication.

We've always told people we met in the hospital, which most everyone has accepted at face value. Everyone except Astrid. She's seen through our half-truth since the beginning. It's surprising to me that she wasn't able to extract the information from her new boyfriend, unless she never considered he might know.

"I don't care anymore. You can tell 'em if you want." Croy is displeased, but has resigned himself to being branded a failure.

I shake my head *no* in hopes this will be the end of it. After all, I have zero interest in outing my husband in front of his judgmental parents. But wishful thinking isn't reality. Astrid is determined to get answers, by any means necessary.

"Matt, tell us how they met, or I'm breaking up with you."

Stunned silence fills the room as Kelly stares through me, contemplating his next move. He's doing everything he can to swallow his anger over what he heard Croy say, and now he has to ingest the truth sitting on the tip of his tongue. "I love you, but..." I'm not entirely sure if he's talking to me or Astrid, so I hold my breath and wait for him to continue. "I think once you hear the whole story, you're going to regret asking."

"Okay, so you do know, and you lied to me. I was joking when I said I was going to break up with you, but I'm beginning to reconsider. I don't understand why the three of you are being so weird about this." Astrid sounds annoyed, but I get the feeling Kelly's stay in the doghouse will be short-lived. After a night of sex and a few lines whispered in his bedroom voice, he'll be back in her good graces.

"Oh, for Christ's sake, Kelly. Tell the damn story. Now's your chance to say exactly how you feel about me." Croy sits back in his chair, prepared to meet the firing squad. "I'm interested to hear your version."

"I haven't said one negative word about you, and I wouldn't. When are you going to stop treating me like the bad guy?" The flames of dinner table candles catch in his eyes, and our fragile reality is a bomb dangerously short on seconds.

"She needed you, and you weren't there." The other occupants of dining chairs become nothing more than furniture as a long overdue conversation plays out between the two men I can't live without.

"You think I don't know that! Do you have any idea how many times I've replayed that night in my head? How many times I've seen her floating in a pool of blood. I thought she was dead!" Kelly's voice is thick with pain and regret, and it stabs like a sharpened spoon.

"I'm not talking about six months ago, you asshole. I'm talking about the last six weeks. She needed you and you left, and then you have the nerve to show up here like nothing happened." Croy's words hit like a right cross, but Kelly isn't the only one damaged in the onslaught.

"I didn't know about any of that until a few days ago. You're the one who took her three hours away from me, you selfish prick! How the hell am I supposed to be there for her when you're always standing between us?" Kelly's words propel him upwards onto his feet, sending the wooden chair knocking to the floor.

"She's mine! I will be standing beside her from here until the end, so you'd better get used to it." Croy jumps to his feet, encouraging the fight to turn physical.

"I should've taken her from you when I had the chance."

"You've got to be joking! You think because you fucked my wife..."

Before Croy can utter another word, I scream, "cranberry sauce," temporarily breaking the tension. I expected harsh truths from his mother, and for a moment I even thought they might come from the mouth of my old friend, but never, not in a million years, did I anticipate being stabbed in the back by the love of my life.

The room spins as I get to my feet, but I'm able to steady myself with the edge of the table. This is not the time for weakness. My character and self-worth have been destroyed. Standing here, in the full aftermath of my choices, I feel exposed and embarrassed. Fleeing is my last best option.

Croy catches my arm as I step past him but before he can mutter another apology, I twist my arm free. "I'm going to need a minute."

"Thank you, lord. Maybe now she can crawl back to whatever loser knocked her up." One final departing statement from his mother is enough to knock the air from my lungs, sending the tears spilling from my eyes.

I turn, no more than an empty shell in self-preservation mode set to drift away, and make one final request. "If you ever loved me, you will not say another word."

I slip into my shoes and grab my coat, sure to leave Astrid's socks behind. I want nothing from them. Not one thought or memory. I want to disappear and forget this life ever happened.

Catching me on the sidewalk, warm arms wrap around me from behind. I spin on my heels, burying my face in his chest, as the last of my defenses crumble. "I'm sorry I messed up everything for both of us."

"Babe, it's nothing we can't fix, okay?" Kelly's voice is as soothing as tea with honey, reminding me of how thirsty I am. "Let me drive you home and we can talk. Please. You're the only person I want to be around right now."

I look at his face for the first time and notice his lip is split open and he's bleeding. "Oh my god. Did Croy do that?" I'm such an idiot. I was so busy feeling sorry for myself I forgot to pull Kelly out with me. I press the sleeve of my coat against his lip, trying not to injure him further. He shakes his head *no*, but doesn't attempt to speak.

I snicker before asking, "Was it Astrid who hit you?"

His head moves slightly, indicating the answer is *yes*.

He takes my hand and we make our way to the car he conveniently hid across the street in the park. I was wondering how I missed that since he was here before we arrived. Now I see he concealed his whereabouts on purpose, knowing I would recognize his vehicle immediately. Being back inside his car is bittersweet. There are a lot of memories here, mostly good, but also a few bad.

The drive home is quiet, in part because his lip starts bleeding every time he tries to talk, and because there is simply too much to say. I feel crushed under the weight of my omissions, and I imagine he's feeling the same way. Kelly pulls into Croy's designated parking spot next to my car and kills the engine.

"I don't have my keys." I'm not sure why this realization is only now dawning on me, but here we are. "I'll be fine if you have to go. It's not that cold."

"I'd rather sit with you if that's okay. I've got a full tank of gas so we can run the heat until a set of keys arrive." Kelly reaches over and takes my hand. "Everything is going to be okay. I promise you."

"What makes you think that?" Our lives are in shambles and he's acting like it's no big deal. I'm starting to wonder if that shot to the face didn't cause some sort of short-term memory loss.

"I love you a ridiculous amount, but it pales in comparison to how much Croy adores you. Now, I can't promise he won't end up in prison for the rest of his life for killing his mom after what she said, but I can promise you I'm never going to disappear again..." Kelly's words trail off in response to my changing expression.

"Wait a second. Go back. What did you say about Croy going to prison?" I pull the phone from my coat pocket and begin to tap my fingers into the glass screen.

: Please talk to me. Where are you?

Croy: Is everything alright? What's going on?

: That's what I'm trying to find out.

Croy: I'm three minutes away.

"Okay, I can breathe now. Why would you scare me like that?" I playfully smack Kelly's arm before laying my head against him. "So, you and Astrid, huh? Not gonna lie, seeing you together felt like a punch in the gut."

"Yeah, I know the feeling. I'm sorry." Kelly kisses the top of my head and wraps his arms around me. "Do you think you could forgive me? I can't handle losing you again."

"It's already forgiven, you know that. I can't deal with losing you either." I look up in time to see Croy pulling into the visitor parking directly behind us, and he's not alone. "I have a feeling we'll get plenty of opportunities to hang out now that you're dating my sister-in-law."

Kelly's door swings open, revealing a torso I would recognize anywhere. Croy ducks his head into the car, with a half-smile. "Alright you two, break it up. Can we go inside and talk, where it's warm?"

"Yeah, sounds good, man. Or, wait… you probably weren't talking to me." Kelly turns to look at me, as if preparing to say goodbye.

"I was talking to both of you," he says with a smile. This version of my husband reminds me of the man I first fell in love with, which is the polar opposite of the person I left standing at the dinner table. I'm learning Croy is far more emotional than I previously realized, and that's not a bad thing. His stability helps to keep me level, but it would be unfair of me to always expect him to be my anchor. After all, this is a team.

I'm not sure how or why Croy is in such a good mood after

everything that happened, but I'm sure he plans on explaining. I can say one thing for certain, of all the relationships I've found myself in over the years, romantic or otherwise, this one has been the most interesting. There have been times during the last few months when I have felt the sting of loneliness, but I've never been bored.

The thought of losing everything we have and everything we could become seems unfathomable. Despite his mother's best efforts, I think this is a battle she's already lost. And for the first time in history, I'm someone's priority.

Fifty~Three

KELLY EXITS the car as I do, but Croy hasn't moved. The two men stand toe to toe, and the size difference would be almost comical if I wasn't struck with a sudden fear for my friend's safety. In a panic, I try to get around the closing door, but Astrid catches my arm.

"Why don't you and I get inside and find something warm to drink?" Her voice is calm and sweet like a siren's song, leading me away from where I need to be.

Was Croy's perceived kindness an act to catch us off guard? Is there a plot between brother and sister that I am woefully unaware of like a trap that's set to be sprung the moment my back is turned? If I walk away, is Kelly in danger? I would hope not, but it's not a risk I'm willing to take.

I move as though I'm prepared to follow anywhere Astrid leads, but turn back toward the guys before ascending the stairs to the condo. Something about this moment feels off. In fact, everything about this day has felt wrong. At some point, I have to speak up and stop the bleeding. But as I approach, I hear Croy say, "I appreciate you bringing her home for me. After what I said, I knew you were the only person she would leave with."

Pressing the length of my body against his back, I wrap my arms around Croy's waist and hug him from behind. "I'm not going inside until you do." My presence in their conversation is nothing more than a voice.

"At what point do you two stop having each other's back?" Croy's question seems rhetorical, but also directed at both Kelly and myself.

In unison, we reply, "Never," and laugh once we've registered the other's response.

I know there are millions of people out there who will never understand how or why I continue to be friends with someone like Matt Kelly. For the longest time, Croy was among that group, frustrated by my inability to let go. But I'm someone who sees the best in people, for better or worse. I like to step back in order to look at the whole picture and surround myself with individuals who add value to my life. One moment doesn't hold as much weight as patterns of behavior, and so it's easy for me to hold on to the good, and let go of the hurt. Perhaps my self-preservation mode is damaged due to a lack of self-care. Irregardless, my love and friendship are not conditional in the ways that perhaps they should be. I give freely and abundantly because that's the kind of person I am. The number of people I've given up on, I could count on one hand, and it wouldn't even require all of my fingers.

My thoughts trail off as Croy takes my hand and the three of us make our way into the condo, where Astrid is waiting with an assortment of coffee, tea, and hot chocolate. Seeing her as the unassisted hostess warms my soul more than my piping hot beverage ever could. I had hoped she was more than a beautiful face, designer clothes, and the lifestyle she's lived since birth, but I hadn't spent enough time with her to know for sure. Seeing her now, at ease in my kitchen, gives me hope for whatever future there might be between her and my dearest friend. After all, a guy can't live on frozen pizza forever.

We spend the rest of the night spinning tales. I'm not sure which garners more surprise, the odd way Croy and I met, or the argument with his parents that took place after Kelly and I walked away from the dinner table. There's a lot of air that needs to be cleared, and stories that can finally be shared.

Astrid beams with pride like a spotlight, as she takes to heart the whole truth about her brother and the manner in which he saved my life. But that light dims when Kelly begins to confess his past behavior. I imagine it's not easy to hear the man you love admit to being a manipulative jerk. And even though Kelly doesn't need me to sing his praises, I do it anyway. After all, if he's irredeemable, then so am I, and I'm not willing to believe that.

We even discuss the largely unspoken issue that has been hanging over all of us, which turns out to be a far more civil conversation than I anticipated. After some convincing from the group, I concede and agree to make an appointment for the paternity test. I've been on the fence about it, but after being outvoted three to one, I figured it's best to know one way or another. If I'm being honest, I've been avoiding the test because I'm afraid of what the results might say.

I need a win, but those can be hard to come by when you're a loser.

It's been dark for hours once Astrid and Kelly announce their plan to get on the road, and while we spoke, a light dusting of snow has painted everything white. "Be careful driving," is the last thing I say, as the door closes behind them. Somehow, these words feel like a bad omen, but I'm going to try not to dwell on it. There is a conversation I've been needing to have, one that silence can well afford.

As Croy makes his way to the couch, I call after him. My question is sure to annoy him, but only because he doesn't realize how badly I need the answer. "Why are you still with me?" I shout with some force.

"Okay, so we're doing this right now?" He responds by turning towards me instead of taking a seat on the couch, heads straight to my location by the door, and backs me against the wall. Croy's arms rest atop my shoulders as his hands press flat against the wall. "Can I be honest with you?"

"I would hope so. That's what I'm looking for."

"I hate when you ask me questions like this. It hurts my soul that you would question my love for you. But I'll tell you what, if you agree to spend the rest of your life by my side, I'll do my best to convince you that you're so much more than I deserve." He leans down, pressing his forehead to mine.

"I appreciate that you're trying to make me feel better, but you know it doesn't make sense." I require more than pretty words and offers of forever.

His response comes without so much as a second's pause. "Being with you is the only thing in my life that makes sense. I'm sorry about what happened at dinner. I got caught in the moment and blurted out something I never should have said. I understand if you're pissed at me. You have every right to be. And if I have to, I'll sleep on the couch. I'll rub your feet. I'll beg for your forgiveness. Hell, I'll even clean the bathroom. But I will not walk away from our marriage. No matter how many times you say I deserve better, you will never be able to convince me that someone better than you exists in my world."

"Your parents are never going to accept me."

"I don't care! I'm done trying to please people who are incapable of being happy for us. We don't owe them anything and we don't need them. I've been on my own for a long time, which is probably why they're so disapproving of my choices, but you know what, I'm done worrying about what they think. From here on out, I'm going to offer them the same level of respect they show you, and if they have a problem with it, I will suggest they take a long hard look inward at their own words and actions before pointing the finger in our direction. They chose to have children. Astrid and I did not choose to have them as parents."

"Okay. Well, goddamn. I guess that answers that." I look into his eyes, where I know I'll always find my place. My insecurities require constant reassurance, but the good news is, I finally found someone willing to remind me that I'm worth the trouble, even when I refuse to believe it. "Let's go to bed."

Fifty~Four

THE FOUR AND a half weeks between Thanksgiving and Christmas have been blissful chaos. With the remaining days of Croy's holiday vacation, we moved everything out of the condo and turned over our keys. I thought when the time came, I'd be sad to leave, but it almost felt like a relief. The new house offers a sense of permanence and purpose, which are feelings I didn't realize my relationship was missing until I had them. You'd think the ring, binding legal marriage contract, and husband would be enough to give a girl a sense of security, but apparently not. The dream house in combination with the perfect husband, now that was the clincher.

Oddly enough, Croy, who's been a homeowner for years, owned exactly zero holiday decorations when we met. A fact I was quick to point out while packing for the move back at the old house in Oak Falls. How a person, single or not, can celebrate Christmas without the warm glow of an artificial tree in their living space is beyond me.

Once we settled in and unpacked, we made time for a shopping spree of epic proportions. The goal was to get everything we needed on Saturday, so we could spend all day Sunday decorating the house. In the end, we stopped at six different stores and spent more money than I care to think about. Croy's SUV was nearly bursting at the seams when we stopped for lunch, and that was before we found the perfect pre-lit Christmas tree. Twelve feet tall and flocked to perfection, our boxed tree was forced up onto the roof, despite my objections. Even with Croy's impressive collection of ratchet straps, I was a nervous wreck the entire drive home. Thankfully, the weather held out, and our new holiday focal point was no worse for the wear.

In twenty-nine years, I have yet to come across anything more magical than a perfectly decorated tree, bathed in the glow of its own radiance. I even made sure to buy a timer, so it's lit when Croy wakes up for work in the morning, and remains that way until we head off to bed at night.

All of the gifts I ordered online have arrived, so the packages are wrapped and ready to go. I even received a last-minute envelope in the mail, which I've tucked into a fuzzy sock and hidden in my underwear drawer. This is going to be our first major gift-giving holiday together, and I'm worried he might outdo me. When it comes to funds, Croy's got me beat. But I tend to be a unique and thoughtful gift giver, so hopefully it's the intent that counts and not solely the cost of the contents.

Starting December first, Croy insisted that the entire outbuilding, which included the gym, pool house, and garage was "off limits". And since he's security conscious, there were already cameras in place before we moved in. So, it's strictly No Peeking. I'm not a total idiot, so I know that's where he's hiding my presents. Unless, he's moonlighting as a serial killer and I'm blissfully naive like some dewy-eyed simpleton filled with child-like wonder and Christmas spirit.

Shit, maybe I should have peered in the windows, or at the very least, listened for screams. Instead, I've been in the house, listening to traditional holiday classics 24/7 and baking an assortment of cookies. I'm going to end up on the news, still wearing my red and white striped kitchen apron that says *I like cheer!* with flour in my hair and a spatula in my hand, yelling about how there are cookies I need to get out of the oven.

Even without Croy being a secret serial killer, this has been a crazy month. He ignored every phone call and text from his parents and refused every invitation to leave the house on Christmas day. From what I overheard him tell his sister, "If someone wants to see us, they know where we live. Our family will be spending Christmas at home in our pajamas from here until the foreseeable future. You're welcome anytime."

After the disaster that was Thanksgiving dinner, Astrid was quick to forgive Kelly, which made my life easier. The last thing I needed was to be stuck in the middle of those two, especially after being sandwiched between him and Croy for what felt like a lifetime.

And in a particularly exciting turn of events, the two loves in my life have called for a cease fire, effective through the end of the year, at which time terms will be renegotiated. So, Kelly and I have talked pretty much every day leading up to Christmas eve, when we secretly finalized our plan.

Kells: I can't do this without you. I love you so goddamn much. You know I need you by my side. Green for Go or Red full Stop?

: GREEN!!! My heart is beating out of my chest. I love you and I can't wait to see you tomorrow.

Kells: Are you 100% sure? If you have any doubts about us, be honest with me. You know me better than anyone.

: Stop questioning everything. This is FATE! Meant to be. Written in the stars. It's glowing Christmas light green, and there is no backing out now.

Kells: You're right. You're always right.

: I'm glad you've finally realized what's been
staring you in the face this whole time.

Kells: I've known since the beginning.

Fifty~Five

CHRISTMAS MORNING IS HERE at last, and my heart is bursting in anticipation of events still to come. Kelly messaged me twenty minutes ago to let me know he's on his way, and I've been trying to mentally prepare myself since the text came in.

I woke up early, attempting to get my gifts under the tree first, but Croy beat me to the punch. What a jerk! You'd think with it being Christmas he could let me have a win, but no. He insists on being the more amazing, thoughtful, loving, and respectful one out of the two of us. Honestly, sometimes it makes me sick. Until I remember he's mine, and then I smile at my stroke of dumb luck.

Croy hands me a cup of coffee at the same time the doorbell rings. Looking at his phone, he sets his mug on the counter and walks towards the front of the house with a grin.

"Your boyfriend is here."

"Someday you're going to realize that joke isn't funny. And I hope it's sooner rather than later." I catch up to him as the door swings open.

Standing there, framed in Christmas light glow, is my best friend, looking photo ready. The temptation to grab him and pull him through the door is raging inside of me, but I stifle the urge, and take a second to imprint the image of him into my permanent memory. He is walking perfection, in a way I've never mastered, and I'm looking forward to a lifetime of holidays spent together.

"Where's Astrid?" Croy leans his head out the door and looks past Kelly. "Found her."

He slips on his shoes and grabs a coat from the closet, before jogging out to the driveway to help her.

Finally, Kelly steps into the house, shaking off his coat and kicking off his shoes before pulling me into his arms. "I've missed you. We haven't seen each other all week." His words fill my heart nearly to its breaking point and I catch myself on the verge of tears.

"I know. Croy's been working from home all week and I couldn't get out of the house. I'm glad you're here now, though, even if you are painfully overdressed. You show up looking like a cover model and I'm in my pjs."

"You look beautiful, per usual." He kisses my forehead and begins backing me away from the door. "Come on, let's get away from the cold. I need some coffee in my life, unless it's all decaf."

We walk into the kitchen and I hand him a mug. "Do you want to make it, or would you rather I do it?"

"I like it when you wait on me. Watching you make my coffee reminds me of a dream I had once." Without another word, he joins me by the counter and pulls me back into his arms. "But this is all I truly want."

"How are you going to get through opening presents if you can't even hold it together long enough for me to make your coffee? Croy isn't blind. He's going to notice if you keep carrying on this way. You need to chill out and act normal." My words come out as a whispered threat.

I expect Croy and Astrid to be joining us at any second, and Kelly is about to ruin everything. We've been talking day and night in secret for weeks, ever since Thanksgiving. That day was enough to shake me, core and all, and for once I saw the future I was meant to have. Everything made sense, once the pieces started falling into place, and today is the day we complete the picture.

The sound of the front door opening prompts Kelly to let me go, while the banter of approaching voices drives him a step back. Croy and Astrid make a detour into the baby's room before joining us in the kitchen. I return to making coffee, but without Kelly beside me a chill runs up my spine.

"I'm disappointed in you, Croy. I expected to see a new car sitting in the driveway with a big ass bow on it." Kelly's gentle ribbing directed at my husband makes me roll my eyes, but before I can say anything, Croy responds.

"It's in the garage."

I turn to face them both, handing Kelly his coffee and shooting Croy a look. "It had better not be!"

Croy winks, more so at Kelly than at me. "I'll show it to you later."

I shouldn't be surprised, or angry. I expected him to pull some shit like this. But when I looked out the front window and saw the driveway empty, I assumed he had respected my wishes. Now I'm not entirely sure if he's going along with Kelly's joke or being serious.

"You're not allowed to be mad on Christmas, my love. Those are the rules." Croy moves to my side and replaces me in front of the coffee maker. "Now go sit on the couch so I can make my sister something to drink, and take your friend with you."

I leave the kitchen, but allow the decision to follow in the hands of our guests. Grown adults can make their own choices in this house, without any prompting from me.

The three of them join me minutes later, and it's finally time for the festivities to begin. I've been anxiously awaiting this morning, excited for the last gift to be unwrapped and every question to be answered.

My mind flashes back to my first day at the jail and even then, I knew Kelly was something special. I was drawn to him in a way that didn't make sense to me at the time, but as our relationship developed, I realized he was meant to be in my life. I trusted him to have my back and returned the favor happily. He never failed me, even though he would argue otherwise.

Fate led us here, back to each other, exactly where we were meant to be.

The four of us take turns opening gifts, revealing items and trinkets that reflect the love we share for one another. Kelly and Croy even manage to exchange thoughtful presents with one another, without a hint of former rivalry.

When it comes time for the last few packages, Astrid excuses herself to the restroom. "Sorry. You guys go on without me. I have to pee."

She gets up from the couch and heads toward Verlaine's room. I suppose that makes sense since it would probably be weird to use the bathroom her brother and I share. Once she's out of my visual range, I turn my attention back to Croy.

He kneels in front of me, holding the black velvet ring box I recognize from the safe. My heart begins pounding in my chest, the way it did the night he proposed, and for a second, I forget we're already married. "What are you doing?"

"I've made a lot of promises to you since we first met, and I intend to follow through on all of them, if you'll let me. This last year, you have given me the life I was too afraid to dream of on my own, and for that, I will forever be in your debt. With you, I found my best friend and my soulmate. I can't begin to thank you enough for being my family." Croy leans forward, placing his hand on my stomach. "A family I look forward to expanding."

"I love you more than you know."

Unable to hold back the tears any longer, I allow them to spill freely from my eyes and wash over my face, as Croy places the ring box in my hand.

"Your dreams have become my dreams, to the point where I forget what my life looked like before you were in it. Please spend the rest of your life with me, and let's build the family we both deserve."

My eyes shift focus, from one man to the other, as he looks on at the scene playing out in front of him. Through my tears, I can see Kelly mouth the words "I'll always love you," before smiling and looking away.

With shaking hands, I open the lid of the ring box, revealing a silver pendant that's been engraved with a name. "JoJo," I say with a laugh, taking the bone-shaped tag from the box and turning it over in my hand. Seconds later, a red ball of fur appears over my shoulder, whimpering slightly as it awakens in my hands.

The white-headed puppy looks up at me with piercing blue eyes before lunging to kiss me, but Croy grabs him before he makes it to my face. "You need to calm down buddy. I don't need you stepping all over your sister."

"Oh, stop it. This little guy only weighs a few pounds. Now give him back and let me love on him." I take the puppy from Croy's hand and begin rubbing him on my face, taking in the new puppy smell. "He's so damn cute. Where did you find him?"

Astrid comes around the back of the couch and scoots in next to me, resting her head on my shoulder. "Matt and I picked this adorable little baby boy up a few days ago and he's been staying at our house, along with his sister."

"What? Is there a second dog in the house?" I scan the room but don't see anything puppy-sized moving in the background.

"She's still in the bathroom, and she's my precious little angel, so don't get any ideas about keeping her." Astrid jumps up from the couch. "I'll go get her."

It takes twenty minutes of nonstop crying and puppy cuddling before I remember I still have to give Croy his final present. Handing Astrid both dogs, I get up to retrieve the thin box hidden in the branches of the tree.

"There was only ever one gift I wanted to give you, so I'm

glad it arrived on time." I hand the box to Croy, who's standing next to me, and stretch up onto my tiptoes to kiss him.

"I have no idea what this could be," he says, removing the wrapping from the outermost layer to reveal a decorative box with a lid.

I bite my lip and step back, joining Kelly on the couch, where we watch, hand in hand, as Croy removes the lid of the box. He takes out a plain white envelope, turns it over a few times, and then opens it. Before looking at the letter inside, he inspects the pair of us with mourning eyes. "This isn't divorce papers, is it?"

Everyone remains silent, waiting for him to continue. Even from here, I can see his eyes begin to well with tears and his hands begin to shake. I want to go to Croy and make everything better, but Kelly wraps an arm around me and holds me in place by his side.

"I can't look at this."

Astrid sets both dogs on the couch and joins her brother in front of the tree, where he looks like he's about to collapse. "Come on, we'll do it together, okay?"

Finding strength in each other, they open the letter and begin reading.

The emotion of the moment is more than I can bear and I begin sobbing into Kelly's chest as he wraps his other arm around me. Even his body seems to tremble, under the weight of the moment, as he works to maintain his composure.

When Croy drops to his knees, I know I can no longer maintain my distance. I jump up from the couch and throw myself on top of him, a heap of blubbering emotion. It isn't long before Astrid and Kelly join us on the floor, all four of us tearfully embracing. It isn't until the dogs join in that the heaviness begins to lift, and we find ourselves laughing and exchanging smiles.

Croy stands and scoops me up in his arms, careful not to step on anyone.

"I love you so much. This was the best gift you could have ever given me. I can't believe you knew and kept it a secret."

"Congratulations, man! You're going to be an amazing father. These ladies are all fortunate to have you in their lives." Kelly says, putting a hand on Croy's shoulder.

Carefully, I'm lowered back to the floor, finding my feet before he releases me. Then, Croy grabs Kelly by the arm and pulls him into a bear-hug, forcing the air from his lungs. The two men embrace until Kelly taps out, needing to breathe.

"I was starting to think you were part of this family as well."

"That depends on your sister's answer." Kelly turns to Astrid and drops to one knee, pulling a ring box from his pocket.

Knowing in advance this event was scheduled to happen, I reserved scarcely enough emotional energy to remain standing. I watch as my best friend proposes to my sister-in-law, officially linking Kelly and I together from here until the end. That is if she accepts.

"That letter gave us all an answer we've wanted, but now I need one more from you. Astrid, I love you, to a depth I never thought possible. You are the center of my everything, and I would die to protect you. I might even start working out with your brother, in case a situation should arise, but that's not important right now. Anyways… Will you allow me the honor of standing by your side, from here until our happily ever after?"

By the time Kelly finishes his speech, Croy is supporting most of my weight, keeping me from falling over. I'm on pins and needles awaiting Astrid's reply, a feeling that is currently spreading up both of my legs.

"Yes, I'll marry you," Astrid says, excitedly, causing my heart to leap in my chest.

Eventually, the four of us fall back onto the couch, puppies in tow, silently staring off in the direction of the tree. Collectively exhausted and dazed, we remain mostly still, allowing the morning to fully absorb, before finally getting up to say our goodbyes.

Astrid and Kelly are off to visit extended family, while Croy and I opt to spend the holiday at home, establishing new traditions of our own. No matter what the years ahead have in store, this will be a holiday morning we remember forever. It will be the story we pass on to our children, via yearly retellings of the Christmas it all began, when we became the family we all deserved.

About the Author

If you've read my books, you probably walked away with a
pretty good sense of who I am, or rather who I used to be.
These days I'm old enough to know better, but it's still
interesting to look back at the years that brought me heartbreak
so deep, the echoes of pain still live in my bones.
Eventually, I managed to find love, purpose, and a handful
of reasons to get out of bed every morning, and I'm grateful
for the life I've built with my family.
Without them, none of this would be possible.

If you've enjoyed any of my stories, please take a moment to
leave a review online. Every little bit helps, and word of mouth
is everything for indie authors.

instagram.com/author_amanda_bryk
tiktok.com/@author_amanda_bryk
threads.net/@author_amanda_bryk